I HAD A GUN WHICH SHOT TO THE MARK,

a straight left that was poison in a fight, and a knack of sitting the saddle on a raging horse. Good society would not have tolerated me for a moment. I wore my hat at a rakish angle, kept my coat open to show a brilliant waistcoat, my riding boots had heels finished off with great silver spurs. Even the butt of my rifle was set off with gold fretwork, and the handles of my revolvers were works of art. Trouble was what I wanted. And in Zander City,

TROUBLE WAS WHAT I GOT!

Warner Books

By Max Brand

Man From Savage Creek
Trouble Trail
Rustlers of Beacon Creek
Flaming Irons
The Gambler
The Guns of Dorking Hollow
The Gentle Gunman
Dan Barry's Daughter
The Stranger
Mystery Ranch
Frontier Feud
The Garden of Eden
Cheyenne Gold
Golden Lightning
Lucky Larribee
Border Guns
Mighty Lobo
Torture Trail
Tamer of the Wild
The Long Chase
Devil Horse
The White Wolf
Drifter's Vengeance
Trailin'
Gunman's Gold
Timbal Gulch Trail
Seventh Man
Speedy

Galloping Broncos
Fire Brain
The Big Trail
The White Cheyenne
Trail Partners
Outlaw Breed
The Smiling Desperado
The Invisible Outlaw
Silvertip's Strike
Silvertip's Chase
Silvertip
The Sheriff Rides
Valley Vultures
Marbleface
The Return of the Rancher
Mountain Riders
Slow Joe
Happy Jack
Brothers on the Trail
The Happy Valley
The King Bird Rides
The Long Chance
Mistral
Smiling Charlie
The Rancher's Revenge
The Dude
Silvertip's Roundup

THE
WHITE
CHEYENNE

MAX BRAND

WARNER BOOKS

A Warner Communications Company

The characters, places, incidents and situations in this book are imaginary and have no relation to any person, place or actual happening.

WARNER BOOKS EDITION

ISBN: 0-446-98344-6

This Warner Books Edition is published
by arrangement with Dodd, Mead and Company, Inc.

Cover illustration by Carl Hantman

Warner Books, Inc., 75 Rockefeller Plaza, New York, N.Y. 10019.

W A Warner Communications Company

Printed in the United States of America

First Printing: May, 1974

Reissued: July, 1979

10 9 8 7 6 5 4 3 2

1

What makes me wonder chiefly is why I am not wandering around Charleston, wearing a rusty black coat, a white Vandyke, and an air of pretending not to know that I am being pointed out as a son of one of the best families in melancholy South Carolina.

I was an anomaly from the day of my birth.

I didn't fit.

When I was born, it was seen that upon my head there were a few wisps of tow-colored hair; the whole family circle nearly fainted. The terrible news was hushed up and kept from the ears of Charleston lest the fatal tongue of scandal should attaint my mother. My mother—who was five per cent dear idiot and ninety-five per cent purest saint!

Well, while I lay squawking in my cradle, the wise heads of the family got together and dragged out the tomes of the family history. I wish I could re-create the scene for you, because I know it just as well as if I had been there!

You see, my family on both sides was drenched with the book-publishing mania. Both the Rivieres and the Duchesnes had always written books—about themselves. There never had been a man, in either branch of the family, since the beginning of print who had not been capable of some sort of wildness in his youth, who had not mulled the deeds of his boyhood over during his middle age, and who had not sat down in a few quiet moments before his end to scribble out or dictate his memoirs.

Usually what he had to write about was a string of sanctified lies. I mean, facts which had become invested with a "certain atmosphere" by frequent tellings and re-tellings, until not even the days which mothered the real events could have recognized their progeny. Careless little boyish remarks became bearded orations in this process of time and tender imagination; yawns became sighs, and sighs became music, so to speak.

To maintain the tradition, here am I sitting in my library doing the very same thing. Only, I think that I have just a touch more of the historian about me, and that, when some critical Diogenes hunts through my narrative for a few honest facts, he will see a scattering here and there, not too completely disguised.

To go back to the family conclave in my infancy.

The library was such a room as would fitly house the traditions of the Riviere-Duchesnes. It was a lofty chamber with dark woodwork and a gloomy red carpet upon the floor. Upon the walls appeared pictures of more or less celebrated ancestors—chiefly more, of course. The first study to which the youth of the Riviere-Duchesne family was introduced was history—family history. There was not a cousin, however distant, who, on appearing in the library which was the sanctum of the clan, could not instantly identify the subjects of these smudgy old oil paintings. Most of them were out of the wig-and-lace period when the gentry all wore high-arched eyebrows and had hands which had never done a lick of work except when the fingers were wrapped around the hilt of a sword.

They had done some work, though—that was to write about themselves:

"For the sake of my dear children, who have pressed me to commit to paper the narrative of my life."

A lot of pressing they needed! I know by my own example. Who could keep me from turning out this history? Only I am frank about admitting that I hope its future abiding place will not be in that musty Riviere-Duchesne house, but in sundry public libraries—the more, the better!

It was the solemn volumes of this library which were sought and pored over by my anxious relatives in an effort to identify other members of the family who had been blond of hair and gray of eye. All the rest were befittingly

6

dark of skin and dark of eye and hair. What is so romantic as a black eye and a white head?

At last—I think it was Uncle Renault St. Omer Louvois, of the Duchesne branch, you know—I think it was this uncle who rushed out of the library as fast as he could one midnight, with a twenty-pound book under his arm. He gathered my anxious father, half a dozen more anxious cousins, and so forth, around him.

Uncle Renny—though I never dared to shorten his name so familiarly to his face—declared that he had trailed the secret to its hiding place. He straightway opened that volume and was instantly immersed in the details of how a great-uncle, or some such relative, had slipped from the straight and very narrow matrimonial path of a proper Riviere-Duchesne. Finding a pretty Saxon in the County of Kent, he had made her his housekeeper and, in due time, his wife.

This was how blond hair came into the stately line.

It was a thing not to be spoken of, the history of the family of this same Kentish girl. It was not gentle. It seems that the rascals had turned out a fine strain of buccaneering swordsmen, who had followed the sea and made nothing of taking the vessels of their majesties of Spain or of France either—not even when it involved the round thumping of a Riviere-Duchesne in command of the "lilies" of France.

However, this was not a thing to be dwelt upon.

What was important was that there was a precedent, some hundred years old, of blond heads in our family. No dreadful whisper could be circulated concerning my seven-times-sacred mother.

The next step was to discover how many times the blond hair had intruded upon what might be called the pure strain, up to this moment. It was then learned that there had been no fewer than three. The reason why their names were not prominent in our annals was that all three had been preeminent rascals!

The first was Terence. At the age of eleven he disappeared, coming back five years later with a rolling gait, a brown face, and a frightful seaman's lingo.

The bad blood was breaking out! Did not the whole

7

world know that the Riviere-Duchesne gentry always followed the land, and nothing but the land? The sea smacks of piracy and merchandise. The Riviere-Duchesnes were *always* people of landed estates. Yet here was this Terence turning himself into a sea-roving vagabond in this disgusting fashion.

Of course, they clapped him straightway into a school. Before a single Latin quantity had been thumped into his head, he broke the nose of his tutor and escaped by night, to be seen no more during half a dozen years. When he appeared again he was a grown-up young man with some sort of a gold-laced uniform on his shoulders. No one could find out just what service this Terence Riviere-Duchesne was in, but it was certain that it was one which paid him handsomely. In prize money, he said. Presently it was discovered that the service he was in was his own. This very proper youth was a pirate of the old school, it might be said; he both picked the pockets and cut the throats of his victims. He died very properly on his own quarter-deck in the act of passing a pike through one of his Britannic majesty's naval officers.

The next blond-headed Riviere-Duchesne was given the name of Oliver. This gentleman did not go to sea. He felt that the land would be much more fitting for his talents. While he was still in his early twenties he was arrested and charged with some prodigious robberies. His escape from justice was due, many felt, to the talents of his lawyer, whom he hired with a fraction of his ill-got gains. A few years later he was accused again, this time of being the head of a whole circle of thieves, whose operations he directed.

This time he was convicted, but he disappeared and was never seen again. All of his great estate was found to be so tied up in the law that it went to his heirs, and those he had robbed could not reclaim a penny of their money.

The third blond gentleman was given the name of Paul. He, too, had felt the sea call in his blood and ran away in his boyhood. He returned to dry land, and, graduating from the United States Military Academy, he immediately resigned to take service with a South American republic

8

which was trying to get used to liberty by cutting throats on all sides with a free hand. Here he disappeared, for the most part. During the past fifteen or twenty years mention was heard of him only now and again. There were vague rumors that a certain enormously wealthy Señor Don Paolo Riviero in South America was none other than our own Paul.

These three precedents did not argue very favorably for my future. Yet my father was a man who took the facts by the horns—and broke the neck of them if he could.

He said it was shameful to dodge the truth; that, for his part, he had no intention of attempting to do so, but he would be very happy to have any one convince him that there had not been *some* good in each of those three persons. For his part, again, he felt that they had simply been blessed with too much energy, and therefore what they had needed was not new natures, but better educated ones.

He said that he would face the fact.

His manner of facing it sent a shudder through the entire family circle. He straightaway called me by the whole group of the three names—Terence Oliver Paul Riviere-Duchesne!

My Uncle Renault used to say: "Even if the blood of a pirate, a thief, and a mercenary soldier are in his veins, why should you immortalize the fact in his very name?"

My poor mother said: "Alas, my dear, if you call upon the devil, is he not apt to appear?"

2

My father, as you have guessed by this time, was a man of ideas, with a theory to fit with every occasion. Therefore, though he did not doubt that the devil was really in me, he determined that the first thing to do was to "face the facts" and be honest and begin with the boy himself.

At the age of eight years, having just been brought in after blacking the aristocratic eye of a neighbor's son, I was taken by my father to the rear of the house. He locked the door, sat down with me, and entered into a long conversation, in the course of which he explained that the reason why he had decided to give me an extra hard beating was not so much because I had beaten another boy—that being not altogether unworthy of commendation—but because this fighting taste of mine was a sign of a certain devil in me.

After this, he collared me and gave me a tremendous whacking. When I had stopped groaning, he carried me into the library. He got out three books, two of them fairly old, one of them fairly new. In those three books he marked the places where the histories of the blond-headed Riviere-Duchesne were narrated. He told me to study them well.

There was no need of telling me that. This was the sort of history that any boy would thoroughly enjoy. I began with a pirate, I proceeded with a thief, and I concluded with a soldier of fortune.

After I had finished these documents, my father showed me pictures of each of the three, pointing out that where the usual Riviere-Duchesne was a tall, well made, handsome dark man, worthy of standing in the train of a king, each of these blond fellows was a slight, waspish man with a mouth too big and a jaw too broad for beauty.

By all these tokens, he asked me to examine myself in the mirror and regard my future well. Because there was undoubtedly a devil of violence and craft in me, and I must school myself with the greatest care. This is to a boy of eight years!

The result, of course, was that I began to consider myself an exceptional youth, furnished with an excuse at birth for every evil emotion that rose in me. If I wanted to steal apples, I said that it was the spirit of Oliver rising in me. If I wanted to carry off the toy gun of another boy, I felt that this was merely the soul of Terence speaking through my flesh. If I wanted to punch the nose of another youngster, I was sure that it was Uncle Paul rising to the surface in action.

My father had only two ways of dealing with this refractory spirit in me. On the one hand he talked to me like a philosopher, on the other hand he tanned me like a schoolmaster of the most rigid pattern.

In the meantime, both he and I could not help being aware that he was regarded by my relatives as an unlucky prophet who had saddled three evil natures upon me with the three names he had given me. No matter what I learned about my faults, I also discovered that it was best to make them *successful* faults. Terence had lived a short life, but a merry one. Oliver had disappeared with a purse fat enough to keep him for the rest of his days, and Paul was presumed to be a man of great note and a general admitted into the most powerful councils of a flourishing country.

So I spent my time learning to ride, to shoot, and to tell only the useful part of the truth. I grew up a perfect young Persian, with the third quality changed as noted above. If I had any grace, it was the saving one of a sense of humor. If I did not take my father and the family council any too seriously, neither did I take my own faults or virtues too much to heart. In fact, I think that I was born with my tongue in my cheek. That was another thing which my father and the rest attributed to a natural perversity.

11

I have gone into all of these details so that you may understand the event that eventually rooted me out of South Carolina and sent me West.

It was a touchy time in that State. I had been born just out of date. Had I been a single year older, I should have marched in the armies of the Confederacy, in that unlucky '65. As it was, I was just fifteen when the war ended, and I had not yet joined the colors. For half a dozen years after that I lived in a society where "all was lost save honor," and the result was that "honor" was always underlined rather ridiculously. When people had nothing left but their gentility, they made the most of their capital. You could not look cross-eyed at any young man in Charleston without having him come up and ask what you meant by it.

That was not so bad while I was still in my teens, because the fights that rose were settled with fists, but when I entered my twenties all of this changed. I was always getting into trouble. The first time that I seriously offended a man he happened to be a boy two years older than I. He had served in the Confederate ranks as a boy lieutenant, was an eminent example of all having been lost but that same precious honor. I offended him by laughing at a stiff, old-fashioned way he had of accosting a girl at a dance and asking for the honor of her hand in the next piece. He replied by calling me aside into a little group of other men and stating in the hearing of all that my conduct was not worthy of being called the behavior of a gentleman.

My first impulse was to knock him down, but I saw by the serious faces around me that that line would not do. Yet I could not help breaking out: "The devil, Arnold! Are you going to make a really serious affair out of this?"

A cold look settled on the face of Arnold Perrault. The same look was on the faces of the others. I saw that they suspected me of showing the white feather in a business which might mean shooting. I had to swallow my irritation. He bowed to me and said that he trusted it would not be too serious to inconvenience me, and that he would send a friend to see a friend of mine.

There you were!

There was a good deal of this nonsense going on at that time.

We met down by the river at the edge of some willows where I had often gone swimming when I was a youngster. The memory of how I had skylarked with this same Arnold in the old days gave me a ghostly feeling.

We were to fire at the word of an umpire. When he spoke, I shot poor Arnold Perrault squarely through the brain!

The matter would have been hushed up, if any but I had been the winner. It would have been just another unlucky hunting accident. Since I was in the matter, it was much more serious.

"The devil in young Riviere-Duchesne has grown up!" was the way people put it. "He has murdered a man—and Arnold Perrault is the man!"

Such talk hummed about until it got to the ears of the police. When I saw two officers coming toward me in the street the next afternoon, I did not stop to ask why they were bent for me so eagerly. I simply jumped over the next fence and started across the fields.

I found a horse at the next lot. It was a tame old brute which had done its share of hunting, once. Now it was pretty badly broken down in front. I threw myself on it and headed it up the meadow, across to the street beyond, via the fence, and then up the next street and over another fence.

Hunting that game old runner out of Charleston, I flew the fences that came in my way, so that by the time they got on my trail with horses under them they had a stiff handicap to overcome.

Eight miles from the start there was hardly another jump left in the carcass of my borrowed horse, so I left him down the road and jogged along on foot to the house of a friend of mine a little farther on. He was not a gentleman, but he was a great hunter, a good shot, and a good "seat." He had taught me what wicked medicine a straight left could be in a hard fight with the fists. He was a friend of mine, and when he saw me come in, hot and perspiring, he merely gave a side glance at my face, then, telling his wife to go into the next room, he shut the door.

13

He was always that way, was McKenzie. He thought with the speed of a prize fighter, and you could never corner him. He said: "What's up?"

"A dead man," said I. "And a friend of mine and a good fellow—Arnold Perrault. It was a stand-up fight, but now they call it murder."

You see, McKenzie was the sort of a man who had to hear all of a story or else none of it. He merely said:

"Well, when I first heard, the other day, that you had done for Perrault, I guessed that it might come along to something like this. That's their way. They don't judge a man by what he does but by what he looks, my friend!"

3

There was a lot of truth in that. I had chances to think it over afterward and decided that McKenzie was one of the wisest of the wise. Just at that moment I wasn't in a humor for listening to anything, or thinking, either. All that I knew of importance was that I wanted a good, sure-footed horse under me. From McKenzie I presently got what I wanted—a tall, hard-mouthed roan with the disposition of a devil and the legs of a bronze statue.

I liked McKenzie. But I liked the roan better than I did the fighting Scot.

I used those four legs of bronze to carry me a hundred miles west, out of Charleston way. When the next morning came, I saw that I had most of my trouble for nothing. I had given that horse a good rest and a good feed the night before, but he had had too much taken out of him. He couldn't respond as I wanted him to when three horsemen came jogging down the road. I felt that I *knew* they couldn't be after me so soon. Yet something about their way of going along told me that they were. When they quickened the pace of their horses, I was sure.

It was the telegraph, of course. The wiser heads in Charleston knew that I had been born and reared, so to speak, in the saddle. They didn't yearn to break their hearts following me straight across country. They did follow me far enough to get the general direction in which I was heading. Then they let the telegraph do the rest for them. They scattered the warning, and they sent along a little offer of a reward that meant a good deal to some of the poorer farmer folk that were out that way. They turned out in force, and I might as well have met with a dozen of them as with three.

They looked at me and then they started to gallop. I tried the roan for a turn down the road, but he wouldn't do. He could still jump, and he was too mean to confess himself beaten. He got over a fence by means of knocking down the top rail, and he floundered through the soft of the field beyond, a badly spent horse.

Even that little jump was too much for one of the three that followed me. His horse was stalled there and that left only two to come hurling after me, yelling to one another. Of course, they saw that they had me as good as in their pockets. They were wild with the foretaste of that reward already sweet in their mouths.

However, I had a friend along in the shape of a strong-shooting old .44 Colt which McKenzie had given me with a grin and this word of advice:

"Don't ever pull it unless you're planning on dead men!"

I was not planning on dead men, but I was planning on my own life, if I could save it. I turned in the saddle and blazed away. It was not very long-distance shooting, but it was from a running horse, and I was lucky when the second shot hurt one of the horses enough to slow it up badly.

That left one rider behind me. He didn't like the hand-to-hand game. He jumped off his horse and began to pop at me with his rifle. It was not one of the new repeaters, and before he had whanged away three times I was safely out of range. But the roan was done for sure.

I left him in a hollow, pretty sure that he would not

15

give himself away by trotting about or by neighing. The trumpet blast of the last day couldn't have raised an echo from that poor gelding that day, he was so done.

Cutting away sharp to the side, I followed a little ridge covered with shrubs and rocks. It gave me cover enough to help me away. After I had gone a little distance, I had the pleasure of seeing two of my men come after and hunt across that hollow at a great rate and straight on, according to my own direction.

Well, I was out of that pinch, but there were two weeks of hard work before me before I got to the mountains. There I laid up for four or five days, resting, because I was fairly well used up. Then I came to another bad pinch, when a mountain constable came in and tried to take me single-handed.

If he had not been such a pig about the thing, wanting to get all the reward for himself, he would certainly have had me. As it was, I managed to get a bullet through his arm while he was unlimbering a big, old-fashioned rifle.

I started farther west on another "borrowed" horse. I kept that up until I was on the shady side of the mountains and still headed farther and farther westward. When I speak of the shady side of the mountains I don't want to be understood as casting any reflections on the society east of the Mississippi in those days. But there *were* some shady spots in it, and when a man had it too hot along the seaboard he hit mainland.

This is just the spot for me to drop in a little talk about how grieved I was to be away from home; how I reflected upon the misfortunes which had overtaken me, and particularly upon the cruel injustice which had driven me away from Charleston.

As a matter of fact, I was not at all troubled by these reflections. I knew perfectly well that if I happened to be the victim of an injustice in this particular case, it was the merest accident. I had made enough trouble in my time to account for almost anything. I was *not* sorry to be away from home. I knew that my parents preferred my brothers and sisters to me. In turn, I did not waste much affection on them.

I was out of place in my father's home. I knew it—

and so did they. I could not listen to them and watch their grave ways without wanting to laugh. When I wanted to laugh, I generally did. There is nothing in the world that people will forgive less readily than a lack of reverence to their persons.

In fact, there was only one thing for which I was genuinely sorry. That was that my bullet had killed poor Arnold Perrault. There was nothing wrong with him except his high-headed pride. I suppose that his was not the most valuable life that was ended by that selfsame pride.

Even this regret was not enough, as you might say, to spoil my appetite for the life which I saw before me. I liked the prospect thoroughly well.

You see, I believed in the treble rascality of the nature which had been wished upon me in the three names with which my father had so foolishly endowed me. I haven't the slightest doubt that a normal name might have turned me out a thoroughly normal boy in every respect. Yet here I was, as I felt, created for the sake of doing mischief in the world and thoroughly prepared to have a good time while I was doing it.

I was twenty-one years old. I had never had a sick day in my life. My nerves were as steady as chilled steel. I had at my disposal a hundred and fifty-odd pounds of muscle and bone which I knew very well how to use to the best advantage—whether the engagement were wrestling or boxing or straight rough and tumble—for which I had a low taste!

Just when a young hero of good mind and morals would have been deploring his fate, I was looking westward with a smile in my heart. I felt just as though I had received a signed commission permitting me to do as I pleased.

When I ran out of money I ran into a job which was running moonshine whisky from a mountain still down to the towns in the valley below. It was as risky a work as you would like to undertake. I liked it well enough, because it gave me a pair of thoroughly good horses to ride, plenty of money in my pocket, and plenty of danger blowing down the wind.

In short, I had found just the place for a young ruffian.

17

And such I was, exactly that and no more, though my name and my antecedents might have stood for a good deal higher social stratum. I changed that name to Rivers. From that time on I was known as Terence Rivers over a widening pool of society.

A young man takes it for granted that the world is so great that no matter in what direction he travels he may keep going forever without ever once finding his own footmarks on the trail before him. Yet after I had been a while in this employment, a nasty wind blew over the mountains the rumor that Terry Rivers was wanted back in Charleston for murder.

I got a lift in wages at once. There are certain occupations where murder is at once rewarded in this fashion, and with a grisly sort of honor. That is the ultimate brand. It distinguishes the wolf from the house dog. In the line that I was following, the real wild strain was what was wanted.

However, this rumor that blew over the mountains crystalized in the shape of a posse that started on my trail. I took my choice of my two horses sold the other for a song and drifted on farther west with a hundred dollars and a bit more in my pocket, a new-style Winchester rifle thrust into the long carbine holster that passed under my right knee and along the side of the saddle, two revolvers beside the pommel of that saddle, and two more stuck away in my clothes.

You might say that I was a young walking arsenal. I was. If I had had handy room for more guns and more than the one heavy-handled Bowie knife at my belt, I assure you that I would have carried more. Those were the days which you read about but to which justice can never be done. Those were the days when the West was really *bad*.

On the farther bank of the Mississippi there were the fine fellows who merely loved adventure in an innocent way, the hardy-handed chaps who wanted to beat raw nature on the frontier and make their living by their own efforts; there were the gay trappers and hunters and their set, and there were tourists, too. Yes, even as early as this there were tourists. But there were not enough of

18

these law-abiding elements to make up for the high season-
ing of deviltry which was spread through the community.

For there were the outlawed men from the Atlantic seaboard, together with many a chosen rascal who had sailed
west from Europe. You could not find any town of five
hundred which did not have in it some French gambler,
some Italian knife artist, some German butcher.

Of all the towns along the range of crime I could not
have picked out a wilder destination than Zander City.

4

I don't know why Zander City should have passed
on. The flower of its wickedness was bright enough to
have given it immortality along with sundry other naughty
towns. It should be living to keep before us, to-day, the
memories of the bad men and the good who died in her
streets, in her back yards, in her saloons and trading stores.
However, civilization did not choose to place Zander City
among the elect. I have seen it recently—just a brown
stretch of flat ground with the dirty waters of the river
walking past on the way toward the Mississippi.

Because Zander City is gone, the knaves and the heroes
who once flourished in her have died, also. At a later date,
no county historian found fellow townsmen to tell reverent
lies, thinly salted with truth about the great men of the
past. The little heroes of Rome all are remembered, but
out of Carthage we know only a Hannibal and a little group
which can still be seen in Hannibal's light.

So it was with Zander City, I presume that most people
have heard something about a few of the leading figures in
my history, such as Major Beals and Danny Croydon, the
scout. Above all, everybody must have listened to tales

about that famous leader of the Cheyennes—Lost Wolf. They used that name to frighten the children for half a generation, and he still crops up in histories now and again. Who has heard of that odd and graceful fellow, Running Deer? Who knows the heroic minister, Gleason, and the rest of those who wore guns in Zander City?

Well, I cannot pretend to be able to recreate the entire picture of the dead days in that town and the people that lived there. In fact, I shall try only to publish the things with which I came intimately in contact.

I had been about a year around the West, by this time. I had had my share of trouble and fighting. I had learned to be glad of three things—a gun which shot to the mark, a straight left that was poison in a fight, and a knack of sitting the saddle on a raging horse.

Those were the three talents which I brought out of Charleston with me. They were all given scope, and the edge of them sharpened by my Western experiences. By the time that I got to that town on the flats, I was what you might have called a tough one.

Good society would not have tolerated me for a moment. I wore my hat at a rakish angle, kept my coat open to show a brilliant waistcoat, and always had the finest sort of riding boots, whose heels were finished off with great silver spurs. Ordinary guns would not suit me. Even the butt of my rifle was set off with gold fretwork, and the handles of my revolvers were works of art. More than this, I carried myself with a very aggressive air which was bound to find trouble in those dangerous waters. Trouble was exactly what I wanted.

When I got off the steamer at the dock at Zander City, I stood for a time to watch men working with ropes to bind the great stacks of buffalo hides into bales for shipping down the river. Then I went on to see what was to be seen.

You would never have guessed what was in the air of that town, at this time of the day. For it was close to noon, and only the face of honest traffic showed itself. Wagons rolled in and out of town, followed by an attending cloud of dust, and a dull murmur of labor rolled up toward that prairie sky. A murmur with sharp notes struck through it from the clang of the anvil in a distant blacksmith shop.

Yonder, many carpenters kept up the burden of the march with a rattle of hammers as steady as the roll of drums.

It was a quietly sleeping town, so far as excitement was concerned. I had seen twenty places more or less of a pattern. The long row of squat shacks which staggered down the street on either side of me was not thrilling—I was not even able to guess what lay behind those dull faces.

Here a wagon went by, and when the teamster swung his whip the lash caught my hat and flicked it into the dust. I caught it up with an oath and glared at my teamster, but he was not even glancing my way as he swayed on in his lofty seat.

I finished dusting that hat off and settled it on my head again. It was barely pulled down when another whiplash curled around it, as a second wagon rumbled past over a culvert. That hat was yanked fairly from my head, tossed high in the air, and sent spinning to the farther side of the road.

It was hard to imagine that two such things could have happened by mere accident. Yet it was almost harder to believe in such skill in a whip hand as must be there, if I were to attribute it to malice.

When I looked wildly around me, I saw all that I wanted to see in order to make myself sure. No one laughed. It was not the time of day when men laughed in Zander City. But there were villainous broad grins of appreciation of the knavish trick which had been played on me.

I was twenty-two years old, and any one at that age is a sensitive fool. I leaped after that wagon like a tiger and sprang up beside the seat—only to have the muzzle of a huge revolver gaping in my very face while a brutal voice asked me what I wanted.

What had happened to me was what usually happened to people who got into a blind rage in the West in those days—particularly in towns where the population had grown faster than the law. I had simply run into a corner where I had to show myself a fool. I was only lucky that instead of merely showing the gun he had not fired it. If he had, what would have been done about it?

Not a thing in the world! I had no friends in that town. No voice would be raised against him. The universal comment would simply be that, being unable to take a joke, I had forced a battle and been destroyed by the teamster in self-defense.

As I stood on the board sidewalk again, I was almost blind with fury. The grins had not abated. No one laughed. That, as I said before, was merely because it was not the time of day when men laughed in Zander City.

I could not endure this. I, a Riviere-Duchesne, had been handled like an idiot in this town of ruffians. I had to have redress. I picked out the largest and most formidable-looking fellow I could see, walked up to him, and demanded to know what he was laughing at.

"I ain't laughing," said he. "You ain't *worth* a real laugh!"

This to me! Shades of the pirate and revolutionary and robber whose names I bore!

My gun came out faster than a thought, and I was curling my finger around the trigger when I saw that the other fellow had not made a move to get out a weapon.

He was never to know how close he came to being wiped out in that moment.

When he did not even alter his smile, I began to realize that there *was* something unusual about the people of this town. They made me feel wonderfully like a small boy who was attempting to play a grown-up role and doing a powerfully bad job of it.

He said: "I don't wear a gun till noon, because me temper ain't fit for it. So run along, son, till noontime, and then come back and get a hole drilled through you, if you have to die young! We got a fool garden of a good size out here. There's always room for one more plant in it!"

By that, of course, he meant the cemetery.

Well, I was completely blind by this time. I tore off my coat and flung down my hat, shouting:

"There lies my advantage of guns on the ground. If you won't fight with a gun, you'll *have* to fight me with your fists!"

"It's before noon," said he, "and I hate to put up my

22

'maulies' before noon! However, if you are *bound* to have your fun, I'll do what I can to keep up my end of it!"

He stepped forth without deigning to strip off his coat as I had done. He stepped forth, a long, big-boned man with the reach and a large share of the strength of a gorilla. Not that there was anything stupidly brutal about this man. He had a long face with pale, thoughtful eyes, wonderfully cold. The instant he put up his hands, I knew that he was a boxer. He was receiving some forty pounds from poor me; he was a trained man, and he was calm as standing water while I was as mad as a raging brook.

I flung out at him with a rush. He stepped back, caught my punches on forearms as solid as bars of iron, and then, in turn, snapped his fist up.

It glanced from my face like a flung boulder, flicking off a bit of skin and flesh and sending me reeling.

"Now, bantam," said the tall man, "have you had enough of this business?"

I merely gasped out: "I'll kill you, you big devil!"

Again I came in at him, completely beyond myself with rage and grief and agonizing shame. I managed to duck under the terrible reach of a driving arm as I came at him. I landed on his ribs.

It was like striking the ribs of a ship! Before I could strike again, a big hand caught me by the shoulder and shoved me away; the second hand dropped upon my chin and blanketed my brain in blackness so complete and sudden that I do not even remember how I felt.

What first brought me to my senses was a burning heat against my face. It was the dust of the street in which I had fallen—a dust baked stove hot, by the direct rays of the midday sun. I got up in time to hear the big man say:

"Now, youngster, the thing for you to do is to skin out of Zander City before some of the *rough* boys find out that you're here. Because I ain't rough. I'm one of the lambs. But there is men in this here town that wouldn't think nothing of eating you *raw*. Now you believe me! The thing for you to do is to just start out back for the part of the country where folks has been letting you pass for a man. Up here in Zander City, disguises like you're

23

wearin' are dangerous. You run along, and while you're running I'll keep these here shooting irons, to save you from getting into any more messes that may be a lot worse than this one!"

I was sick; my knees were swaying under my weight, and I could hardly see a foot before me. So I knew that it would be folly for me to attempt to strike back at the big man now.

Going to a box which I saw, I sat down on it until my head had partially cleared. Then I got up and started back for the boat. I was determined to kill that tall man if it were the last act of my life, and kill him before that day was ended.

5

When I got back to the boat, I got ashore the rest of my belongings. One of them was a long-legged Kentucky thoroughbred with the bone and substance that comes from a diet of blue grass and lime water. It had cost me a lot of money and trouble to take that bay gelding up the river with me, but I never regretted it, because Sir Thomas had speed and endurance and something that is better than both—brains! He knew how to sprint like a racer; he knew how to hold himself in and work calmly through a long day over dusty, narrow, broken trails.

When I looked into the wise eye of Sir Thomas, I felt better. I patted his neck and leaned for a moment against his shoulder.

That steadied me. There is nothing that brings assurance back to a man so quickly as the feeling that he has really gained the mastery over some twelve hundred and odd pounds of high-spirited horse. I patched up my bruised face, brushed the dust from my clothes, and shoved into my holsters my second pair of guns to take the place of the ones which the big man had taken from me so shamefully. After that, I saddled Sir Thomas and went back into Zander City, sitting in that saddle with a devil raging in my heart.

I got back quickly enough to the place where I had been made a double jackass for the first time in my life— once by a common teamster and once by the most extraordinary fists of that tall man.

When I arrived on the spot, I looked around hungrily. I was not long in finding a few faces of men who had seen me there before. They felt that they knew me well enough, by this time, and they not only smiled openly at me, but they went so far as to shrug their shoulders and sneer.

I picked the biggest of the lot and rode up to him.

"Were you here ten minutes ago?" I asked him.

He looked me over with his contempt like poison on his face.

"What if I was, son?" said he.

"If you were," said I, "the first thing I have to do is to teach you manners."

"Why, darn my heart," said this fellow, rearing himself up from the old, crazy apple barrel on which he had been sitting, "either the kid has a little spunk or else he's just crazy! How will you teach me manners, youngster?"

"With a whip," said I, and I gave him the lash squarely across his face.

There are ways and ways of using a quirt. You can simply sting a horse or, if you are an expert and keep the right sort of a heavy, supple lash, you can cut the skin. I had the right sort of a lash, and I was an expert. A crimson stain followed that savage cut of mine.

He screamed with pain and surprise and shame, all mingled. With one hand thrown up before his face to ward off another of those terrible blows, he reached for his revolver.

I could have killed him three times while he was dragging out that gun, and in my left hand I kept the gun ready to open fire the moment that a gun should be necessary. I did not see any necessity for it as yet. I knew how to handle that long-lashed quirt, and I fell to work with it now. The second slash wound the thin tentacle of oiled leather around the gun wrist of that man. The backward drag of my arm drew the lash off again with a force and a speed that ripped the skin from his arm and yanked the gun fifty feet away.

That would have finished most men, but he was a fighting machine, that big fellow was. Only, he was not the same sort of fighting stuff that had mastered me on that same spot not many minutes before. He came in blindly to tear me from my horse and rip me to bits in his big hands. I literally cut him to ribbons with that dreadful quirt as he came storming in, recoiling, and plunging again. I hate to speak of that scene now. At the time, every stroke gave me infinite pleasure. Finally, he had enough and turned and fled with a scream.

I sat there and watched him go, with the devil sinking back in my heart a little appeased.

When he had disappeared I looked around me with care. I found that no one was sitting down. Nor was any one smiling.

I selected my nearest neighbor, and I rode up to him, saying: "A little while ago I was beaten here by a tall fellow. If you saw that fight, I want you to tell me the name of that man and where he can be found."

The other was a fellow of middle age. And I suppose that he was past his fighting prime, or perhaps he had never had one. He merely nodded.

"You mean The Doctor, stranger," said he.

"Is he a physician in this town?" I asked.

"I dunno that he ever spent much of his time *curing*," said the other, and he smiled faintly, with much meaning.

"Well," said I, "I want you to tell me where I can find him."

He shook his head.

"Be glad to oblige you, stranger. But I dunno that I can say that. The Doctor comes, and The Doctor goes, pretty much as he doggone pleases."

"What got him that name?"

"Why, I suppose that it was the sort of scientific way that he had of cutting up gents."

26

"I follow the idea. Now I want you to tell The Doctor, if you see him, that I am going to be back in this same place at three o'clock in the afternoon of this day, and that I expect to find him here. When I find him, I am going to shoot him through the head if I can!"

I reined back Sir Thomas, and he gave way, prancing, because that was the only direction in which he didn't like to travel. And I said to that choice cross section of Zander City's finest ruffians and cutthroats:

"And if there are any friends of The Doctor in hearing, who want to tell me that he is anything else than a scoundrelly blackguard, I would like to have them step out and speak, because just now I happen to be in a listening humor. Do you hear? Do you all hear me?"

They heard me, but that was not all that they were to hear. For I rode up and down that place on Sir Thomas, cursing Zander City and the men thereof to their faces, telling of the regions from which they had come, and of the place to which they were all inevitably bound.

They listened to me seriously, never smiling, but with their heads cocked a little to one side as though they were preparing to pass critically upon the quality and quantity of the cursing which I was doing at that moment.

Not a one of them answered me. So I left them and retired to a distant saloon. There I stretched myself out in the shadows of a back room which was filled with reminiscent stenches of stale cigars and lager beer and terrible whisky. I gave a dollar to a loafer to watch the door, to warn me if any one tried to come in, and, in the meantime, call me at ten minutes before three o'clock, unless I was disturbed before that time.

At ten minutes to three I had to be shaken by the shoulder before I could waken. My nerves are not now what they were then. At the time it had seemed to me a perfectly natural and normal thing to be doing—to take a restful little nap before swinging into action. For two hours I snored in that back room; then I got up and shook myself together.

When I started out, after paying the loafer, the bartender significantly pushed a black bottle toward me. I put a dollar on the bar and asked for a glass of water and a towel. I used the water to pour over the back of my neck and head, and the towel to rub myself dry again. There is nothing better than a dose of this sort to pull the wits together and brush the cobwebs out of the brain.

I was ready for my work when I stepped out of that saloon, and untethered Sir Thomas. Then I walked down the street with that good horse following me like a big dog. I wanted to have an even steadier base than Sir Thomas himself when I unlimbered and went into action against The Doctor.

As I went along, I rather regretted that I had not made inquiries about The Doctor at the saloon. On the whole, it was perhaps as well that I had not learned all of the details of his heroic reputation before I started against him.

At the same place where I had first encountered the big Doctor, I slowed up, going along at a casual gait. I had an audience, now, and it was the sort of a scene in which I liked to figure. I suppose that most young men are the same. If they are going to be virtuous, they want to be virtuous to the playing of a drum, and if they are going to be wicked, they want to be wicked on a broad stage, with plenty of audience standing about. I couldn't have been half so savage if there had not been a crowd on hand.

Big Sir Thomas walked quietly along behind me, keeping his eye thoughtfully on everything, after the fashion of a thoroughly good horse. I strolled down the center of that street, searching for The Doctor everywhere.

I went a hundred yards down; then I came a hundred yards back. No Doctor appeared. Then an idea like a hot hand caught at my brain and made me dizzy. The idea was that The Doctor had been afraid to come out to face me!

Back in my head there was something that told me that any such thought was perfectly silly, because The Doctor was not the sort of man to sidestep trouble in any form. If he were deadly with his bare hands, I had a very great confidence that he was probably just as sure with powder and lead—or the cold edge of a knife.

When my second turn brought me back in front of that watching crowd, I stopped and said: "Gentlemen, I've

28

announced that at this hour I intended to meet The Doctor. I've published that intention through Zander City and still there does not appear to be any Doctor here! I don't want to accuse any one on a slight cause. But I have to tell you that I think that The Doctor is afraid to show his face to me."

No, they were not smiling. I was just spectacular enough to catch their fancy, and I suppose the ugly tale about the horse-whipping of the second man of that day had come to their ears, also. They watched me with a contented silence—the silence of rough men who suspect that there is some one a little wilder and rougher than themselves in the offing.

Moreover, The Doctor was not there, and that fact gave a good deal of point to me and what I had to say.

So I could swagger my fill there and enjoy my big moment without danger. Danger just then was exactly what I wanted. I wanted to get the poison out of my system, and I could do it only by soundly thrashing some man as I had been thrashed.

After a pause, I said: "Failing The Doctor, I'd be glad to see and talk with any other fellow in this crowd who calls himself a friend of The Doctor and is willing to stand up in his place. I'm not proud. I'll take a substitute!"

It was the sort of a joke that went down with such men. They acknowledged that bit of wit with a deep-throated chuckle. Then they waited, and I saw eyes glancing askance here and there through the crowd, as they picked out various acquaintances of that celebrated man.

It was a pleasant climax.

I saw three or four fellows gathering their resolution to come out and tackle me, unknown problem that I was in Zander City, because they were known friends of The Doctor, and they felt that they were being forced to show their hands in public or be considered cowards.

However, that consummation was not to take place. The situation still hung in suspense, and action had not yet been precipitated, when a voice and a rumor spread from the farther end of the street, bringing to Zander City news of such importance that I was forgotten. The Doctor was forgotten, and all other such minor details of life were brushed to the side in the minds of the worthy citizens.

Here was a bit of history shoved under their eyes, and history of exactly the type that they were the best fitted to criticize. The voice that called from the distance said: "They've caught Running Deer, and they're bringing him in alive!"

Who Running Deer was I hadn't the slightest idea, except that I knew enough to recognize the title as that of some Indian chief. Then came Running Deer himself at the head of a procession that I could never afterward forget.

6

Except for a loin strap, he was naked; his long hair was decorated with a single feather very much the worse for wear. With his hands tied behind his back, he was mounted upon his favorite war pony, a shaggy little beast with thick legs and a roached back that looked like nothing at all, as the saying is. In spite of this poor outfit, Running Deer looked exactly what he was—the most brilliant and the most famous of the young Cheyenne war chiefs.

Taking them from first to last, I suppose that the Cheyenne was the finest fighting man among the Indians of North America. They were big, strapping fellows; they felt that, man for man, they were the heroes of the world. They carried the impress of this self-confidence in their faces.

Running Deer was an exception among an exceptional lot. He was made like a Greek athlete of the youthful type. He looked like his name, composed specifically for grace

30

and speed, and he had a handsome face. Change the color of his skin, and any white mother would have been glad to have him as one of her children.

This seemingly good-natured red man was taken down the street in the midst of the most triumphant cries and cheers. Those rough fellows, who had been standing about as though they despised everything in the world, now acted like a lot of boys. They capered in front of Running Deer, yelled, and waved their hands. The Cheyenne kept his head high and his eyes straight in front of him. You would have thought, if you looked at his face alone, that he was the conqueror, returning from war, followed by his men and their captives, so contemptuous of his conquered foes that he would not allow that contempt to appear in his features. You would have thought that these yelling whites were the applauding men of his own tribe who had come out of the village to greet him, and that he was mildly displeased with them because they had remained at home.

Then you looked down and saw that he carried no weapons, his hands were tied, and a rope on either side attached his pony to the saddles of two of his captors. Another pair followed behind him with their loaded rifles carried slung under their armpits, so afraid of the tricks of this savage that they were constantly ready and really waiting just to blow him into the next world at a stride.

You had to look at that picture in this way—very closely and seriously—before you could see all the meaning that there was in it.

The longer you looked the more you could see the horrible antipathy of race for race, for instance, with a million years of precedent and custom behind either side —a million years which would have to be unlived before the two could understand one another. The whites looked upon the Cheyenne as if he were a brute fashioned in the shape of a man more or less by accident. The Cheyenne, behind his mask of indifference, regarded the whites as snakes whose fangs it would be a virtuous act to draw.

I write these things with half a century between me and that day. I cannot pretend that I had all of those thoughts at that moment. There wasn't much difference between me and most of the men of that crowd. If anything, that difference was morally in favor of them.

When I saw Running Deer I was chiefly impressed by the fact that he looked like a first-rate fighting man. I said to a fellow near me, as I drew to the side of the street to let the procession pass:

"Who is this Running Deer?"

He flashed one glance at me, irritated to have his eyes dragged away from that picture just then, wondering, too, how any one in the world could fail to understand how important this day was and what was the identity of the Indian.

Then he said: "Running Deer? He's Lost Wolf's best friend—if *that* means anything to you!"

It didn't, of course, more than a mere name. I had heard of Lost Wolf here and there—but in what connection I could not recall. From the intonation of the frontiersman who furnished this information, and from the manner in which he looked on Running Deer—half exultation and half awe—I was prepared to guess at some really tremendous personage in Lost Wolf.

The chief distinction of Running Deer was merely that he was the best friend of *another* Indian. Then what an Indian that second one must be!

I decided that I must elicit more information before I died with curiosity. I could not see this Running Deer now. He was merely a floating shadow of a man. All that I was searching for with greedy eyes was Lost Wolf— the man behind the man.

There were about sixty frontiersmen going by. They were riding either singly or in pairs, a wild motley of men and weapons and horses of all kinds and nationalities. Since there was a good deal of distance between the riders, it took a time for the train to go by.

As it wound along, I shifted my position a little and murmured confidentially in the ear of a companion:

"There'll be a rumpus when Lost Wolf is brought in!"

He looked at me with a cross between suspicion and astonishment.

"Do you think he'll *ever* be brought in?"

"Why not?" said I. "The best redskin in the world has

to go down at last before white men's wits and ways, I suppose. Don't you think so?"

He continued to stare at me, but only with half an eye. The rest of his head was returning to the procession which still filed past, every man sitting particularly straight in the saddle, as if all sixty of them were extra proud because he had had a hand in the capture of a single savage. Which they were, too. Cheyennes were a brand of savage which could not be duplicated in any other part of the world.

Then my new companion said: "Since when did Lost Wolf have a red skin? Can you tell me that, stranger?"

It seemed peculiarly difficult to get any information about this chief out of the crowd. I stepped deeper among the men. I said to the first one whose eye I caught in passing:

"The Cheyennes are a great lot, with two chiefs like Running Deer and Lost Wolf!"

"Good heavens!" this man said in great dismay. "Have they made that fellow a chief, now? When did you get that news?"

He was immensely excited and sought to stop me and get more of the details of this bit of gossip, but I hurried away from him.

I decided that Lost Wolf was one of the queerest creatures in the world if he were an Indian so great that his mere friendship distinguished another brave and made him great. Yet if he were without a following as a chief and if he were even without a red skin—what was he, then?

If I had been curious before, of course, I was in a flame now. I decided that it was hopeless to try to draw out information from these people except by inference and innuendo—getting them to talk about something about which they thought I already knew. That is still the best way with your true Westerner, who still hates to explain the simplest matters to a stranger.

I mixed still deeper in the crowd, and as half a dozen riders went by on the tall, grand-moving horses which were being brought from the East to the plains, just as I had brought Sir Thomas, I said casually to a companion:

"It's a queer thing that those little, ratty Indian ponies can keep away from real horseflesh like this! Still Running Deer and Lost Wolf and their kind must know how to make the most out of those runts!"

This time the man who had caught my words turned around and swore openly in amazement.

"Stranger," said he, "who ever has seen Lost Wolf on anything but the finest hoss that ever stepped on grass?"

I slunk away.

From that moment I began to almost give up hope of ever learning anything about Lost Wolf. No matter what I suggested—and surely everything that I had said had been most probable—I seemed to be wrong—utterly and laughably wrong.

However, in a half-despairing fashion I determined to keep up my crossfire in the hope of raising a little news about the great and absent Lost Wolf.

I retired with Sir Thomas. As the last of the riders went past and most of the crowd followed, I began to pat the shoulder of my beauty, saying quietly to an old chap near by—one philosophical enough to let the others follow the procession without paying any heed to them:

"Well, partner, they'll remember this day, I suppose, now that Running Deer has been brought in!"

"Aye, they'll be apt to remember it!" said he.

It seemed to me that there was an evil light in his eyes. Therefore I added: "You act as though you were in doubt about it being a good thing to bring him in at all."

His eyes glinted at me aside from under his shrubbery of brows.

"I doubt it, right enough," said he.

I waited, sure that he was now excited enough to follow up his last remark without further urging on my part, and I was right.

"Oh, they're pretty happy to-night," said he, "but *I* say that they're a lot of fools! Sixty brave men with the wits enough to get Running Deer, but without the wits to take his scalp and leave him dead out there on the plains!"

"Why," I said, surprised by this calm brutality, "would that really be the best thing?"

He snapped out: "Suppose that you found a bear's cub,

would you take it home and then leave the door open after you got inside your cabin?"

He waited, glaring.

"Well," he added, "how can the door of this town be shut? Will you tell me that? Shut fast enough to keep out Lost Wolf, when he comes raging and ramping into town?"

He was very much worked up and he went on: "There's gunna be dead men around these parts before the morning ever takes a squint at Zander City. But *I* ain't gunna be one of them. I'm gunna be off in the tall timber. I'm gunna jog right along!"

He started up and hurried off as though there were no time to lose.

I gaped after him in amazement. One would have thought that Lost Wolf was resistless wildfire!

7

My personal grudge and rage against the big Doctor was gone, by this time. Not that I had any reason, of course, for hating him the less, but because I had come on the trail of something much larger than he or I. I had before me the graceful figure of Running Deer, whom sixty frontiersmen could rejoice in capturing because he was the friend of Lost Wolf—who was neither chief nor even redskin!

I could learn what had happened this day concerning Running Deer, at the least.

Rene Laforce, that brutal and famous scout from Canada had been in Zander City the day before, when news was brought in that a party of Cheyennes had swooped down on the pasture lands near the town where a large number of horses were grazed, carrying off seven or eight score of them.

Laforce had reputation enough to be given command of the party of riders which started in hot pursuit. They rode fast enough to come up to the heels of the Indians. There were only some dozen or fifteen of these, but, like true Cheyennes under a dauntless leader, they had turned back and started to put up a running fight to keep off the whites, while two or three of the Indians kept the stolen horseflesh on the move.

The leader of this rear-guard action, which cost the men from Zander City three or four casualties, was the brilliant figure of Running Deer. Hard luck followed him at the last, however, and it was chance rather than the skill of the whites that brought him down. The pony he was riding stumbled, catching its foot in a hole in the ground, throwing the young chief so heavily that he was stunned. The Cheyennes turned back to fight for him, but they had no chance. A wave of a score of triumphant men whirled around Running Deer. With this living prize the party turned and started back toward Zander City.

Here was Running Deer among us, and yonder on the prairies was his friend, Lost Wolf.

"But," said I, "I don't see why Lost Wolf is so much to be feared, if he allows his friend to be carried off like that."

I was told that Lost Wolf was not there; that he could not have been there, for had he been present the men of Zander City would have had to pay dearly for their captive.

Here I was met by a current of rumor which I myself had lucklessly started—that Lost Wolf had been made a chief among the Cheyennes!

Too much filled with shame to remain to hear any more after this, I simply hurried along to get as near as I could to the place of activity, which was near Running Deer, of course.

He had been put inside the store of one of the biggest traders in the town. The walls of that building were composed of heavy logs. As it was in a central location, it was felt that a sufficient guard against Lost Wolf would be erected in this manner.

I stepped in and visited an offhand street council on the way, where the matter was seriously debated back and forth. The leading orator of that group maintained that the only politic thing to be done was to turn Running Deer loose as soon as he had procured the restitution of the horses which he had stolen. Because, this town politician of the frontier maintained, Lost Wolf, who up to this time had never taken arms against the whites, would now certainly go on the warpath to avenge the death of his friend. And bitter would be the visitation of his vengeance upon Zander City and all the men thereof! Nothing less than the immediate wiping out of the town was prophesied!

From that place, I went on to the store where the chief was kept. I had no sooner presented myself at the door than I was not only admitted where the rest were kept back, but I was presently offered a position of trust. They wished me to become a member of the group which was guarding the distinguished prisoner.

No young man can refuse anything that smacks of distinction. When you are past thirty the edge of the appetite for fame is a little more slack, whether it has been gratified or not. Up to that age there is nothing like a pat on the shoulder from the right hand. So it was with me, and presently I found myself one of half a dozen men who lounged in the store.

They were experienced men of the frontier. I could see that at a glance. There was responsibility in their faces and pride in their manner, so that I was very glad to be counted one of them. At least, my foolishness of that day, including my trouncing at the hands of The Doctor, had brought me *this* much reward. Zander City was willing to recognize me as a man of might!

I had only a moment for the faces of the other guards, however. They had accepted their task philosophically, and, like men who know how work should be done, three of them were lying down and resting, though not one was asleep. Of the other three, two sat on opposite sides of the spot where the prisoner was tied securely to one of the heavy upright posts that supported the roof of the store. These two, it might be taken for granted, would spot any approaching danger. The third member of the watch faced the prisoner himself, keeping a watchful regard upon the young chief.

A very neat arrangement, if you think it over for a moment. I would not have given a damaged nickel for the chances of Running Deer to escape.

He was the fellow that I wanted to see at close hand, however. My first glance had given me a flashing and a brilliant picture of that captive. Now that I could examine him at my leisure, I saw that I had underestimated him rather than put him above the facts.

He was lean from the labors of a long trail. You could have counted his ribs with the greatest ease. That leanness, like the thin sides of a wolf, rather seemed to make him more formidable. Since all superfluous fat was gone, I could follow the outline of every muscle. He was robed in active strength. Ten thousand whipcords seemed stretching and stirring under his skin whenever he moved.

Yes, he looked the part of a man who would be all teeth, if he were cornered. I remembered at that moment stories which I had heard from men who declared that one white man was enough for any half dozen Indians. I could recall that they had said these things in the quiet warmth of their hearth, long after they had left the ardors of the frontier behind them.

Two men like Running Deer would have coped with any pair of whites that I had ever known!

I could see a broad bruised place on his temple, as large as the heel of my palm. It was greatly swollen. From the skin, which was perfectly black, a number of bristling bits of grass projected. Grass, bits of gravel, and all had lodged in his flesh in his fall, and no one had thought of cleansing the wound.

I stepped closer to him and laid my hand against his forehead. It was what I expected—burning hot! What with exhaustion and the mental strain of his captivity and his hurt, he was in a high fever.

Well, I was as calloused a youth as you could find in a long hunt, but I could not help a feeling of compassion for the Cheyenne in his misery. What touched me

38

most was that an accident had felled him. I knew that the best horse in the world may go down, and the best rider in the world may be thrown.

I remembered, too, having been lost in the country and going without water for twelve hours of a hot summer day. One glimpse of the dried, cracking lips of the Cheyenne told me what he was suffering.

Getting him a quart tin of water, I held it at his lips. He made no move to accept it. I thought I understood him. Perhaps he suspected that the white men would make short work of their problem by poisoning their prisoner. So I tasted the water myself and then offered it to him again.

I shall never forget how his dark eyes flashed suddenly up to me while the dark copper of his skin turned red. He drank, paused with heaving sides, and drank again. He emptied the measure of water and leaned back against the post with his eyes closed—almost overcome with the relief which that draft had given him.

"Why," said one of the guards, "it looks like the Deer is pretty dry. I never thought of that!"

"Let him dry up," said another. "He has given some of our boys worse than that!"

I looked over at the speaker and he looked straight back at me in a very ugly fashion. He was a true-blue Indian hater. You could tell that at a glance. In that day, you were apt to run across one of these fellows in any part of the country, men who had had nothing to do with Indians except when the latter were in their most devilish moods. They could keep your hair bristling all night with tales about atrocities which had been committed by the tribes. A lot of them were true, but nearly all a bit exaggerated.

Very frequently the cause of trouble between the races came from the white man first. Of course, his rascality usually took the form of some merely civil crime—such as giving the redskin light weight and short measures in his trading, or, again, by breaking a little promise. What Indian would think of a lawsuit? He despised methods of talk. He knew nothing but the warpath and the scalping knife to make wrong right.

Not that I am apologizing for the Indians. I don't pretend to know everything about them. Even at the last I was never able to speak any Indian tongue with a real fluency. And who can know any people, really, unless he has mastered their speech thoroughly? I am only frankly setting forth the Indians whom I happened to meet, and what they were at the time I met them, some bad and some good. I have an idea that if one were able to draw a middle line between the two extremes one would find that the Indian's character was just about like the character of a child—a child with the power of a man in his hands!

When I listened to the last speaker and looked across the room to him, into the rage and the scorn that was in his eyes simply because I was daring to extend a little charity to that poor devil of a prisoner, I can assure you that all the doubts I had myself about Indians were banished for the moment under the determination to give still further offense to that Indian hater.

I cast about for a means of giving that offense. That was my motive rather than any Christian charity for the sufferer, I have to admit.

First, I cleaned out that wound of the straws and the bits of gravel. It was horribly inflamed from this dirt and from the long ride in the heat of the sun. On the whole, it was simply remarkable that that man was not raging in a delirium, such was the condition of that wound.

The relief was so great, as I reduced the swelling, that the poor devil broke into a perspiration. I gave him a mere taste of brandy to brace him up a bit. That brought another snarl from the guard, but he had heard enough about me to keep from accusing me to my face. He merely contented himself with muttering and glowering at me.

When this work was ended, I cast about me for some other means of angering my friend, the Indian hater. The sight of a pile of jerky in a corner of the store exactly fitted in with my wishes. I picked up a couple of big strips of that meat, and since the Cheyenne's hands were both tied behind him, I fed him that meat, mouthful by mouthful. He ate like a savage wolf at the edge of death from starvation.

40

All this time he had said not a word. Except for that first upward flash of his eyes, I could not tell whether he were moved or not by my kindness to him. As a matter of fact, as I have already said, I did not care. I was aiming at provoking that other frontiersman, and, indeed, he was raging with anger before I had ended.

Just then, big Laforce came into the store. The aggrieved Indian hater registered a murmured complaint against me, and Laforce instantly granted the complaint.

Perhaps you have heard of Laforce. He was one of the biggest and ugliest men that ever lived. His face was perfectly normal except for one feature. That was an extraordinary growth of flesh about the chin which made him simply horrible to behold.

This Laforce told me, politely enough, that now that he had returned they could dispense with my services, for which he thanked me. Since there was nothing to be done unless, like a fool, I began by questioning his authority, I simply walked out of the store, rather well pleased with myself. Because I was such a fool in those days that next to making a friend I was gladdest of making an enemy, and I succeeded much better in the second line than in the first.

The instant I was out of the store, I was glad that I was in the open, for word came that a message had reached Zander City from Lost Wolf himself!

8

I have forgotten the name of the man. I remember that his arms from which the sleeves of his shirt had been entirely ripped away, were covered with great red freckles, though there were no freckles on his face, the skin of which had been burned by wind and sun until it was leathery.

When I first saw him, he was not doing any great deal of talking. I was one of a hundred or so who crowded around a spot under a big awning which one of the traders had stretched across the front of his shack by way of making a convenient spot of shade. Under this shadow a man was stretched. He had ridden this far into the town of Zander City; there he had tumbled from his horse. Perhaps he would not have received much attention had it not been that he managed to croak out two or three words that brought him instant notice.

He managed to speak the name of Lost Wolf, and that did handsomely for him.

They got him into the shade and there they examined him, finding that he was in a sad way. All except a rag or two of his clothes had been ripped from his body; those that remained to him were tattered. He was oddly injured. Splinters had been driven under his nails. His body was pock-marked with deep burns where other bits of wood had been thrust into his flesh and ignited.

There were other injuries of a minor sort which had appeared on him, and the people looked upon these with the most intense interest. These were the signs of Indian handicraft; and since it was also known that this very man had been in Zander City that morning, it was taken for granted that the Cheyennes were hunting close to the town.

Then someone remembered out loud that he had seen this fellow leave the town in company with the big Doctor before noon of the day! It made my flesh crawl. No matter by what stratagem this poor devil had got away, it was not likely that the Indians would fail to keep a secure hold upon the big Doctor. I did not like The Doctor, obviously. At least, he was more than a name to me, and being that, I could not wish him to be finished in the same manner that this chap had begun.

Brandy and a bit of food worked wonders with him. Presently he was able to sit up and look around him, and although he was so weak that his head hung over one shoulder, he grinned in a half-witted way for pure joy that he found himself recovering his wits among his own kind.

After that, he was able to talk. He said that he had started out with The Doctor, leaving Zander City at an hour which was shortly after my encounter with the latter. They had ridden along for not more than a single mile when a group of men started out at them from shrubbery beside the road. Three of them fastened themselves upon him and mastered him and his guns before he could make powder and lead talk for him.

A single man dashed at The Doctor, and the smaller victim declared that he could not believe his eyes when he saw The Doctor simply lifted from the horse like a child and then gently tied up in a knot!

Now, I was no Hercules, but for my hundred and fifty pounds I was a strong man and I knew how to use that strength to the greatest advantage. Yet I had been a child in the hands of the big Doctor. How was I to believe that another person had been able to treat The Doctor even more contemptuously than he had treated me? There was no such doubt in the minds of the others who were listening to this narrative, however, and a shout came from half a dozen at the same moment: "Lost Wolf?"

The man with the freckled arms nodded. He rested a moment to recruit his strength, while the crowd was spellbound.

He went on to narrate how he and The Doctor had then been carried off to a hollow in the plain where there were half a dozen other braves, and three or four squaws who had been brought along to perform all of the drudgery for the entire party. Lost Wolf now left the camp and rode off for a time. During that interval the women became ugly and finally picked on him, because he showed some fear of them. The braves grew tired of defending him, and they stood by to enjoy the brutal spectacle of the torture.

Here the story ended abruptly, and the teller almost fainted. The sight of that swollen body and the fever places where the fire had burned him was enough to explain why he could not tell about what had followed. He said that he would unquestionably have died in the hands of those female fiends if Lost Wolf had not returned suddenly to the camp and found what was happening. He had the prisoner freed at once, dressed his wounds, and then directed him to return to Zander City, and tell the inhabitants of the town that he was being sent in as a ransom in part for Running Deer, and that the ransom would be completed by the delivery of The Doctor if the town would give up Running Deer in turn.

You would never believe what a commotion that made in the camp. The whole population began to boil over the fire of that question. Even the gamblers came out in their frock coats, the rascals, and gave wise opinions. It was one of them who suggested the course that was finally followed. They declared the proper scheme was to keep no faith with such a man as Lost Wolf but to promise anything, get The Doctor back, and then keep Running Deer, also, until some sort of a court of justice could sit on him.

Perhaps you know what such a court of justice would do? It would find out that a war party had been led by Running Deer, and that during the expedition some whites had been killed or shot down and badly wounded—"with intent to kill!" Because Running Deer was in command, he would be held to be equally guilty, and therefore he would surely be condemned to death without delay.

Justice, I suppose, was in such a judgment, but not the sort of justice that one needed on the prairies, dealing with such a wild people as those. You would not dream of trying to pass a mustang through the tricks of a high-school horse; then why will you expect subtleties of civilization from a redskin?

Not that I attempt to solve the problem. But, at least, I know that the conduct of the people of Zander City was very scoundrelly on this occasion. The tortured man had been told by Lost Wolf how the negotiations might be continued, which was to send a single group of three riders to the top of a hill about five miles from the town, where they would be eventually met by three Indians. There they were to make the contact and exchange prisoners.

So the party set out from Zander City and I was one who watched it pass. I was one, also, who was by when the minister appeared and tried to interrupt proceedings. It was the first time I had ever seen Charles Gleason, and he was a man worthy of being marked. He looked what he was—a reverent worker for the good of others, and never a thought for himself. His seamed, worried face was in a flame when he broke out through the edge of the crowd and stopped the procession down the street.

I heard him cry, when his first protest was overruled: "Men, you forget in the safety of the town that there *is* a God; but when you are on the prairies again in the danger of this same Lost Wolf or of others of his kind, you will remember it again, and then it will be too late. You will want His mercy then, when the Cheyennes are surrounding you and you begin to die under their rifles. But remember the treachery which you plan on this day, and believe that you have already had your reward on earth. You will have no help from Him!"

He carried on some more in this strain, and the party halted there and listened to him quite respectfully, which was a great surprise to me, for they were a good ways from the church-going type. Then a pair of them made some sort of a rejoinder, and they passed on by him and left Zander City.

They accomplished their errand. I was not along, and so I can only repeat what was told to me by those who were at the place. They declared that after the three of them had been for a short time on the appointed hill, they saw three riders coming toward them. These developed to be Lost Wolf and two Cheyenne braves along with him.

He asked what they would do about the bargain which he proposed, and he was told that the town thought well of it. If he would send in The Doctor at once, Zander City would presently return Running Deer to him. To this, Lost Wolf replied that he would not doubt the honesty of the men of Zander City, but that he would live up to his half of the bargain. If they did not do the same on their part, he would make them regret it afterward.

I heard this report. Still I could not believe that Lost Wolf would make such a one-sided offer with no surety whatever. That was exactly what happened, not more than an hour after the return of the three, while the sun

45

was still a few minutes above the edge of the western horizon, The Doctor came back to the town.

He came in a hurry, too, and he went smashing to the center of the town where the street council was still in progress. There were men other than the minister who were in favor of living up to the bargain that they had made, but they were voted down by others who pointed out that so long as they had a good guard kept upon Running Deer, they did not need to be afraid of Lost Wolf.

When The Doctor came in, he thanked the men of the town in a way that showed that he knew what had been spared him, if he had been left with the Cheyennes. When he heard that Running Deer was *not* to be sent back according to promise, I have never seen such a change in a man. He had been standing head and shoulders above the crowd up to that moment. Now he seemed to wilt down into it.

Then he said in a voice that I could hear even at the farther side of the crowd, where I was struggling vainly to come closer to him:

"Gents, I've got a shack in this town—you know the place and the stock that's in it. I refused twenty-five hundred dollars for it this morning. Is Harry Sampson here now that made that offer?"

Harry Sampson spoke up and said that he wasn't in a mood for buying just now. The Doctor bellowed: "Boys, this here is a forced sale and a real one. I'm not going to be in Zander City half an hour from now, because when the boat sails down the river at sunset, I'm going to be on her. Who'll buy my shack and the stuff that's in her? Come on, now, because I mean real business!"

Somebody chipped in with an offer of five hundred and the boys laughed. The Doctor said that that was good enough for him; that he was bound to go.

"Look here, Doctor," said somebody else, "if you're afraid of Lost Wolf, you're a fool. There are enough men in this town to protect you from twenty fellows like him!"

"Are there," asked The Doctor, "as many real men as that in this town? Then you know them, but I don't. I haven't seen that many in all the time that I've been out

46

here in the West. But I *have* seen Lost Wolf—and I've felt him!"

He laughed, and that laughter of his was worth hearing. I can tell you that there wasn't any mirth in it. What most paralyzed me with astonishment was that a man like The Doctor would stand up there, without shame and confess his fear. Just as you or any other man would be willing to confess to your fear of a lion or a tiger, say!

The sale went on. Harry Sampson broke in with a bid of a round thousand; he was bucked up to thirteen hundred and got the shack at that price—hardly more than half of what had been refused that same morning.

I saw The Doctor collect his money, break from the crowd, and rush for the river dock where a load had been jammed aboard the same boat that had brought me to Zander City that same morning. I had no great temptation to step out and bar his path. I had found him a desperate and dangerous fighter when he was perfectly calm and at rest. I had no desire to cross him now that he was maddened with terror.

He got onto that boat, and he was so happy about being there that we saw him do a war dance on the deck.

When that steamer was out of sight around the first bend, there was a consultation in Zander City. The sun was just down, and the sinking of it seemed to take a lot of courage out of some that had been very bold, just before. When fear had shown in such a man as The Doctor, it opened the way for fear to appear in others, too. Ten minutes later it was unanimously voted that Running Deer should be delivered, true to the terms of the contract!

9

I wasn't surprised that they changed their minds. I would simply have been *very* much surprised if they hadn't, because this affair of The Doctor's flight was enough to send a chill through me. If you had seen him and *felt* him, as I did, you would have agreed with me, I have no doubt.

It was a great sight to see Running Deer brought out from the prison in which he had been kept. No doubt he had despaired of life a hundred times while he was in it, but when he came out, he was as calm as stone. They had given him a buffalo robe—so much had he risen in their estimation and value since it was known that he was to go free—and they restored to him his war pony. He rode out of Zander City at a walk, though a shudder must have run through his flesh when he found his back turned upon such enemies as he could not help knowing that he had in that town. I watched him out of sight; then I started hunting for a place to spend the night.

There would be plenty of ways of spending the evening, as I could see. The moment the sun went down Zander City began to light up; new voices were heard, and like rats out of holes, where they had been hiding during the day, men came out to work for their living by lamplight—at card tables, and the like. Zander City had looked rough and tawdry, only, in the sun; when the lamps were lighted there was a lure about it.

One forgot that the prairie was a flat sea of land all around; one remembered the great arch of the sky above, and looked toward the stars.

There would be plenty of ways of spending the evening,

and I was anxious to enter a dozen doors that I marked as I went down the street, because I liked cards as well as the next man, and had already won and lost my little fortunes.

Nobody but a fool spends the evening without having provided for the night. I began to hunt for a lodging. The first "hotel" at which I inquired was built nine-tenths of canvas and one-tenth of unplaned boards, and I was showed to a little cubby-hole about two by six. I could have that bed in the night. It was occupied in the day.

This was not for me. I was never rough enough to enjoy that sort of thing. I continued my search until one rough proprietor bellowed at me: "What d'you take this for? The minister's house?"

That put an idea in my head. When the minister's house was pointed out to me, I saw a good-sized, well-built house with a neat garden around it, and was glad of the sight, I can tell you. I had no doubt that the very thought of a minister's presence was enough to scare most of the choice spirits of the town away from that house, but I was not of that kind. I had sense enough to realize that a minister is just as human as the next man, and I was willing to put up with a little cant for the sake of a fair deal of cleanliness and good cooking. Also, I did not see how any man of God could possibly charge such outrageous rates as the professional hotel keepers of Zander City.

I went up to the door and knocked. It was opened to me by a girl in blue calico—the prettiest girl in the world! I only had a flash of her eyes opening at me, and I heard her say that she would ask her mother.

Then her mother came; she was *not* the prettiest thing in the world. Oh, she had been handsome enough in her time, I have no doubt, but where girls come by their beauty I never could understand. I have never seen a case of true inheritance. Now and then, heaven opens on a birth and gives a girl child the golden touch.

So it was with the minister's daughter, Peggy.

When I saw Marcia Gleason for the first time, I simply wanted to turn around and run. She had been working in flour. It was still in the creases of her fingers; it was dusted over her forearms. They were big arms, but the fat could

49

not completely disguise the muscle that lay beneath. The breadth of her knuckles was convincing, too. Instantly I made up my mind that I did not have to ask who was the master in this house. At least, I did not care to have any trouble with the *mistress thereof*.

She said to me: "Yes, young man, I take lodgers and boarders, now and then, when I get ones with good recommendations, and I don't mind saying that it's a pretty hard job to find that same in this town. Who sent you to me?"

It angered me a little. I have known a great many people who like frank, outspoken women. I hate them. When a woman loses her sweetness, she might as well cease life, too. Because all that she becomes then is a sort of imitation of a man, and they are not the stuff of which men can be imitated well.

At any rate, this Marcia Gleason loomed over me with her talk about recommendations, and such things, until I was an angry man, I can tell you.

I said: "I was sent here by a hotelkeeper in the town who said: 'You must be looking for the minister's house.' So I took him at his word, and here I am."

She opened her eyes a little at this and gave the door a half swing, as though she would have slammed it in my face.

Many a time thereafter I have heard her wish aloud that she *had* slammed it in my face, because that would have shut out a great deal of trouble from the life of her family. However, she didn't quite make up her mind.

When a woman is a bully, she is three times as cruel as any man. This woman was a bully, you see, and it rather amazed her to hear such talk. Because you can depend upon it that the more vigorously masculine a woman is, the more certainly she will demand that she be treated like a lady of the gentlest breeding! Your Western women have their grand qualities, but that's apt to be their defect.

She jerked the door wide and said: "Come in, young man."

I followed her into the parlor, and she sat me down in the first comfortable chair that had received me since I left Charleston. Then she leaned her elbows on her knees and her chin on her fists. She said:

"You've had education, I see. You speak well enough. So what are you doing out *here*?"

"Watching the natives and their queer ways," said I.

"You act," said she, "as if you meant to include me in the list."

"Madame," said I, "I am afraid that you are suspicious."

"Humph!" she said, doing her thinking shamelessly aloud. "Sometimes these frank men are honest, and sometimes they are the worst crooks in the whole lot. I suppose that you haven't got any recommendation?"

"I didn't think that recommendations were needed on this side of the Mississippi," I told her. Then I got up to leave.

She said: "You can stay! I like something about the sassy way that you have with you. But hold on. Let me have a look at your horse!"

She went to the front door and looked at Sir Thomas. By her exclamation I knew that she understood horses. It warmed my heart toward her not a little.

She said: "That puzzles me more than ever. No man in Zander City ought to have a horse as fine and as fast as that unless he is a born gentleman and can afford the luxury—or unless he *needs* to have all of that speed at his command!"

She turned around and glared at me in her frank, manly way. "I wonder what *you* are?" said she.

"I don' know," said I.

"Humph!" said she. "You won't give me a single trick, I see. And I'll have to take you into the house if for nothing else than to find you out. You can bring your things in, I suppose!"

I went out to get my pack off the back of Sir Thomas, and I heard Mrs. Gleason sing out: "Peggy, go open the windows in the side bedroom."

"They have enough money to keep a servant—a little negress or a half-breed," said I to myself, and I trudged up the stairs with my pack.

When I got to the side bedroom, the girl of the front door came out into the hall and gave me a sort of half-frightened smile of apology, as though she had been intruding by entering a room that was to be mine!

That was Peggy!

I dumped my pack on the floor of that room and kicked the door shut. Then I slumped down on the bed with my chin in my palm and groaned. I could feel it coming over me; there was the same sickness in the pit of the stomach, waviness in front of the eyes, and fluttering in the heart. That sounds like a description of homesickness, perhaps. It will do equally well for love.

I had been in love nearly every year of my life since I was twelve. Each time, it was just the same. I would have married any one of the lot, and after marriage, I suppose that I would have sworn that I never could have been happy with any other woman. Then along came a trip to a new county, or her other and older beau showed up. So I was left heartbroken until another pretty girl came along.

I have this satisfaction—they were all pretty, they were all gentle. Too, they were all tender. A score of them would not have been able to rake together enough brains to overstock any one head. All the same, each of them was wonderful, feminine—with the golden touch which can burn a Troy or build it again.

As I sat on the bed, I said aloud: "That is her mother's work—calling a young nymph, a goddess, a perfectly sweet thing like that by such a name as—Peggy! Peggy for that!"

So spoke I, aloud, but in my heart of hearts I was groaning because I knew that I had been touched to the heart by the fatal arrow again. Already I was such an old hand in these affairs that I did not even waste time hoping; I simply wondered how long the ravages of the disease would continue before it had worked out its strength. Because I was never what you could call a successful lover. I lacked the flash and the fire of the perfect liar. That is what one needs to be in order to win one of those flowers of whom I am speaking—that, or else wear a uniform, coming newly home from the wars with a bar or two on the shoulders and a casual air of speaking of the deaths which have rubbed elbows with you now and anon.

I lacked those graces; therefore I merely sat there and half closed my eyes, wondering, bitterly, how long it would last.

10

A long time! I was sure of that when I saw her at the dinner table. She waited on the table, and, as I watched her slip from her chair to go to the kitchen for this or that, my heart was snatched further and further away from the region of common sense.

There was ways and ways of rising from a chair. The usual way begins with a backward hitch of the chair and a forward bend of the body that almost throws the chin against the edge of the table. Then there is a convulsive heave upward and a screech of the chair, as the legs are ground shuddering against the floor.

There are other ways, too. But only once or thrice in a lifetime is it given to see a person who can dip into a chair and out of it with no more effort than a swallow dipping down and up in mid flight. When you find that rare being who can stand up without fracturing a smile or breaking a sentence, stand and watch and drink in the sight with reverence, because it is one of the world's rarest and most beautiful wonders, too.

All of this was Peggy Gleason. Except that one cannot say it in prose.

Prose adds one to one quietly and methodically until it reaches its comfortable thousand or two, after a time of labor. Verse hitches together one and two, and suddenly out of a few units strikes forth a million. Out of the dry stalk of a few words it evokes a blossom, an eternal flame. One needs such a medium for talking of Peggy Gleason.

I hardly dared to look at her, for I felt myself growing pale, but I kept up the end of a conversation with the minister and his wife—chiefly with his wife. For he was weary, poor fellow, and once when he closed his eyes and leaned back in his chair there was such sorrow and exhaustion in his face that it looked like a death's head.

Some men are like that. Nothing lives in their faces except their eyes. There's the soul which keeps on burning and throwing out a light against all reason, defying the mechanical laws in a thousand ways.

Charles Gleason was that sort of a man; I could not get a spark from him, except a kind word or two of greeting—even when I told him that I had been standing by and had heard him protest against the cheating of Lost Wolf. He merely smiled faintly to thank me for that praise. That shrew of a wife of his broke in:

"Young man, I'll wager that you kept that admiration of yours thoughtfully silent when a word or two spoken out loud might have bucked up my Charlie in the face of the crowd!"

Trust her to find a tender point in any conversation and then put her heel down upon it—and grind!

The minister merely said he hoped she would stop. Then he said that it had been a sweet moment to him when they had decided to keep to their contract with Lost Wolf.

"The scoundrels were afraid not to!" said Mrs. Gleason.

"No, no, Marcie," said he, "but the good that was in them was only stifled for a moment. The evil chokes back our better impulses too often. And it's only on second thought that we do what is right. If only we can be brave enough to change our minds!"

I quote that to show you the difference between the man and his wife. He was all gentleness; she all hardness and sharpness.

"Nonsense!" said she. "Sometimes you positively talk like a fool, Charlie! There's nothing in the world to control these ruffians, except a loaded gun or a horsewhip!"

I felt that that was rather a cut at me, and I glanced across the table. Mrs. Gleason was not staring back at me, as she would have been sure to do in case she had meant a stab at me, but was looking down thoughtfully.

The minister smiled sadly and shook his head. He would not argue beyond a phrase or two. Though, as long as I was with them, I never could make out whether it was because he had reasoned out the truth about her, which was that argument had no force against her prejudice, or that he simply had not the strength to waste upon her.

She ranted a while longer on the subject; then she whirled on me and cried: "And I suppose that you have come up here ready to shoot it out with the first man that argues with you?"

I told her that I was not raised to treat discussion in that fashion, and that I trusted that I should not have to use a gun.

She nodded approvingly at me. She even said: "I believe that, young man. I believe that there is no such tomfoolery in you. Because I've noticed that when a man is so bold with his words as you are, he's not so apt to be ready with his hands!"

That was the way with Marcia Gleason. She could not pat you on the back with one hand, without knocking you down with the other heavy fist! Confound such women!

However, I made the most of this cheap inning and pretended not to have understood that there was a sting in her words. I said I hoped that I would have no trouble while I was in Zander City or in other parts of the West; that my one desire was to live peaceably.

This speech was a good deal applauded by the minister.

He said: "Now that is what I call sense—good Christian sense. The bigger part of our young men can't think of anything, except to make a name for themselves with guns in their hands! But the quiet way and the way of the law is the best way, after all!"

That was a type of the speeches of Charles Gleason. He was one of the best men in the world and one of the dullest. I suppose that you have wondered at that fact as often as I have—why is goodness so often stupid?

Mrs. Gleason could only mumble, but a minute later she was haranguing her husband, telling him that he must go over and lecture their next-door neighbors and get

55

compensation from them. The new dog had broken into the yard and killed one of the Gleason chickens. Mr. Gleason endured this tirade in a weary silence—or at most returned only a curt word or two now and then.

I watched the face of the girl, and I pitied her. She had a good deal of this sort of thing to endure, I presume, and yet she could never have grown accustomed to it. All during the altercation her glances were going back and forth from one of them to the other; her eyes were big in sympathy, or shrinking in concern.

I wanted to use a horsewhip on that mother of hers. I wanted most of all to ask some oracle how it was that such a woman could have had such a child.

Just then I was given something else to think about because a neighbor's wife came to the kitchen door of the Gleason house to borrow a cup of sugar and lingered there for a few moments to gossip. What they gossiped about I was not left long to wonder at, because Mrs. Gleason came back with her face white with anger. She sat down and fixed an eagle eye on me.

"You are the young man who never wants to use a gun?" said she.

I looked up at her and saw that my finish was about to come, and that she intended to lay me out. I wanted to get up and run out of the room, but I couldn't run away while the big, startled eyes of Peg Gleason were there to watch me.

So I sat and endured.

"You want no trouble!" said Mrs. Gleason with a bitter irony. "But an attack on a harmless teamster doesn't seem like trouble to you, I presume, and neither does a fist fight with that great lank brute, The Doctor, seem like trouble to you. To say nothing of horsewhipping the gun out of the hand of a man and then flogging him. Charlie, what sort of a man have you let into our house?"

This was a specimen of her logic. She was not blaming her husband because *she* had let me into the place! Oh, she was a cheerful lot!

"And then," cried Mrs. Gleason, while her husband and daughter laid down knife and fork to stare at me, "and then parade up and down through the streets of

56

the town and challenge The Doctor—*or any of his friends*—to dare to come out and fight you to the death with—oh, young man, did you think that we were *fools* in this house, to swallow your lies and—"

"Marcia!" said her husband.

"Mother!" whispered Peg.

"A falsehood is a falsehood," said Mrs. Gleason, "and I have the right to call it by its own name!"

"Madame," said the minister, "you are using such language while you sit at my table?"

"And where should I be sitting?" said Mrs. Gleason. "But this young rascal—"

"Peace!" said the minister.

He hadn't raised his voice, but there was a cutting edge to it, I can tell you. His eye was just about thirty degrees colder than the freezing point. Mrs. Gleason gave a wail and stammered something about scoundrels dragged into the house against her will by a stupid husband. Then she ran from the room, and in the distance could be heard sobbing—or groaning—with rage. I couldn't tell which.

It wasn't a pretty scene. I got up and bowed to Mr. Gleason and thanked him for his kindness.

"But," I said, "I *did* lie to your wife, or before her, and I suppose that I'm not a bit more peaceful than most other young men in this town. I won't stay here to trouble her, of course!"

Mr. Gleason hesitated, looking at me with much trouble in his face. The girl cried, in a whisper of horror: "Father, you will not let him be driven out!"

She, poor saint, had taken pity upon me. She wouldn't have me thrown out into that rough town. Her eyes were shining, and her lips were trembling with emotion. Her beauty and her gentleness made my brain swim.

"You are right, Margaret," said her father. And I thought that this name came like a benediction from his lips. It fitted her so much more musically well than the curt nickname. "You are right. I do not wish to have you go, Mr. Rivers. Promise me that you will remain here with us. Mrs. Gleason will be eager to make you amends."

I should never have remained, of course, except for the girl. I knew that Gleason was speaking out of a sense of the purest duty, only, but that made no real difference. What I wanted was a chance to remain close to Margaret Gleason. At the cost of a great deal of shame, I remained.

But Margaret? There was no sense in her that a proud man should not have done as I did on this occasion. No, she shone with respect and with admiration as she watched me.

I was a dazzled man, with a heart crashing and thundering in my breast, when I went upstairs to my room, at the last.

11

There I sat by the window for a long time, wondering how this miraculous chance had come to me, for I knew that I had stirred the heart of Margaret Gleason somewhat as she had stirred mine. I did not have to learn of it in words, because there was not sham in her sufficient to mask what she felt. She let it fly up into her eyes; it was visible as a flame in a lamp, showing me all that was in her soul.

That utter simplicity in her filled me with fear—fear, you understand, lest I should ever be a thing to her other than perfectly respectful and reverent. Next of all, I wondered what it could be that had touched her? Certainly no words that I had spoken and nothing graceful that I had done. I hit on it at last, and when I found the thing I laughed silently, with amazement and with shame and with pity.

It was that recital that her mother had poured forth to abash me—that wild tale about fighting The Doctor, and then about challenging the entire town. That had been the appeal to beautiful Peggy, of course. It was just the flare of something novel which attracted her, and out of her own childish imagination she made me a hero.

I wasn't flattered a great deal. I don't know why. It simply shamed and abashed me, for I knew in my heart of hearts that I had intruded myself into her attention by false pretenses. Yet I sat trembling and almost sick by that window for hours and hours with the thought of Margaret, like a sword of joy and of pain thrusting through and through my brain.

But I slept, too—a sound, deep sleep that let me waken fresh enough in the dawn. I went down the stairs to the garden and there I met Margaret Gleason running around the path beside the house. She stopped with the air of one about to run away in fear, but, as I stepped aside for her and smiled, she smiled back at me and hurried on.

Her apron was filled with fresh-cut flowers, but that was not the fragrance that made me lean dizzily against the side of the house.

When I went on again I encountered the last person that I wanted to meet; that was Mrs. Gleason on her knees, thrusting a trowel into the garden mold with an arm so stout that the blade was fleshed to the handle, at every stroke. I would have turned away, but she, who saw all things, even when her back was turned, called out to me:

"Come here, young Mr. Rivers."

There was not more ceremony than you would use in speaking to a dog. I had to obey her or else appear a sulky fool. Just the same, my dignity was grievously offended. I stalked around and stood before her.

"Hold that bush by the head while I pack the mold around its roots," said she.

It was a rose bush, and the thorns sank unexpectedly into all the tender places in the palm of my hand. However, I would not have murmured, not even if my hand had been cut off at the wrist.

She moved that bush from one place to another, and she kept me holding the infernal thing while she sifted fertilizer and soft loam around the roots of the plant. At last she finished and looked up at me for the first time.

She merely said: "Well, you have done a good deed

for *once* in your life—or helped in the doing of it, at least!"

I did not smile. One did not have to smile when one talked with Mrs. Gleason, and that was a blessing. One could look her in the eye.

"Dear, dear," said she. "*how* you hate me! So did poor Charles when he first met me—the lamb!"

I grew red at the thought that I, too, might develop a weakness for this huge, burly woman. She saw my color and laughed loudly in my face.

"Well," said Mrs. Gleason, "you are a little pale. I see that you did not sleep too well last night in your new room. Was the mattress hard?"

"No," said I, "the room does very well."

"Sometimes," said she, "there are thoughts that make harder lying than a stiff mattress. Much harder!"

She looked at me sharply in the eye, making no secret of the eagerness with which she was scrutinizing me.

"I thought," said she at last, "that the damage was all on one side, but I see that it's not, and that makes the trouble doubly bad!"

I told her that I didn't know what she was talking about.

"And you don't care, either, I suppose," said she, "but you very soon will before you are more than a minute older, Mr. Reeves."

"Rivers is the name," said I.

"Rivers—Reeves—Robbers—what's in a name?" said she. "Well, young man, my daughter had a restless night, too."

No one could have thought it. No one could have been prepared for such a thing. It took me, as the saying is, between wind and water, and I was instantly a sinking ship. I could not control my color, my eyes, or my facial expression. At a glance, she could see my heart.

I wished that there had been poison for her in it!

"It is working in you, I see," said this most disagreeable of women. "Now and then it strikes a man. With all of her simplicity Margaret seems to work quickly enough. And so, sir, you are one of the unlucky ones!"

I was so angry that I could not help blurting out:

"Madame, may I ask how it is determined beforehand that I am to be unlucky—unless *you* are the only judge?"

"Meaning that I hate you?" said she. "No, I don't hate you. I like you better than I do most youngsters—a great deal better, because there is some spirit in you. Just the same, I don't like you well enough to want to see you the husband of a girl like Peggy. Not I!"

"I have not asked for her hand," said I. "It seems to me that you are carrying very far forward, Mrs. Gleason."

She merely laughed at me. She didn't care a whit for her own dignity, so long as she could succeed in stripping away the dignity of all the people with whom she had anything to do.

"Well," said she, "I don't have to call myself a prophet when I say that you *will* be asking for her hand. But it won't do, Mr. Rivers. I want to tell you in the first place," she went on, with a hard glint in her eyes, "that Mr. Gleason and I are not fools. We have not had a diamond put into our hands in order that we should throw it away."

I could not help breaking out at her. *Any one* with the least spirit must have done the same thing. I said:

"Mrs. Gleason, I don't know what you mean by that sort of talk unless you imply that I am without decent honor. I don't like this mode of talk and I don't intend to remain here to listen to it any longer."

I made a step away from her. She stopped me with her abrupt, masculine voice.

"You'll hear the rest of what I have to say. As a matter of fact, I'm only sorry that this thing has happened. I don't really wish you any harm. The lie you told me last night was a small thing—by way of making conversation, one might say. But I know that nothing *I* can do will stop you paying your attentions to Peggy. And I know, furthermore, that there is nothing so certain to make a fool out of a girl as to give her the idea that her lover is being persecuted. No, young man, I am not going to persecute you. You are welcome to stay here, I suppose, until this disease has worked its course in Peggy, poor child! It is the first time that she has ever been infected, and I trust that the sickness will wear away soon. Heaven alone knows what there is about you that could have upset her so much, and so soon!"

I suppose that you have never been baited like this—at least, not by a woman. The only real answer was to strike. But a woman knows the immense bulwark behind which she can shelter herself.

So I said: "Frankly, the damage was done by your own silly talk."

She fired up at that. "My *silly* talk?" cried she. "And pray, young man, what might you mean by that?"

"You are so busy holding up the mirror for other people that you never take a look at yourself," said I. "It was your nonsense that you talked last night at the table, when you were denouncing me. You made me out a sort of hero. And while you were scoring me, every word that hit me, was lifting me a notch higher in the eyes of Margaret."

Her eyes flashed, and her lips parted to speed a smashing rejoinder at me. Then she went blank as the realization of the truth came home in her. She drove the trowel almost out of sight in the damp ground with a stroke of her powerful arm, exclaiming:

"By heavens, that *is* it!"

I smiled sourly down at her. She went on:

"While I painted you a villain, the other side of the picture was a hero!"

"Exactly," said I.

"Ah, well," said she, "I must find a way to undo that harm."

And she added: "Unless you go on and actually live up to that reputation!"

"And get myself killed in the act?" said I. "Thank you! But I prefer life!"

"Mr. Rivers," said she, "I thank you for your candor. In the meantime, I have talked this matter over with my husband."

I made a wry face, but she went on with a man's grin.

"Oh, he has good sense, even if he is a minister. He and I have agreed that the best way is to keep you right here in the house as long as you'll stay."

It was another side of her nature. The brighter side of the dollar, as you might say.

"Very well," said I, "I take that for a challenge. I am to stay here and court Margaret—openly?"

"I suppose that that is the name for it," said she.

"And who is the referee to say when I have won?"

She became very grave.

"I think that we will all know when the thing is inevitable," she said.

It sobered me to see the roughness in her disappear and the mother in her flash to the surface. I bowed to her and was about to try to make a graceful little speech when she cried: "Here comes that odious Tom Mitchell! I hope that *he* is not one of your new-found friends in Zander City!"

12

He was not. He was not my friend or any one's friend. When I saw him sauntering up the street, I was able to catalogue him easily enough as that worst type of border ruffian. I mean, the type who wraps himself in a pretense of culture and good manners. His pretense did not go very much further than the trim of his long mustaches, which he curled out instead of allowing it to droop straight down. In addition to that, he wore a beard and a wide-brimmed black hat that furled up a little on one side where he took hold of it, when he raised it. He bore himself with dignity, and yet he was not such a complete picture as he would have liked to think.

He gave his hat a flourish when he raised it to Mrs. Gleason. That old Tartar simply grunted and went on with her gardening. Then Mitchell called me over to the fence and introduced himself, saying that he had heard a good deal about me since I came to Zander City the week before. I told him I had not been there twenty-four hours, and he pretended to be surprised, saying that I had done more in that time than most people accomplish in months.

Well, this crude stuff didn't interest me, but I tried to be polite, while I wondered what he was trying to get out of me. Finally it came out. He said that when the final agreement was made with Lost Wolf, the point had been stressed by the whites that in giving up a chief so famous as young Running Deer, they were more than surrendering the face value of two fellows like the Doctor and his companion. Lost Wolf had agreed and declared that the town should not have cause to complain of his gratitude. Now word had come in to Zander City from him, that he would be prepared on this day to make good his word. He only specified that Rivers should be the man who must come out to receive the gratuity for Zander City.

Mitchell pretended that I should regard this as an honor, but I asked him point blank what reason there was that Lost Wolf should wish to see me rather than any other. Mitchell had the coolness to say that, unquestionably, it was because he had heard so much about my actions in Zander City. I merely laughed in the face of the rogue. He had the grace to blush, but he said that he hoped I would go out and negotiate with Lost Wolf, because the friendship of that chief would mean a great deal to the entire town.

Why I agreed I hardly know. Unless it was that irresponsible impulsiveness which is apt to take possession of young men. I knew a good deal about the cruelty of Indians. I had heard plenty of stories about their treachery and their atrocities, but as a matter of fact I was overwhelmed with an immense curiosity. The wife of Bluebeard never felt so keen a desire to see the secret chamber as I felt to see this man who had mastered the giant Doctor as easily as I might have mastered a child.

The men of Zander City wondered at me for a perfect fool, but before that morning was two hours older, I had mounted my horse and started out from the town. When I got well out from Zander City in the westerly direction I had been told to pursue, my nerve began to fail. I told

64

myself that Sir Thomas would be able to snatch me away from any danger that was not *too* imminent. I could trust to his speed on this day, as I had trusted to it so often before.

Five miles from the town, nothing had happened worth notice except that I scared up a great buffalo wolf out of a shrub that I passed near and sent the monster loping across the plain. There must have been a hundred and fifty pounds of him, and as he labored across the plain the loose flesh and hair along his back rolled into a bunch above his shoulders at every stride. The strangest feature of him was his color. I have seen pale yellow wolves, but this one seemed extremely close to pure white.

I watched the beast running away from me and then reached for my rifle because I wanted to have that strange-colored pelt. The minute I had the rifle out of it sheath, the wolf darted aside into the brush. When I rode hastily up to the spot, it had disappeared. Another instance of what every old hunter knows—that hunted animals know the meaning of a gun.

So I went on my way. I had not gone another mile before I saw a mounted figure on the top of a swell of land just in front of me. An Indian, he appeared, with one hand lifted high above his head in token of greeting.

Even at that distance, I knew that this was Lost Wolf. There was not apt to be two such figures on the whole range of the prairies. I brought Sir Thomas down to a walk and came up at this pace, straining every nerve to alertness, and sweeping the whole prairie before me in a great anxiety. At the first token of danger, I was ready to wheel Sir Thomas on a tight rein and spur him away like the wind for Zander City.

When I came closer still, I saw that even the speed of Sir Thomas was apt to be useless. This solitary rider was mounted on a red horse—a true blood-chestnut with the mane and tail more red than chestnut. It was a stallion, with the look of a king and the lines of a thoroughbred. Some people have said that that famous horse was a mustang, and a throwback to the beauty of the original barb and Arab stock which the Conquistadores brought to the New World. I think that I know enough about horseflesh to deny that suggestion with authority. In every line he told of the finest blood that ever appeared in the horse world—the blood of the English race horse. He had the legs, and that is the great answer. I have seen beautiful Arabs and great barbs, but I have never seen one of them with the ground-devouring legs of the thoroughbred. He had the big flat bone, too, and the power in his shoulders and haunches might have carried two men as easily as one.

He needed a good part of that extra power, you can be sure, for the horse was the only proper pedestal for the man. Except that you would have called the horse a plain beauty and the man was a plain terror. He would never have done in a romantic book for the hero. He was a big, ugly devil with two hundred pounds of wild-cat muscle to make his devilishness more effective.

He had straight black hair that reached his shoulders. He had broad, high cheekbones of true Indian pattern. He had jet-black eyes and a broad mouth. These were all the true features of the Indian; so was the polished copper appearance of his skin. But I could understand, I thought, why he was not considered a redskin in Zander City. Indeed, it was quite possible that there was white blood mixed in him. His chin was the blunt, broad chin of a pugilist. I have never seen such a chin in barbarous, colored races. His forehead would have done for a philosopher or a poet.

I saw those things, however, rather because I was staring at him very hard, trying to solve the mystery which was gathered around him in my mind. Put him among a thousand Indians, and the best judge in the world could never have picked him from the ranks unless he had been warned beforehand what to look for.

You wouldn't look too long at the face of this man, I think, any more than you would spend your hour examining the carved handle of a pistol. What counted was the barrel of the gun. What counted in a plainsman was the strength he had that would execute his designs. This man had the strength: Two hundred pounds of it, distributed from head to foot unevenly and not prettily. His shoulders were too broad; his arms were too long, and

66

his hands were too large. His legs were a tangle of power; still they did not match the torso. His waist and hips looked pinched and starved compared with the upper man. I don't mean to give the impression that he was a deformed creature or a freak. I simply mean that you would say, instantly, that here was an Indian who would not be so much at home running across the prairie as he would be on the back of a horse. The red stallion was not merely a pedestal. He seemed actually like a part of the man. One saw the glorious strength and beauty of the red horse, the savage, indomitable face of the rider, and the corded might of the shoulders and the great arms of Lost Wolf.

I had looked upon The Doctor as one of the most formidable men in the world in hand-to-hand battle. Now, that I had looked upon this denizen of the prairies, I knew at once that we had not heard any fable in Zander City. This fellow could easily lift The Doctor into the air and break him in two before he touched the ground.

He did not wear the universal buffalo robe, this being the warmer part of the year. He was contented with a deer skin, covered with beautiful dapplings, fastening under an armpit and over the opposite shoulder, leaving it to flow down gracefully over the back of the saddle. He wore nothing except moccasins and a loin strap. In his hair were thrust two or three long eagle feathers, with their tips dyed purple, yellow, and red.

He held a rifle which I recognized as one of the new-model Winchesters which were making such a sensation on the prairie lands at that time; a pair of heavy Colts were thrust into the saddle holsters; and a great hunting knife attached to the girdling thong of his loin strap, in front of the right hip.

Altogether, he looked completely the savage, and completely the king. He might not be a chief, but a chiefdom could not have added to his dignity.

My first shock was his voice, which addressed me in perfectly pure and grammatical English. He said: "I am glad that you have come; but there is another who will be happier than I. Will you come with me, friend? I am Lost Wolf."

All this was said gently, while his black eyes searched

67

me through and through, with a friendly glance. This greeting was enough for me. I was mightily afraid of this terrible giant, of course, but I decided that so long as I did not offend him, I could trust him as thoroughly as any white man I had ever met in my life, perhaps a little more so. I was also convinced that if I *did* offend him, it would not take much to bring that sheath knife glancing from its case to my throat.

I decided to be on my watch every instant and use all the courtesy that I could, mingled with dignity. And so we started across the prairie. Before we had gone a hundred yards I pulled up my horse with an oath and snatched out my rifle.

"Lost Wolf!" cried I to him. "There is a white wolf, the first I have ever seen. Shall we shoot it?"

"Do not shoot," said Lost Wolf, "because that is one of my friends."

13

It sent a chill through me, as you may imagine, hearing a man speak in this casual manner of a brute beast as though it had a human soul in it. I remembered that, according to the name, this was a wolf who sat on the horse beside me, and I wondered just how far some native superstition might account for the attitude of the prairie dweller.

I lost sight of the white wolf a moment later, however, and so we went on for a few moments in silence, Sir Thomas striding large and free, as though disdaining to be held equal with any other horse; the red stallion drifting across the plain like a blown wraith, effortless and unconcerned. One can tell a good deal about a horse by the way it stands, but this lazy galloping stride of the red horse was a revelation to me, and I knew that I never could trust to the speed of Sir Thomas as long as this monster was in the race.

We made a smoke on the horizon, now; it grew in distinctness until we could see the camp there, and a black scattering of animals near by. Another rider came out to meet us. I recognized Running Deer.

Then the explanation flashed vividly over me. Running Deer was the chosen friend of Lost Wolf. I had done certain small offices for Running Deer. Therefore the Wolf would make his gift to the town through my hands.

The frigid calm of Running Deer, which I had seen when he was a captive in Zander City, was quite dropped from him now. He shook my hand and smiled upon me with the affection of a brother, speaking rapidly in Cheyenne, which Lost Wolf translated.

"Running Deer is a happy man to see his kind friend once more. He has not forgotten the thirst which was eating his heart in the circle of the white man. You gave him to drink. He has not forgotten the pain of his wound which you dressed and cleaned. He has not forgotten the weakness of hunger, but you made him strong with food."

A very formal acknowledgment, as you must admit, considering the meager nature of the service which I had performed for the captive Indian. However, they took me on to the camp and I was greeted like a long lost brother.

Those red rascals had gathered together a dozen men who were all, as I took it, people of importance in their tribe. As each of these men came up, I was told his name and he made me a little speech filled with compliments and hope for a happy future for me.

It was desired that I should have many squaws and not a laggard among them. It was hoped that I would have so many sons that I might be a great chief, having only my own family to command. It was fervently wished that there might be a lasting peace in my tepee, and that the herds of my horses would increase.

Not in heavy, formal language—but simply, directly, gravely. Not book talk at all!

Every time one of those chiefs came up to me, he gave me something. These were not presents for Zander City. These were presents for me, in person. Because young Running Deer had sworn that he would have died of sickness and hunger and thirst, had not I helped him, and, having helped him, I had brought him good fortune, also. That was believed, too. Luck was not just a shuddery superstition but fact with them.

They brought me their gifts and made a little speech about everything that they gave me. You can believe me when I tell you that an Indian is free-handed, but he likes to have the value of his present thoroughly appreciated in the first place.

The second man to come up brought me an Indian pony with a white blaze down the face—an ugly, Roman-nosed brute with the eye of a living devil, which he was, as I found out afterward. The lead rope of this pony was given to me, and the donor stood back, making me a speech in which he told me that the wind was in the feet of that horse, and his slowest gait was a good deal faster than anything this side of a thunderbolt. However, such a horse was only proper for a great chief and hero like me.

When he got through with this rigmarole, the pony put in a gesture for itself, by backing away and trying to hammer my head off of my shoulders with two flinty, little heels. I managed to duck in time, and the pony was led away.

Nobody laughed. The chief who had made me the present stood by with a rather expectant attitude. Nobody had ever coached me in this sort of business, but I knew that the redskin expected some sort of a return for this gift. I instinctively dipped my hand into my pocket. It brought out no more than a little pearl-handled pocket knife. I was about to put this back again in haste when I saw a greedy gleam in the eyes of the Indian.

I remembered that the intrinsic value of an article has no meaning in the mind of the Indian. All that he demands is that his fancy should be tickled.

Well, I opened up that little knife and made a speech about it, because I didn't want the horse to be lied about any more fluently than the knife was. For all I knew, good rapid lying on the spur of the moment might be a most highly valued talent among these barbarians. How was I to know that that little caricature of a pony which had been presented to me really deserved the good things that had been said about it? It could beat any race horse for two hundred yards. It would stop from full speed in twice its own short length. It could dodge like a rabbit and it could endure until doomsday. Besides, it had wits in every hoof and could be depended upon not to put a foot into an unhandy prairie dog hole, breaking its neck and its rider's head at the same stroke.

I could not know these things about the wicked, little fiend, so I laid it on about the knife. I showed the pearl handle, first of all, and discussed its dazzling whiteness and translucency. I showed the little gold-looking studs that fastened the pearl sheathing to the iron core of that knife. And I opened the five little blades, one by one.

They each had a peculiar virtue, according to me, and could be used for most particular ends, if one only understood. What fascinated that hard-faced chief with Heaven knows how many human scalps drying above the smoke of the fire in his tepee, was the absurd little blade which was a file for finger nails.

When I showed him the use of it, he tried it, and gave a start and a cry as the rasp shuddered against the nerves of his finger-tip. And after that, he forgot all dignity, sat down on the spot, and began to saw away with the new tool!

The next chief had a painted buffalo robe. It was rather hard to make out what the paintings were about, but I knew that those robes had a good big value in any trader's store, because there was a demand for them all over the world. People liked to buy them as a sample of "fine arts in their infancy." As a matter of fact, they looked like nothing at all, most of the time.

When I got that painted buffalo robe—and it was a grand one of its kind, probably costing the artist more trouble than half a dozen war trails—I fetched out a silk handkerchief that I had bought six months before in New Orleans. It was checkered all over with bright colors, and the silk had a glossy surface which set those colors off to a great advantage.

That silk handkerchief was considered a more than satisfactory return for a magnificent buffalo robe as supple as chamois, and covered with twelve months of suffering called "art."

So this show went on! Every one of the twelve had a gift for me that was a staggering value; yet I managed to fetch out of my pockets something with which to reward them. Before it was ended, all of them were as busy as bees, envying one another, because not one of them could decide who had the real prize—whether it were the match safe which opened with a spring, or the matches, themselves, which were a new kind and burned with a blue spurt of flame, or the toothpick in its silver case—or half a dozen other little trinkets.

I had gone out with only the casual lining in my pockets that any man might bear around through city streets. With it, I was able to take as barter enough loot to set me up in business as a trader! Yes, it was an amazing thing, and before the end of the show, young and hard as I was, I was beginning to pity those poor people.

I kept waiting for Lost Wolf to see through this ridiculous nonsense, but he didn't! Not a whit. He waited until Running Deer had made personal acknowledgment to me in the form of a very handsome and brand-new rifle that must have cost him a great deal of money. When I tried to press a return acknowledgment upon Running Deer, he very gracefully declined to take anything in exchange, except that he declared he would be very happy if I would shoot the gun to see whether or not it were a good medicine.

I could not very well refuse, and the Indians stood back, expectant and curious. Few of the redskins that I met were much with a rifle. Uusually they could not afford ammunition for practice. Besides that, their nerves lacked the peculiar steady coldness which a marksman needs. However, they were vitally interested in *any* trial of skill, and they stood about with expectant faces to see what I would do with the gun.

I wanted to excel myself, you can be sure, because I

knew that a first impression is about two thirds of the battle with Indians. I was simply an ordinary good shot, with nothing marvelous about me, at all. On that frontier it would be hard to find one man in ten to beat me. But out of twenty there was almost sure to be one who had a natural gift for powder and lead.

However, I caught up the rifle and looked around me for a mark, but saw none that pleased me—simply because all were so distant. Running Deer, at this moment, raised a hand, pointed up, and smiled at me, as much as to say: "There is a target ready made for you!"

A target, certainly! It was a big hawk, sailing low and slow to be sure—but even a good hand with a shot gun would not have cared to try for such a target. With a rifle it was a pretty foolish thing for a person of my caliber to attempt such a thing. However, I smiled in turn, as though to show that this would not be a serious effort, and jerking the rifle to my shoulder I fired a bullet which I merely hoped would whistle close enough to him to frighten him away.

The thousandth chance was working in my favor. That hawk dipped straight down for the ground and struck at our feet with a thud.

The Cheyennes were really thunderstruck; they forgot their dignity and rushed at the bird, chattering over it while they passed it from hand to hand. Even big Lost Wolf showed some emotion.

"Brother," said he to me, "I had rather have you with me against the Pawnee horse thieves than seven men!"

14

That was the making of me, so far as the prairies were concerned. The story of how I snap shot a hawk out of the sky was whistling fast as a speeding bullet, almost, from place to place. It is an actual fact that it was back in Zander City before I was!

That silly accident and the fact that in a mad bravado I had dared the best men in Zander City to step forth and shoot it out with me, gave me a background of reputation. Yet I never had the name among the whites that I had among the redskins, with two such personages as Running Deer and that famous Lost Wolf to report favorably upon me.

In the meantime, Lost Wolf got out his own present, and it was one which made the rest seem very cheap by comparison.

Running Deer, with a brand-new rifle and a belt of good ammunition, had given me a present which was at about the market price of five pretty Cheyenne girls for squaws. What Lost Wolf produced was fairly staggering. It was art that *was* art. It was a whole suit of the finest kind of deerskin completely worked over with beads. The fringing of that suit alone was worth a day's wonder. When I had the leisure to examine the work which had gone to the embroidery of a single cuff, I was fairly staggered at the sight of the solid yards of workmanship which overlaid the rest of the leather. Yet it was not weighted down with this decoration. The beads were so small and of such fine quality that they looked rather like gay and delicately rendered color work. Only the patience of a barbarian could have completed such a labor.

This was what Lost Wolf offered to me, and the Cheyennes stood around with glittering eyes as they saw this treasure. What its value was in Indian terms I could not guess, but I knew that it ought to be under glass in some museum where thousands could see and wonder at it.

There was expectancy in their eyes, too, as though they wondered what I would produce to match this marvel, but I saw at once that even if I had had all of my trifles to heap together and offer, even barbarian ignorance would have been able to smile at the exchange, so I determined to offer something of a different kind.

I said to Lost Wolf: "With a treasure like this, a man could buy a village and all the horses and all the guns in it. I can only offer you a true friendship in return, and if you ride on the warpath and need another gun to fight at your side, call for me."

Lost Wolf said something in Cheyenne which must have been a translation. It brought a grunt of pleasure from the others. Then he said to me: "Brother, men are not bought and sold with guns or beadwork; a good friend is more to me than all the gold in the purses of the white men. But the Cheyennes have heard how a kind hand worked for Running Deer and they will not forget."

He said it solemnly, and what happened after that was simply an anti-climax—though it amounted to the delivery of forty-two horses which these reckless marauders had stolen from the town and which they were now sending back by men to make up the promised difference between the value of Running Deer and that of the two whites who had been used to ransom him.

Finally, they mounted their own ponies and gave that herd of horses a running start toward the town. Once the herd was under way, each of the braves in turn came by me with an ear-breaking yell and a brandishing of rifles. Five minutes later the Cheyennes were a mere dust cloud in the distance.

A full twenty men were waiting for me near the edge of Zander City. When they saw the troop of horses, they were so busy selecting the stolen horseflesh which belonged to them, that they entirely overlooked me. I managed to get through the town and back to the house of Gleason, the minister. I was as happy as a child over my presents and my experience. I felt that not very many men had been lucky enough to see the redoubtable Lost Wolf at close range, in this fashion, and live to tell of it afterwards as *I* seemed to have a good chance of doing.

When I got as far as the room which had been assigned to me, I spread out my trophies, which had been a bundle as heavy as I could carry up from the back of Sir Thomas. I was interrupted by noon and the dinner bell of Mrs. Gleason. When I came down, the story was there before me. The minister was filled with it. Even Mrs. Gleason relaxed enough to smile at me once or twice.

"After all," said she, "it's what the Indians need—to see what white hands *can* do with weapons. It will help to keep the murdering villains in order for a while."

"Hush, my dear," said the minister. "Friendship and charity are what we need above all else. Friendship and charity, I tell you! But I think the fact that a man from the town was brave enough to trust himself to the honor of the Cheyennes will make a great deal for better relations all around. Young man, I congratulate you!"

"I wish," said Margaret, "that I had been there to see the hawk fall!"

After lunch, I asked them up to my room and showed them the plunder which I had brought back with me. Mrs. Gleason was the most impressed, but particularly she wondered over the beaded suit. She suggested that I put on the jacket, and when I did, the sleeves hung down far over my fingertips, and the shoulders flopped clumsily about me. It had been made for big Lost Wolf. There was no doubt about that. With a redskin's usual disregard of utility, he had made me a present which I could never use. Indeed, there would hardly be another man on the prairies that that suit would fit.

After that, I had to tell how they had come to shower such treasures upon me, and so the story of Running Deer and my care of him had to be told. I told it as briefly as I could; Mrs. Gleason grunted and the minister smiled and Margaret fairly laughed with joy.

Mr. Gleason wanted me to walk to his church with him after lunch, and I did. On the way, I asked him what he knew of Lost Wolf, and he gave me more details than I could have hoped to hear. For he said that Lost Wolf was in reality as white as either you or I. He had been adopted in infancy by the Cheyennes. Just as he grew to young manhood, he fell into the hands of that famous scout, Danny Croydon, who taught him reading and writing and gave him the basis of a good education. The youngster might have turned thoroughly white had it not been that he was cheated by Major Beals, an Indian fighter, out of what he considered his legitimate due—a Pawnee chief as prisoner. That had disappointed the young fellow so heartily that he decided the redskins were more his people than the whites, and he had gone back to the barbarians to live.

I asked Gleason, since it was explained that Lost Wolf was not a redskin, why it was that he was such a great man, but yet not a chief. Gleason was able to answer. He knew a great deal about Lost Wolf, he said, because he was a great friend of Danny Croydon, the scout, and Danny was still able to keep in touch with the white-red man.

As for being a chief, Lost Wolf could never pretend to that dignity because he was not the type to be followed by the Indian braves. The Cheyennes are as reckless as any natives in North America, but even the Cheyennes preferred a leader consummate in caution. Whereas this was where the white of his nature ruined Lost Wolf. He was admittedly the most dexterous man in the Cheyenne nation in planning a campaign and organizing desperate enterprises, but the execution of them could not be intrusted to his hands for the reason that when the time came for the final stroke, Lost Wolf was carried out of control of himself by an irresistible desire for smashing tactics. When he saw a point to be gained, he wanted to lead a charge straight down the throat of danger. The result was that he had been the leader in only one great expedition.

With a hundred braves he had ranged far, far to the West, and had come into the land of the Blackfeet, who promptly gathered in numbers and, uniting behind him, cut off his retreat. After that, the maneuvers of Lost Wolf were beautiful to relate. By marches and countermarches he scattered the Blackfeet until there was only a band some fifty per cent greater than his between him and safety in the east. That band he attacked and simply pulverized. Every man in his band counted at least one coup and took at least one scalp. But Lost Wolf paid dearly for this success with the lives of twenty-five of his men.

When he came back to the home lodges the rejoicings at the scalp dance could not drown the wails of the widows and the bereaved parents. He had brought safely home nearly three-quarters of his warriors, and he had struck a truly great blow on the march. But the Cheyennes were not willing to endure such a loss no matter *what* the gain.

"That's the white that's in him," said Gleason. "He wants to stand out and let the other fellows have a fair fling at his face. Your Indian gets his greatest glory out of a night attack, and the safe throat-cutting of a sleeping warrior. A woman's scalp looks as well as a man's, and a child's is as good as a woman's in Indian logic. That's why their ideas can't fit in with those of Lost Wolf. If they only knew what a treasure they have in him, and if they would pour all of their power into his hands, he would sweep their Pawnee and Sioux enemies off the plains in no time and make things extraordinarily hot for the whites.

"But as it is, he has to be simply the greatest brave and medicine man in the tribe. If he would be willing to wrap himself in a little more mystery, he could paralyze the entire tribe! His great friend is Running Deer, and Running Deer is the most successful chief in the whole list of the Cheyennes because he takes the advice of Lost Wolf in everything except the final battle. There he does things in his own Indian way."

This, in short, was what Gleason told me about Lost Wolf. I went on into the town with my mind crammed and my imagination fairly boiling. An hour later I was sitting at a card table. By the time that evening came I was offering the painted buffalo robe as my stakes. The game fairly had me, and for three days I did not leave that room. Twice I got down to the beaded suit alone; twice I offered it for a thousand dollars as stakes, and twice that stake turned my luck. The second time my luck held. I sat through a few more feverish hours and finally got up from the table with over nine hundred dollars, which was three times as much as I had ever called my own in the past.

When I reached my boarding house, I shall never forget the faint little cry that came from the lips of Peggy when she opened the door to me. I looked more than half dead; she helped me up the stairs to my room, and then I fell on the bed and was unconscious with sleep. When I wakened the first time, Gleason was in the room, and I was vaguely conscious of the harsh, sharp voice of the minister's wife clacking in the hall beyond the door.

"No," said the minister, "he's not drunk, but exhausted. He hasn't been drinking a great deal."

Then I was lost in utter sleep, which was not broken for a long time. I lay on that bed on my face, just as I had fallen there, with one arm thrown over the bundle which contained the beaded suit that had been my luck.

What I knew next was the voice of Peggy and I came staggering back to my senses to find that there was food beside me and the trembling voice of Peggy hoping that I was better. Better? I was well! I was nine hundred dollars in pocket, and that was wealth, to me. Nine hundred dollars closer to my great hope—which was the day when I could afford to ask this same Peggy to be my wife. So I laughed, wildly enough to send her hastily out of the room. I ate and slept again. For, during three days, sleep had been a stranger to me.

When I awakened again, it was the dark of night, the deep, thick, middle of the night though there was not silence, as yet. For from the beginning of darkness to the coming of dawn, life had no rest in Zander City. The gaming halls worked, and the saloons were crowded.

I lay on the bed listening to those vague murmurs, split across, from time to time, by yelling, drunken laughter or loud and excited shouts in the far distance.

I was still dizzy, but I had rested a great deal. There was not the dreadful faintness at heart which had seemed to me like death coming at the end of my vigil at the gaming table. Every moment my brain cleared, and then something stirred.

I knew that some one was sitting silently with me in the dark of the room.

15

I did what any other person would have done in that year of our history, in such a case as mine. I reached for a revolver and snaked it quietly out of my belt. At the same time, I heard a deep bass voice say:

"It is I, my friend."

Lost Wolf had been sitting there in the dark and the silence of my room, waiting patiently for me to awaken! Well, it was a good deal like opening one's eyes and finding a tiger purring at one's ear. I was frightened, but I stood up and told him that I was glad to see him. We shook hands. There was no light on him except the dimness of the stars beyond the window. He looked bigger and more formidable than ever.

I exclaimed: "Lost Wolf! You are in danger in this place. Surely you know that!"

"Danger?" said he. "Yes, there is danger here, but there is danger there, also." He waved his hand in the night, gesturing toward the vastness of the prairies toward the west of the town. Suddenly I was aware of the life he led, surrounded by fear of death at all times of night and day, breathing danger like the air. What was it to him whether he stole into Zander City, where a hundred hands of white men would so willingly turn guns in his direction, if for no other reason than to have a share in the finish of so notorious a character as he?

"I am glad to see you," I said, "but I wonder what has brought you to me here?"

He was as direct and simple as a child, saying, "I was in great need of a friend, and though I have many friends among the Cheyennes, this is a thing in which I must have the wits of a white man to help me. So I have come to you, remembering kind words which you spoke to me."

The first thought that jumped into my mind was a thoroughly unworthy one. I suddenly remembered the Indians—and this fellow had to be considered on that moral level—were capable of almost any sort of ruse to get people into their power. I should not have doubted that something I had done might have displeased this man to the bottom of his stern heart.

For instance, he might well have heard how I had put up his gift in the gaming house and used it as a gambler's stake. Such light usage of his gift might, I thought, very well infuriate him to the last degree. But while I stood there with this black thought rushing through my mind, there came a tap at the door. I turned to tell Lost Wolf to hide himself. He had already disappeared, so I went to the door and opened it a scant inch.

"Yes," I said.

It was Peggy Gleason; the door gave back in my hand. I let the sight of her come beautifully upon me. She had a small night lamp in her hand; the massive single braid of her hair was slipping over her shoulder, and her dressing gown was girded around her like a monk's robe. She looked half boyish, and by the contrast, more delicately feminine.

She said: "I heard your voice and I was afraid that there might be a fever—after your long sleep."

"I was talking in my sleep," said I. "It is an old trick of mine. But your knock wakened me."

That was all there was to that little interview, except that as she went away, she paused an instant to smile back to me and wish me a good night. It was hardly a thing large enough to be worth describing, this night visit from Peggy, unless it were to illustrate her gentle kindness, which I knew already. The results of that visit were so great that, in a way, you might say that the lives of all three of us had a new beginning in that moment—I mean the life of Lost Wolf, my life, and that of Peggy. In that instant, one terribly powerful chain of interest linked us all together. So long as we lived nothing could remove that tie, for good or for evil.

How much evil I could not guess!

When I closed the door and turned back to Lost Wolf, I had to pause a moment. Then I said:

"How long will this work take, Lost Wolf?"

He did not answer me. I stepped closer and saw, through the shadows, that his arms were folded. He was looking through the window toward the shining of the stars. I recalled him to himself, and he said in answer: "Is your time short?"

As I hesitated, he went on: "Because you wish to come back to make her your squaw?"

Why was I not frank with him? I cannot tell, except that men will always make foolish mysteries out of their affairs with women. If I had spoken then and told him the truth, it would have meant more than millions to me in the time that was to come!

I said nothing, then, except to murmur that as long as he had a real need of me I would be glad to come with him and work for him. You see, my doubt of him had disappeared quickly enough, and there was left in the place of doubt only an immense feeling of flattery that so great a chief had called on me to help him in time of need. To prefer me, say, to such a man as Running Deer!

If I had been only a whit older, I would have been wise enough not to entrust myself to such a chance where he was almost certain to find out that I was far less than I had seemed to be. Just young enough to be utterly rash, the thought of voyaging across the unknown prairies, with such a companion as this famous man, was a great deal too much for me. I would leave to luck, my chance of living up to my former reputation. I think at that moment that even the love of Peggy Gleason could hardly have bought me from this promising expedition; so great was my folly!

He said: "This is the manner of answer that I knew I should have from you. Now, is it not strange that a man should be able to look into the eyes of another and instantly know a brother?"

Suppose that a lion sat down by a rat and said: "Brother!" Or that an eagle dropped down at the side of a canary and said: "Brother!" Well, that was a good deal the way that I felt when this cruising terror of the prairies, this chimera that frightened the children to sleep in a hundred border towns, called me: "Brother!"

What worried me was really not so much that he seemed to misjudge my fighting prowess, as that he seemed to be mistaken about my moral character. You can fool a man about your marksmanship a great deal more adroitly than you can deceive him about your good nature, let us say. At any rate, I could see that this hero of the plains had attributed to me the sort of a soul that I simply didn't possess. I was worried at the thought of what might happen, when he found out the truth. I had no illusions about myself. I knew that no stretch of the imagination could set me forth as a good man.

I was not even a good Charlestonian!

But where was the trip to be? And what was to be done? That did not seem to interest Lost Wolf. His idea was that he must get my consent to what he wanted. It did not seem to occur to him that what was actually done with my time might interest me—any more than it would have occurred to Aladdin to bother about what the slave of the lamp would feel if he were ordered to finish off forty-nine jeweled windows, or only one.

Lost Wolf had decided to put me on the elevated plane of a hero, and therefore all trivial details were dismissed.

What he had to say next was that his horse had been left on the edge of the town, that he was a trifle short of rifle ammunition, and that he would be glad, when I rode Sir Thomas out of Zander City a few minutes hence, if I would bring along an extra hundred rounds.

That was the breath-taking way of Lost Wolf! He didn't hesitate. He was, as matter of fact, about embarking me on a terrible adventure at midnight, as you would be if a friend stepped in and asked you for an afternoon stroll in the park.

A few seconds later, he had melted through the window.

I leaned out and watched him hand himself down—a great bulk of a man, as light as a feather, with the muscles of those huge arms to lower or raise himself. An instant later I was really getting ready to join him on the expedition.

The only time I paused to regret, was when I passed the door of Peggy's room. I stopped there to close my eyes and sigh with the pain of true love—true love that would go gallivanting away across the prairies in this fashion, away from the girl! Well, I think that my love was as true as most, and just as full of aches of the heart.

Half an hour later, I rode out of Zander City on Sir Thomas, bound for I knew not what. Lost Wolf waited just beyond reach of the lights of the town; we rode away side by side. Before dawn we were forty miles away; we halted to cook a breakfast that would have been dried beef had not a rabbit foolishly tried to jump across our way. There was only a flash of it as went from bush to bush, but at that flash, Lost Wolf drew and fired.

I hardly guessed what he was about until he rode into the brush and came out again bearing the dead rabbit. The big slug from the Colt had fairly centered that jack.

While that meat was roasting, and while we ate it, I had a chance to meditate on such marksmanship. This accurate revolver work was a great deal more astonishing than my chance rifle hit had been. Lost Wolf took it quite as a matter of course. I needed no more than this to convince me that my companion was a white man, no matter how he chose to stain his skin, for I think that no Indian that ever lived would have used a gun with such speed and surety. I did not need any more than this either, to tell me how he had built up so great a reputation on the prairies.

In the meantime, having eaten, Lost Wolf had settled back cross-legged by the dying little breakfast fire. Now he lighted his pipe and smoked it, with his eyes half closed in weary enjoyment. As he sat there in that fashion, looking down, I could see the lines of exhaustion in his face. The flanks of the red stallion told the same story, too, and I wondered what great thing had happened that could have brought him on the warpath, that could have made him seek the help of a stranger and a white man.

He began to talk, and I shall give the words he spoke as nearly as I can. They were put into form, for no man can live among the Indians for very long without learning some of the talents of the born story-teller.

16

"A man's life," said Lost Wolf, "is like a circle of tepees that make a village. The chief's lodge is in the center, and the town is built around it. It is so with the mind of a man. He has a central soul, and around it there are outward parts of his brain. Each of these is shut away from the others. I shall open one tepee in my life to you, and you shall see everything in it, from the fire to the entrance flap and from the buffalo robes to the arrows where they hang. All of this part of myself, you shall learn."

So spoke Lost Wolf, with his eyes half closed, looking at me, yet seeing not me but the story which he was telling. He said:

"When I was a young boy, before I was in young manhood, and when my strength was first coming upon me, I was on the bank of the river with the other young boys and the young men of the village. We wrestled on that bank of the river, and one of the boys who was fifteen years old, and who had ridden on the warpath that year for the first time, took hold of me, expecting me to curl up before him.

"My strength, as I said, was coming upon me, and my strength was greater than that of other men. There was something in my hands which other hands did not possess, and there was something in my heart which despised showing fear of any man.

"When Black Elk laid hold on me, I gripped him in turn and in his face I saw his surprise and then his fear. Yet he threw himself at me in the hope of making me weak with fear. So we grappled but the grip of my finger tips went through his flesh and found his bones. I heard him draw in his breath and moan softly with pain and the fear.

"When we fell down, I was on the ground, and he was on top, but it was as though you threw a dog on top of a fighting wildcat. I was tearing him so, that the courage was departing from his heart. Then he gasped out, at my ear:

" 'Do not throw me under you and master me, or I shall be disgraced, and the warriors will laugh at me. Have pity on me, and I will be your friend!'

"When I heard him speak like this, I *did* have pity on him. I was ashamed, too, to hear one who had ridden on the warpath speak in this manner. I thought that I would let him pretend to have the victory, so I let myself fight less hard and presently I lay weak under him. He got up, took me by a wrist and an ankle and threw me into the river, with a shout, telling me not to pretend to fight with men hereafter.

"I dived under the water and swam there a long time before I came up, because I was very angry and did not want to let others see my anger. I used on the water the strength that I might have used on Black Elk.

"On the other side near the bank, I rose and sat there in the sun for a long time, while the boys and the men shouted and laughed at me. No matter what one knows in one's heart about oneself, laughter is a burning fire, even when it is only a fool who laughs.

"So I burned, as I was lying on that bank, and most of all I was mad with rage when I saw Black Elk, laughing loudest of all and scorning me.

"That night, there was a scratching outside the tepee in which I slept. When I crawled out, there was Black Elk, waiting for me. He said that I had saved him from shame and that he would never forget me and that he would be a friend to me in times when I least suspected that I needed a friend. He gave me, too, a nice basket of berries.

"We ate the sweet berries and sat together, and I told him that I did not care how much the people had laughed at me, because there was no poison in laughter.

"After this, I did not see Black Elk often. He knew that I had seen his shame, and he knew that I understood his weakness. We avoided each other. A time came when I was to go out and try what the spirits would tell me of what my life was to be. You, my friend, have not heard this thing, perhaps.

"You must know, then, that in some things the white man is wise, and the Indian is a child; in some things, also, the Indian is wise, and the white man is a child. Such is the way the Father made us, giving each a strength and a weakness. To the cat he gives both teeth and claws, but he does not give strong legs which will carry it over the ground to hunt at great distances. To the dog he gives strong legs and good teeth, but he does not give the claws which rip out the life of an enemy. With men, too—where one is strong, another is weak.

"The Indians who are brave have one strong way which the white men have not.

"When you are young, if you wish to have revealed to you a great thing about your life, you must simply go to some dangerous place and lie there for, four days—two days upon the right side and two days upon the left side. There must be no eating of food during all this time, only water may be drunk. One must not stir or rise or even sit up, because in that way there is undone all the good work that has been accomplished before, and the fast must begin again from the start. There is nothing like this among the white men, which shows that they have all their wise book, and yet they do not know this great thing!

"I had come to the age when I thought that I was old enough and strong enough and brave enough to go and watch by myself for the four days. The man who does this thing must put himself where the bad spirits can harm him, if they have the wits to find him and the power to hurt him. For the bad spirits do not wish that a man should really learn wisdom at all, you see.

"Finally I said to myself that the best thing would be for me to go either to the place where the buffalo go toward the water, and lie down in the trail, or else it would be best for me to go to an island where the under-water people might come and reach their hands to me and draw me down under the water and strangle me there, if they were strong enough.

"So I went where the river spread out in a little lake, and I swam to an island and built there a little shelter just big enough to cover me when I lay down. I lay there for four days, two days upon one side and two days upon the other side. All the time I had the hope that the dream would come to me. Sometimes the dream comes in the shape of a buffalo that speaks good words; sometimes the dream comes as a voice that rises like a mist out of the river. One never can be sure how it will come. I lay there, not daring to move.

"The wind blew very cold. Sometimes it carried nothing, sometimes its arms were white with snow or black with rain. I was drenched and then I was almost frozen. Sometimes I could feel my heart failing in me, and I thought that I should die. Still I lived, growing weaker and weaker. I would lie there for hours and wonder at the way the bones were pressing through my side against the ribs of the hard earth, and I would watch my hands growing weaker and thinner with every day.

"In this fashion I spent the four days, but no dream had come to me. At last, I sat up weakly, knowing that I had failed! For one does not always succeed. And sometimes, even when the dream comes, one needs the help of a great medicine man to tell what it is all about. My four days passed with no dream at all, though I had done everything that should be done, for I had gone out in the coldest and the most dangerous time of the year and I had been far away from my village and I thought that I was all alone!

"When I recovered myself a little, I killed a deer that I found. For two days I roasted and ate the meat of that deer and grew strong again. Then I started home toward the village. On the way, something stirred behind the hill on the farther side of the river. I hurried after it, and I came upon a man. It was Black Elk. Then it was all clear to me, and I shouted at him:

" 'It is you who have spoiled my work. I have lain there for four days, thinking that I was alone, but all the time you were watching me!'

"I knew that he must have come only out of friendship to keep me from harm. But that was a fool's way of acting, because if the under-water people had found me, how could *any* man have helped me against them? And if the bad spirits in a herd of buffaloes had come to trample me, how could any man have helped me? Bullets and knives cannot hurt such spirits. Only enchanted arrows are useful against them, though this you may not have known before.

"Black Elk said to me: 'Do not be too angry. Because I have done better service for you than you think.'

"I spoke to him scornfully: 'Are the spirits afraid of you, then, Black Elk?'

" 'You cannot make me your enemy,' said Black Elk. 'No matter how you talk to me. But tell me—how was it known in the village that you were to keep the watch here?'

"I told him that it was not known to any man.

" 'You are wrong,' said Black Elk. 'It was known in the village well enough to come to my ears, and it was known there well enough to have the story carried away to other peoples, and to your enemies. I shall give you proof.'

"When I heard him talk like this, as a man talks when he really knows, I said that I would go with him a little way. He brought me to a place on the lower part of the island.

"He showed me where he had watched over me, watching me from a slit between two rocks. He showed me, too, the bodies of two Pawnees lying on their backs, looking almost alive, because the great cold had kept them so well. There was an arrow broken off, in the back of one, and there was a knife cut across the throat of the other. Black Elk had taken them by surprise.

"I could remember that in my watch, it had seemed to

me as though I heard the twanging of a bowstring, and I had thought that my dream was about to begin!

"When I saw what Black Elk had done for me, I knew that he was a great friend, that he had saved my life. I took his hand to thank him, but he said that he was only giving me a little payment in return for a great thing that I had done for him, since it was much better and much easier for a man to die than it was for him to be shamed, and then to continue living.

"All of this was true, nevertheless. I knew that Black Elk was my true friend. I determined that I would keep him as a friend so long as I lived.

"For a friend is like sweet sugar—very good to the taste, but easily lost and melted away in any storm. It is easy to find a friend, but it is easier still to lose him!"

17

When Lost Wolf had continued to this point in his narrative, he forgot me and even his pipe. He allowed the smoke from its bowl to dwindle to a tiny, dying wisp before he roused himself and said again:

"You too, have had friends and have lost them?"

I gave a quick glance back through my life. I had thought that I had had friends, but I certainly had had none that would have watched over me during four days in the winter snows, to see that I made a fool of myself safely!

I had to reply to Lost Wolf that I really had never had what *he* would call a friend. But that I had had acquaintances that had passed as friends with me and that I had truly lost them easily enough.

"So," said Lost Wolf, "we all come to learn that a

fool and a coward and a beggar is nevertheless worth something when he becomes a friend. Black Elk was weak, but he was not so low as this. I prized him."

He made another pause and then struck into the burden of his story once more.

He said:

"When we came back to the village, we did not hunt out one another thereafter. But I saw a meaning and a kindness in the eye of Black Elk when he passed me. War came, and battles, and when the fighting came, he saved me, and I saved him. So our friendship became more silent and more strong than ever before. From that day, if Black Elk stood behind me, I knew that a friend guarded my back.

"A little time ago that guard was removed, and I was left without him. It happened in this way:

"Across these plains which are the homes of the Cheyennes and of others of my race, the white men send out caravans which go slowly toward the West. Yet if a hundred wagons start, only twenty-five come back. Where are the other wagons and the other men? They are not lost. Some have died, and some have been broken, to be sure, but most of them remain on the land. Houses are built, and then farms and ranches; towns grow up. Wherever there is a white town, it is like poison in a well. The Indians cannot live near by. They draw back, and the white men are left free to spread still further and further.

"We see these caravans passing and passing, and we know that with each of them that passes, we are nearer to the end!"

So said Lost Wolf, stopping to tap the dottle out of his pipe and refill it. Then he selected a live ember from the fire, caught it up with a smooth speed, laid it over the bowl of his pipe, and began to smoke again. It was rather weird to sit next to one who, I was assured, was a white with a dyed skin, yet hear him talk as if the Indians were really his blood brothers. Since he chose this attitude, I could not very gracefully ask him to take the white man's viewpoint as the natural one for him. So I said at last:

"But perhaps the other Indians do not see this?"

"They do not," said Lost Wolf. "For if they did, they

would soon rise and ride like one man, not against each other, but against the whites."

"Then, would they win?" I asked.

Lost Wolf turned a displeased eye upon me.

"I am not a child," said he. "And I know that all the red peoples gathered together could not fill one of those great cities beyond the river. No, we could not win. We might sweep deep into the country of the white man. We might carry him from his lands clear to the edge of the great river, but we could not cross. The more we killed, the more certain we would be to die. No we could not win, but it would be a death such as a man should die, fighting such numbers. As it is, we must grow smaller and smaller, and weaker and weaker while the white man gathers us in his hand!"

He shook his head very sadly. It was easy to see that the tragedy of this idea cut him to the heart.

He said at last: "But the others do not see what I see. The caravans make them smile. They say that more guns and more fire water are coming to them, and more colored cloth and beads. Well, they smile and do not understand, but Lost Wolf, he sees and knows it all!"

He struck his broad, gleaming chest with his fist, and the thump resounded. Certainly there was a vast gulf between Lost Wolf and those of his true kin.

"It was one of those caravans that took Black Elk. He rode out with a painted buffalo robe to trade with them. It was a great caravan, and he expected no harm from them. From little groups of white men, one can expect much mischief. When there are many of them together, the leader may be a great fool, but he is usually a good man."

He paused to puff, and I was glad of that pause, because there was truly meat enough in this last speech to keep me busily conning it for some time.

"And what happened then," said Lost Wolf, "I cannot tell. I only know that Black Elk rode out to trade with the caravan, because I spoke to him, as he passed out of the village at sunrise. He would come back by the noon of that day, he said. When the noon came, there was no Black Elk. In the afternoon, I myself, rode after the caravan. When I came close to it, men shot rifles at me, and I had to ride back again. Then I learned that the caravan would not allow any Cheyenne to come near them. Since there were a hundred and fifty rifles in that wagon train, the Indians did not try to stop them."

I did not know for sure, but I had a vague idea that the fighting power of the Cheyennes must total far, far more than a hundred and fifty rifles. I asked Lost Wolf if the mere number had stopped him.

He said: "If I called to Running Deer or to other brave young chiefs, they would surely call out the warriors on the warpath. What can stand before the Cheyenne nation. They are more numerous than buffalo. They are stronger than young buffalo bulls. They are more fierce than buffalo bulls charging an enemy. If I called upon them for help, I should have to sweep away all that wagon train, and not only the guilty man or the guilty men who have killed or who keep Black Elk, but also all the hundred and fifty rifles and those who shoot them, and the women, and the children. And there are infants who cannot walk, all in that wagon train like a town on wheels."

When he finished that speech, I wondered at him more than ever. It was truly like meeting a considerate lion or a gentle tiger, this man with the stained skin, who could keep some consideration for the welfare of others, the innocent and the helpless.

"I could not go into the train to find out the guilty people, and I could not send in any other Indian. So I had to find a white man who would try the thing for me. Will you go in among them, then, my friend?"

It did not look like such a desperately dangerous bit of work, hearing him outline the case in this fashion. What developed was simply that Lost Wolf expected me to go into the caravan and join myself to them, which could probably be done by a man with a good horse and a good set of guns, with the greatest ease. I was to work in the caravan until I found out the reason for the disappearance of Black Elk. When I had done that, I was to do the hard part of my task, if possible. I was to lure the guilty man or men out of the range of the rest of the caravan and bring them in touch with Lost Wolf. That was all he asked. He was only too glad to handle the job of vengeance.

Since there was very little chance that I could be able to bring the guilty one out of the caravan, I was, in case of failure, to try to finish off the ringleader with my own hands, and then come back and report the state of things to Lost Wolf.

That was the simple scheme which we planned together as we sent our horses across the prairie for nine days. Prodigious days of marching were these, for Sir Thomas was in the finest fettle. He unrolled the miles like a spinning log behind a steamer. Still, though he worked hard, he could not embarrass the red stallion. That beautiful giant made simple play with the miles. Every evening we camped with the circle of a new horizon around us.

The early afternoon of the ninth day Lost Wolf pointed suddenly ahead; a few moments later, straining my eyes, I saw a faint, rising dust cloud against the edge of the sky. I would have said farewell to Lost Wolf, but he would not let me ride in at once.

He said: "In the middle of the day, when the sun is bright, the minds of men are brighter, too. And they are harder. Would you go to your friend to ask for help while the sun is hot? No! Because then he thinks of how hot he is, and how he is troubled with many sorrows. He is remembering that one squaw is lazy, and one is sick, and one is old. He is thinking how his eldest son died, or else he remembers the bad hunting of that month. He thinks of all these things while the sun is high.

"When the sun sets, and the fires are burning, and the supper is cooking; when the smell of roasting meat is in his nostrils, he is stronger and freer. His heart is lighter, and he remembers how his hand counted the coup, and how his knife took the scalp of a great enemy. His heart is warmed; he pities the poor.

"He gives food to his dog, and he is gentle to the stranger. He pities all men who are hungry, because he is, himself, about to eat! Therefore, waiting until the sun has set and the wagons are drawn out in a circle. Still, after this, there will be a rising of smoke. The meals are cooking, then, and after that, as the sunset dies off, the fires begin to shine more brightly than the light of the dead day.

"That is the time to ride in among them. The first taste of the cooked meat is in their mouths. Tears of joy are in their eyes. With their own hands they will unsaddle your horse. They will guide you to the greatest fire. They will give you a robe to sit on. They will put before you the choicest meat."

I couldn't dodge that sort of wisdom. It was too apt and to the point. I shook hands with Lost Wolf and left him sitting erect on his great horse, with his arms folded so that the great biceps bulged against the arch of his chest.

The long line of the caravan had died out against the sky line, and I was to work gradually after it, while Lost Wolf trailed still farther to the rear, where he was to wait and wait for my coming.

Lost Wolf disappeared behind me; the caravan loomed before me. I brought back the pace of Sir Thomas to a walk.

18

A walking pace, you may very well think, was a good time for reflection. During this interval I should have become aware that I had planned to play the spy upon some of my own kind and to betray one or more of them into the hands of a pseudo redskin. I thought of nothing of the kind. I had about as much tender conscience as a shark in a hungry sea, at that time of my life. All that held me was the prodigious excitement of the thing that I was about to do.

It loomed bigger and bigger in danger, the nearer I

drew to the wagon train. As I drew nearer I was more and more amazed by the great size of that company. A hundred and fifty rifles had been the estimate of Lost Wolf but I knew afterwards that he had much underestimated that number of effective fighting men. There were well-nigh a hundred and fifty *wagons,* to say nothing of the numbers who were attached to the train on horseback only, just as I had intended to attach myself.

When I first had a good view of it—that is, when I had come close enough to let my eye pierce through the misty cloud of dust that rose around it—I saw a fine little city on wheels. It was drawn up in a great circle, the wagons on the outside, their heavy bodies and their great wheels serving as the main articles of the fortress. Under, behind, and between the wagons was piled the bulkiest part of the load, so as to fill in the interstices between the wagons and make a more solid bulwark for the defenders.

One could hardly exaggerate the importance and strength of such a fort. Against similar groups of men and wagons, whole fighting tribes of Indians had thrown themselves vainly, receiving a sound scourging with powder and lead, in return for their daring. Lying at ease behind such secure breastworks and with a brace of rifles loaded at hand, to say nothing of six-shot revolvers, in case the Indian charge actually broke in upon the wagons, one plainsman was enough to turn back ten charging Indians, whether they were Cheyennes or some lesser warriors. The tribes had come to hate the sight of these hard nuts, no matter how much sweet and tender fruit was inside the rind.

I got an idea of the strength of the caravan, too, by the number of little hunting parties that broke away from the caravan from time to time and scoured off across the plains, letting the horses stretch their legs after walking all the hot day. There were lots of those parties out for a crack at game of any kind. If one of these groups had run foul of Black Elk, it would be easy to explain how the Indian had come to disappear.

I laid farther back from the caravan, therefore, and waited according to instructions until the light of the day was more dim and the gleam of the fires began to be more perceptible. Then I rode briskly in on Sir Thomas.

When I got within about a hundred yards of the circle of wagons, a pair of shadows rose out of the ground before me. The glint of the rifles in their hands made me draw up as fast as I could manage the head of Sir Thomas.

"Who are you?" asked one of them.

I had been so startled by them that it angered me a little. "I'm a troop of Federal cavalry come to arrest this wagon train," said I. "Who the devil are you?"

He was a great, loose-made, leather-skinned frontiersman, made on such a scale that his heavy old-fashioned rifle appeared like a thing of painted wood in his hand.

He grinned at my impudence instead of bringing me to task for it, as he might well have done. He asked me what I wanted, and I said that I wanted a free meal, which seemed to please him again. He sent me in to the circle of the wagons with his companion as a guard. For his own part, he lay down again in a little hollow of the ground, which he had deepened by a little scooping out. He was one of the outposts which this well-governed caravan maintained through all of its march across the prairies.

When I got past the wagons and into the heart of things, I found enough to fill my eyes. There were picked men in this party. They had not asked the poor and needy to come along for the sake of additional strength in numbers. Instead, they were able to pick and choose and select only people with money to embark properly on such an adventure.

The result was that all of these wagons were big and newly made, of good steel and hickory, which makes a combination pretty hard to beat! There were no oxen in the entire length of the train, which I will wager was almost a record for that time of the century when it came to prairie traffic. All were good, rangy mules of Spanish breed and horses that were a pleasure to see. They would not be in such fine fettle before the trip West was over, but in the meantime, they were getting along very well. The fat of their home corrals and mangers had not yet been ground off by the labors of the trip, and they had not met the heavy grades and the bitter weather that would strip them of all except bone and the essential driving muscle. In the evening, they were as playful as colts in a pasture. Their harnesses were new and strong. Their shoulders were not yet broken or raked raw. On the whole, it was as neat an outfit as you would ever care to see, but for all of its neatness it was to meet with disaster before the end. Luck was that way on the prairie. Sometimes it let the best organizations split on the rocks of hard times. Sometimes the most ragged aggregations of rascals and beggars got through swimmingly to the Pacific Coast where they were all to take their places as Argonauts and forefathers of a wealthy and happy race.

There is no use talking about what happened to that organization later on. I was not with them long, and what was of importance to me at the time, was the fine way that everything was done around that caravan, the upstanding look of the men, and the general shipshapeness of everything. To see that train and the animals and men and fittings you would say: "I am glad to belong to the same nation!"

I was brought to the captain of the caravan. Every train had a wagon boss who looked after the government of the troop just about as absolutely as the captain of a ship. Once men got embarked in such a region of strangeness and in such dangers, they were sure to be willing to prefer absolute monarchy to the best democracy that ever was devised. A democracy is apt to be more honest than intelligent, and it takes entirely too long to come to decisions and to act upon them.

This captain of the caravan I interviewed that once only. I have forgotten his name, but I remember that he had a fuzz of brown beard growing all around his jaw bone, and running up the sides of his face so that it gave his head a round, owlish look. I think he grew that beard to give him an older appearance, because as a matter of fact he was not much past the late twenties.

He had the brains; it wasn't the fineness of his equipment or the number of his wagons that earned him such respect. He had only four mules, one wagon, and a single rifle. He was one of the poorest men in the outfit, in fact, but before he had been in the caravan a week, he was in the inner councils, and when the cruise began, they put him in the cabin, as you might say.

I could tell why the instant that I was brought before him. He was a little chap, looking, as I said before, a good deal like an owl, and not a very old owl. He had a squawking, foolish-sounding voice that grated on the ears. However, what he said had a lot of point. I began to say that I had got lost, after being out with a hunting party a few days before, but he cut right in and stopped me.

He said: "Young man, you don't look the kind to lose your mates—if you wanted to stay with them. You'd better let me know the truth about this, if you expect to get any good out of me and the rest."

I saw that the lie which I had thought up so carefully was not worth its salt. Of course, I couldn't tell him the truth. I rambled right into a new invention and said that I had got into trouble at Zander City ten days before, and had to ride out of the town—I had cut across the prairies until I came on their trail and followed it up.

He said: "Do you mean to say that you have ridden from Zander City to this place in ten days?"

"In nine days," said I.

He got up and walked around Sir Thomas. "Maybe you have," said he. "That's a licking good horse. What's the latest news from Zander City?"

I told him that the last important thing had happened three days before I left. That was the capture of Running Deer and his ransoming again by Lost Wolf. The little chap seemed a good deal excited at this, wanting to know more about it. Just as I was finishing the story, he cut in again in his sharp way and asked what I expected from the caravan. I said that I didn't expect anything, but that I would be very glad to just ride along with them, and I thought that I would be able to earn my keep as a hunter. At any rate, it would be pleasant to me to have company.

He studied me for a minute, and once or twice he looked away from me with a frown. I could see that he didn't trust me and that he was on the verge of sending me away. He would have done it if it hadn't been for the cold look of the wall of black night outside of the circle of the wagons and their fires, and all the warm and comforting noises and smells in that camp. No, if it had not been for the wisdom of Lost Wolf in sending me in at just that season of the day, that wagon boss would have fired me out of the camp in an instant, because he didn't like my looks—not a little bit.

He spoke up in a sort of growl at last and asked to see one of my guns. I handed him a Colt. He broke it open and looked at the mechanism. He said, as he handed it back: "I don't mind saying that I have my doubts about the reason that brought you here; but you're gun is clean, and I suppose that you can stay with us so long as you behave like a decent man. Will you tell me any more about what made you leave Zander City?"

"There is a dead man," said I—"or a man that I think is dead!"

It was the truth, of course, because both Lost Wolf and I had no great doubt but that Black Elk was dead. However, that wagon captain put another meaning on what I said and thought that I was confessing a murder. He jumped up and held up his hand. "God forgive you," said he. "However, I am not the judge. God forgive you. I, at least, shall not betray you. But I warn you that you will be watched!"

Yes, he was a thoroughly good man and a wise man, too. It was the time of the day that had told in my favor. In another moment, the captain had introduced me to the next circle about a fire and asked them to give me something to eat.

19

I drifted half the way through that camp, before the evening was over, just lounging from camp fire to camp fire, listening to the drowsy talk of the men. I got nothing about Black Elk out of them—not even a whisper.

After a night's sleep, I was up with the first in the morning—that is to say, I was up the instant that the light of day began to color the East. I joined a party of a dozen young men that were off scouting for game. By luck we hit the sign of buffalo inside of two miles and ran bang into them, in twice that distance. It was only a small group. We slaughtered seven fine animals, and all except one of us turned in at the work of skinning and butchering, while a messenger ripped back to the caravan to tell of the pleasant little haul.

That was all it was. Seven buffalo, scattered among a hundred and fifty wagons, did not make much fare. However, it was welcome—all fresh game was welcome for the reason that such a big party stirred up hardly any more game than a little caravan—but absorbed the kill just that much faster, of course.

Out of that hunting, a good report of my riding and shooting went back to the caravan to the wagon captain, I have no doubt, because after that I could feel that I was not being watched so close. I was left free as my own master, and I spent my time for eight solid days in ranging through the caravan and becoming an expert in striking up chance conversations.

Still the subject of Black Elk was never mentioned, and I wondered at it. You can hardly imagine a prominent Indian brave being scooped out of existence without his demise making a pretty lasting impression on a lot of men, most of whom were of average moral sense, at least. When I came on the evidence that I wanted, it was by the purest accident in the world.

We had been out hunting, and we had not bagged a thing. The horse of one of the hunters stumbled, throwing him heavily. The rifle which he was carrying flew out of his hands and hit a sharp-pointed rock, so that the butt was shattered to bits. I was sorry to see that. He was a thin, pale-eyed fellow named Dick Henline. He and his brother, Larry, were about the steadiest shots and the best hunters in the whole caravan, which was saying a

101

good deal. I told Larry that I was sorry that Dick had had such a fall and broken his favorite rifle.

"Oh," says Larry, "Dick will be out again tomorrow morning. He'll have another rifle."

I asked if he owned two guns, and Larry said, with a peculiar grin: "Well, the second rifle is a borrowed gun, after a way of speaking."

The next morning, when the hunters started out foraging again, there was Dick Henline, sure enough, riding with the rest of us, armed with a fine rifle. I had a fairly close look at it, and in spite of the peculiar way in which Larry had spoken of the gun the night before, I could see nothing about it that was worthy of curiosity except three deep notches cut into the butt of the rifle, just below the point where the palm of the right hand would rest.

There was no doubt about what the notches meant. There was a brutal fashion in those old days of signing on a gun the number of victims that had gone down before one's weapons. But it was not the sort of brutality that one would have expected from a quiet man like this Dick Henline. If there were brutality in him, you would expect a different sort—the sort that tortures in silence, you might say. Then, of course, it popped into my mind that this was a borrowed gun. But Larry said that the gun belonged to nobody in the world except to his brother and to himself. The next idea was that they had bought it or *taken* it from somebody else. When I had a chance after the return from the morning hunt, I asked Dick Henline to let me have a look at his rifle. He handed it across.

It was just like any other, except for those three notches gashed into the stock, and the addition of a little design scratched into the wood. That design was the sort of thing that a man might scratch out while he sat waiting for evening, say, and the coming of the game. It was a rude sort of a figure of a man, pretty thoroughly obliterated and almost rubbed out by the chafing and the wear of hands against the polished wood. Anybody might have done such a thing, though it was rather hard to imagine the designer being out of his teens.

What was of more importance in my eyes was that there was a little smear of color in the design—a little touch of red had been worked into the grotesque, little, ruined figure of a man. That settled in my mind *one* point about the gun. No matter who it was that owned the weapon, it was not a white man who had made that sketch originally. A white might have been childish enough to have made the scratched sketch on the wood, but no white that I knew or could imagine had ever been so simple as to color the little drawing with such care. Red, yes, and a little shadowing of blue too. I knew that the hand of an Indian had been at work here.

That explained the three notches, too—Indian ideas, Indian workmanship!

Of course, you suspect that I thought of Black Elk at once—and I did! I spent three days while that caravan wound steadily across the prairie, in trying to learn from one of the two brothers how that rifle had come into their possession. All of my hints, and all of the efforts that I made were useless. I professed a great admiration for that rifle, and I pretended that I felt that the rifle shot much straighter than any other that I had ever used, but these hints got nothing out of them. They willingly let me use the rifle, of course, but they had no desire to talk.

Finally, I determined that only one course remained to me. That was to lose the hunting party the next day, and then try to find big Lost Wolf behind the caravan. When the next morning's hunt began, I slipped off with the rest and then pretended to have something go wrong with my cinches, just as the party got underway along a hot trail of buffalo.

Of course, they kept straight along, and as soon as they were out of sight, I jumped into the saddle and cut straight back along the line of our route. I traveled a half hour before I stopped, raised both hands to my lips and gave a long, screeching cry that Lost Wolf and I had agreed upon between us, as the token which we would use.

I repeated that cry two or three times and listened with a downward ear after each time. Then I heard a cry in answer come quivering to me out of the edge of the horizon. After a little time, Lost Wolf came slipping out of a cut in the ground.

He rode up to me at the full gallop and lifted his hand

in a greeting to me. I saw, as he came nearer, that his stern face was thoroughly lighted with enthusiasm. He expected that I had news of importance. In answer to that expectancy, I simply put into his hands the notched rifle.

The heavy gun trembled in his grip and he said to me: "You have killed the rascal, then?"

That told me everything that I could have asked—this was indeed the rifle of Black Elk.

So I said to the big man: "I have left that pleasure for you."

"You are more than my friend," said Lost Wolf; "you are my brother. Is there more than this one man?"

"There are two, I think."

"That is much better. Bring them back to me. Bring them back to me, my friend!"

I told him that I would do what I could, and I headed back to locate the hunt which I had just left. That was not hard to do. I came up with them as they were half-way back to the camp and I suggested another excursion. But they had had enough hunting and did not wish to wear out their horses with the day's march before the caravan. One of those day's marches was a trifle in most wagon trains, for they went on at a snail's pace. This was an exceptional outfit, and for a few hours every day, they maintained a good average.

That day I stuck close to the Henline brothers, and during the noon halt I decided to put the direct question to Dick. So I asked him point-blank if the notches on that rifle did not prove that it was an Indian rifle. The readiness with which he answered made me wish that I had tried direct questions before, instead of so many hints. He merely laughed and said that rifle and a painted buffalo robe with it had cost him only the price of one loading of his own gun. He and his brother, it developed, were plainsmen of the type who considered an Indian on the level of a snake, and who liked no game and no pelt so well as that of a redskin.

In the morning as the pair rode out hunting from the caravan, they came over the top of a hill and found a solitary Indian about to cross a shallow stream in the

104

hollow beneath them. The noise of the water completely shut from his ears the sound of their approach.

It was a perfectly simple matter to the Henlines. Dick was the one who won the toss of the coin to see who was to have the pleasure of turning that rider into a "good Indian." He pulled his rifle to his shoulder and fired. The body that tumbled from the saddle went whirling down the stream, spinning around and around in the force of the current.

"And that was the last we saw of it," said Dick Henline. "Larry wanted that scalp to add to his collection."

"You like Indians pretty well," said I.

"Oh," said Dick Henline, "I guess we like 'em well enough, all right. We had a kid brother. They got him!"

He pulled his forefinger slowly across his throat; then he dragged it around the crown of his head in a most eloquent gesture. There was really no doubt about where the heart of the Henlines stood in this Indian business.

No wonder that no other people in the caravan had known anything about Black Elk. For this event was no more to the Henlines than if they had met an ant—and stepped on it. That was all!

That evening, I suggested a hunt as soon as the caravan halted. The pair assented at once, and we went whirling back across the hills with me in the lead for three or four miles.

Then I drew up my horse and sprang down, shouting: "Ride along, boys—I'll be up with you soon!"

I pretended to be busy with those cinches again, while from the corner of my eye, I watched the two of them plunge over the top of the next swell. It was not deep enough to swallow them. The horses were lost to my sight, but suddenly there were two shots ringing, and I saw two bodies pitch out of sight. Then two riderless horses were in view on the farther side of the hollow, galloping wildly.

I had no regret—only a vast deal of wonder that one man could have met those two hardy fellows and snuffed them out so quickly.

20

The smoke had hardly ceased curling from the muzzle of the rifle of Lost Wolf when I came over the swell, in turn, and saw the two dead men lying face downward in the grass, just as they had fallen from their saddles.

I told him what I had heard from Dick Henline, and leaning on his rifle, he listened and watched the dead. Only when I related how the dead body of Black Elk had floated down the swirling stream did he look up at me with a single flash of the eye.

There was no doubt that justice had been done to the pair, and yet I did not like it very well. I would have felt better if the shooting had been done by my own hand, rather than by that deadly rifle of big Lost Wolf.

He did not touch the fallen men. He simply took up the rifle of Black Elk from one of the hands that would never lift it again. Then he whistled, and the great red stallion came galloping out of a covert toward him.

It was arranged that I was to go back to the caravan, explain that I had lost the two while out hunting, and then continue with the wagon train for another day, at least, to allay suspicion. Then I was to cut back across country toward Zander City. The first time I camped, if I built two small fires close together, the twin columns of smoke would bring Lost Wolf to me.

I was glad to leave the spot where the two dead men lay. I turned Sir Thomas back and went slowly toward the caravan. On the way, by happy accident, an antelope shot out of a dry gulch and scooted across my way, not fifty yards distant. I had no time to draw my rifle and unlimber it at such an active target, but I snatched out a

Colt and blazed away. The third shot cut the rump of that antelope, making it leap high in the air, a distance which a race horse could hardly stride. When it came down, my fourth bullet luckily struck its head. It fell dead.

So I had all the better excuse for coming in quickly to the caravan.

When I got there I explained casually that the cinches had loosened, and the saddle had turned a little on Sir Thomas, and that by the time I had rearranged things and remounted, my two companions were away and out of sight. So I had gone hunting for myself, found this antelope and then decided to turn back toward the camp. No one asked any questions, but when the supper time was over, I thought that I might as well hobble Sir Thomas outside of the circle of the wagons.

That was what those of us did, who preferred letting our horses have a good chance for grazing, even if there were a danger of having them driven off by Indian horse thieves. A Pawnee thief, for instance, will extract a horse from a crowded camp as quietly as an expert pickpocket will take your handkerchief out of your pocket.

I left Sir Thomas outside of the circle, and I cached my rifle and the bridle inside of a little clump of brush, in the dusk when no one could notice what I was doing.

Then I went back, rolled up in my blanket, and closed my eyes.

The camp was quieting. That wagon boss kept a very strict rule and didn't allow any great deal of noise after the night was fairly settled on the caravan. He said that the daylight was the time for talk, that the night was the time for sleep for horses and men, and he intended that they should have a chance to get it.

I was almost asleep when a man leaned over my blankets and stirred me. It was big "Jock" McKay. He was related to the Henlines through marriage, I think, and he was the one who had persuaded them to go west with this caravan in search of new homes. He wanted to know why his cousins were so late in returning, and I pretended to be very sleepy and very irritated. I cursed the Henlines for having ridden away from me during the hunt, and I said that I hoped that they had lost their way on the prairie.

McKay shook his head, saying that they were not the kind to lose their way, but that they had probably followed a trail too far, for they were eager hunters.

I was sound asleep when the next interruption came. It came in the form of a voice that said solemnly: "Stand back. Give him a chance to wake up and get his wits."

That was big McKay. I knew his voice, and I guessed what the trouble was even before my eyes were open. So I stretched and then sat up with a yawn.

"The boss will be on top of some of you for making this much noise after dark," I said.

Then I saw that the wagon boss, his arms folded and his sharp eyes fixed on me, was in the front rank of the men who encircled me.

He said: "We have some questions to ask you. And the first question is: When did you shoot that antelope?"

I answered according to my first story, word for word. "After I lost the two Henlines, I went off hunting—"

"How long?"

"Oh, about an hour before I found the antelope."

The wagon boss sighed, and big McKay growled. After that there was a heavy silence, and off in the distance I heard a sudden rattle of a halter chain where a mule was jumping out of the way of an angered horse.

Somehow, that sound put the thought of prison and chains into my mind. No, there would be no prison and chains from the sort of justice that *these* men would mete out. They were not the type to burden their hands with offenders of the law. Because a caravan follows the same strictness of legal belief that prevails on board a ship. What is simply frank talk in a town is mutiny on a ship. So it is in a caravan.

Then the captain said: "Get up and come with us."

I got up, and as I started to accompany the captain, I saw two men fall in behind me without orders, and one of them was McKay. I didn't have to ask why he was there, and I didn't have to turn to see whether or not his gun was in his hand. I knew well enough!

The whole camp was stirring—but silent. There was a press around me of almost every man in the place. But

108

there were no children. I noticed that. Off to the side I heard a man bark very sternly: "Get out of this, kid!"

"What's the matter?" whined the boy's voice. "I only want to see—"

"What you want to see ain't good for you. Get out and go back to bed!"

A little chill wandered up my spine, circled my neck, and lodged in my throat. It became a bit harder to breathe.

Then we came to the place. There was already a circle of men standing around it. They opened and let me come up. While I looked down at the center of the circle, every eye rested on me and bored heavily and steadily against me.

Dick and Larry Henline lay there, dead and quiet. Their bodies were half covered with a canvas, but the upper edge had been turned back so that I could see their faces. Then the wagon boss said very gravely: "Why did you kill them, Rivers?"

I had nothing to say. For one terrible moment, with those steady eyes probing at my face, I was afraid that I would stand mute with my guilt showing. In a moment again I rallied, and I was able to look more calmly around me at the others.

I said: "I didn't kill them."

There was no standing upon courtesy among these men. McKay said: "Then why do you lie?"

"About what?" I asked him.

The wagon boss took up the conversation.

"A little while ago, your back trail was followed. Your horse has a queer shoe on his right hind foot that is easy to trace. We followed that horse's hoof prints right up to the spot where the two men lay dead. Will you explain that, my young friend?"

"Young? He might as well have called me his 'dead' friend.

I looked around me, and the wagon boss said: "Take his elbows."

The huge grip of McKay seized my right arm instantly and thrust the elbow behind me. Another caught my other arm. I merely smiled at them as they crushed the flesh against the bone of my arms.

"Do you think I can fly?" I asked them. "Do you think that I can run out of this camp and saddle a horse and get away from the rest of you?"

The logic of that seemed to appeal to all of them. The grips of the men who held me loosened a little.

"Speak up, man," said the wagon boss. "I told you when you joined us that I had my doubts of you. And you gave me a pretty black reason for your flight from Zander City. I can tell you what, Rivers: If you don't talk pretty eloquently now, and explain how your horse was in at the death of the boys, though *you* saw nothing of it, we are going to supply you with a good reason for leaving this earth and taking a short road for heaven. Do you understand me?"

I did, and it threw a mighty chill into me.

So I said: "Will any of you tell me what on earth could have been my reasons for wanting to kill those two men?"

"How do we know where you and they may have started a feud in the past?" said the captain.

"There are twenty men who can tell you that I never knew those two men before I met them in the caravan," I assured the captain. That seemed to stagger him for a moment. I went on: "I told you that I had to cut and run because I had killed a man. I wanted to go on with this wagon train until I got to a place where I could start life over again. Is it very likely that I would have cut off my only chance of company across the prairies? Is it likely that I would want to ride a thousand miles alone?"

The captain had something that made him thoughtful. I think that this argument might have changed his mind if it hadn't been that big McKay broke in at this point.

"I've never heard of a judge and a jury that had to find reasons for why a murderer put away his man. We don't know *why*. Larry and Dick Henline were two white boys, and I'm here to answer for that. What devil put the idea into the head of this chap, I don't know. But where his horse was, he was. And his horse saw the killing of those two men. Can you beat that?"

No, you couldn't very well dodge such logic as this. It had what you might call the ring of honest money about it, and I felt the noose around my neck.

"McKay," said I, "I want to ask you a question."

"Fire away," said he, and drew a little to one side of me. His grip on my arm relaxed. That of the other man was hardly touching me and so I turned fairly around on McKay. I did it as quick as I could jerk my body around, with my left foot jammed hard into the ground. With the sway of my body and the strength of my arm and my desperation, I jammed my left fist into the face of big McKay.

21

Men do not gather thick behind such a man as big McKay was, because his style of shoulders is apt to spoil the view that stretches before them. When McKay went down, there was a gap through the crowd, and into that gap I leaped as fast as any cornered fox that sees an open corner for escape. I was running at full speed, I suppose, before I had taken two steps.

Great arms reached for me. I spun out of them and was flung against another man. He and I went down in a heap—but it was a heap that rolled in the direction that I wanted to go, and in the split part of a second I was on my feet again.

I dodged two who lurched for me. Guns were impossible in such a crowd; even knives were too dangerous. Someone swung a gun butt at me, but it thudded upon another head, and the unlucky victim went down with a groan.

Then I was out through the densest core of the crowd, leaping through the scattering of people near by. A very wide and loose scattering, too, with women here and there. They gave way before me. I had a gun in my hand, and the flash of a gun in the hand of a man suspected of a double murder is poison to the hesitant, I can tell you.

They gave me plenty of space, and I got to the ring of wagons.

I leaped the hedge of goods between two wagons and so was on the outside of the ring, but now I found that I was on the opposite side from Sir Thomas.

It was no good to try to get away on any ordinary horse. McKay and others in that wagon train would make a mighty vigorous attempt to get me, I knew. I had to have a fast horse and a strong horse under me, if I expected to save my neck. So I legged it down the edge of the wagons a little faster, I think, than any other mortal ever stepped since Hector highstepped around the walls of Troy, with Phoebus to help him on his way.

They were after me fast enough. There were young men in that camp that would have handicapped a greyhound a hundred yards, and caught it before it was over the first hurdle. At least, so I thought as I felt them actually gaining on me!

When you run away, blind eyes are planted in your back. They feel the coming of the pursuit. They feel it and they shrink from it just as flesh shrinks from the edge of a knife. Every time those lusty youngsters behind me gained, I found strength in my despair to let out an extra link and draw away again.

I was around that wagon circle and sprinting for the shrub in which I had left the rifle and the bridle—but what was my chance for stopping to pick them out of the bush when hands were reaching for my shoulders as they twitched back and forth while I ran?

I jerked up my revolver. I could not dare to pause even for a partial turn of my body. I just fired over my head. The blaze and the crash of the explosion, however, knocked the wits out of the leader of the hunt. He tripped and went down with a yell, and by the noise, I suppose that two or three more spilled over him. Those behind slowed a little, yelling: "He's killed Tommy Matthews! Shoot the dog!"

In the dark of that night? Well, I was at that bush and I had the bridle and the rifle out, by that time. I only spared time to loose off one shot from that Winchester. A shot aimed at the stars. At the tension those fellows were under, I don't doubt that a good many of them were willing to swear the next day that they heard the bullet whistle an inch from their ear.

In that moment of pause I managed to spot Sir Thomas. As I ran on, with the pursuit beginning to roar and rush behind me, I shifted rifle and bridle to one arm, jammed the revolver into the holster, and caught out my hunting knife from its sheath. So I reached Sir Thomas and never was there a more welcome sight to me than that fine fellow with his head up, snorting, as though he wondered what was up tonight. He was ready for anything that might be coming his way. Oh, he was a glorious runner, and I was aching to feel the wind of his gallop in my hot face!

One slash of the knife reached the hobbling rope, and it parted. I did not wait to put on any bridle. Sir Thomas stood facing the crowd, but I simply leaped for his back and flattened myself on it.

I saw the crowd before me boiling up out of the darkness, but that was all I had a chance to see, for Sir Thomas had dodged like a scared rabbit, almost jerking me from my hold. Swerving away from the mass of that crowd, he quickly lighted out for the open spaces.

No spaces could be too open for me! You can write that down in capital letters! I loved the naked look of those stars as I had loved nothing else in the world. Sir Thomas, shooting me away toward safety with the great pulse of his racing stride, seemed to me a more delightful companion and friend than any I had ever known in a human form.

They were mounted behind me, but they were mounted about thirty seconds after I had my start. Half a minute was more than any horse could afford to give that blessed Sir Thomas.

For about three miles he simply spread himself and ate up the distance. Then he slowed a little. When he did, I managed to throw the reins over his nose and pull him up to a halt. I got off and let him blow. While he cleared his lungs and got a good whiff of fresh, cool air, I worked the bit between his teeth.

A man with a bridle on a thunderbolt could not have felt a great deal safer than I did after that. I jumped on his back, once more, and started him off again at an easy trot. As he trotted along, getting his second wind more strongly at every step, the men from the caravan came roaring out of the darkness again on my trail—half a dozen of the fastest horses in the camp, all bunched and running hard together.

Well, I loosed the reins, and Sir Thomas nearly jumped out of his skin. That bit of pause and then the easy trotting had made him a new horse, let his muscles relax, and eased up his nerves. He shot off with a gait as though the hard prairie were rubber and he were bouncing along over it. For ten minutes they kept at the race; then they began to shoot at me, and I knew that they had given up. I switched Sir Thomas eastwards toward the direction in which I hoped to pick up big Lost Wolf.

I knew pretty well what would happen. Most of those men who had ridden out after me could not afford to delay the caravan by continuing the chase and burning up their most valuable horseflesh in my pursuit. They would draw back to the caravan and once there, the best friends of the Henlines, and my worst enemies in the wagon train—if I had made any with my cocky ways— would band together and make up their minds as to whether or not it would be worth while to follow my trail. The odds were a little better than even that they would feel that it was a hopeless job that lay before them. If they *did* pursue me, they would have a very bad start, and they would have to wait until the next morning before they made any serious attempts to work out the problem of my trail.

Taking no pains to cover that trail, I simply rode straight on in the belief that the best thing that I could do would be to put mileage behind me. After I got to the side of Lost Wolf, he would probably arrange matters so that the trailers would wish they had never come after me!

At a very moderate gait, with the stars to keep me straight for the east, I jogged away until the gray of the morning came. By that time the springing step of Sir Thomas had put a long, long march between me and the starting point. There I got off and made a camp. I had only to scrape together some old buffalo chips to make my fire. While I squatted there, a rabbit stuck its foolish head above the prairie line and got a rifle bullet through the eyes, as a reward for curiosity.

I roasted the rabbit; then I divided my fire into two parts. While I ate I watched the little twin columns rise into the morning air, turning very white as the rising sun struck on them.

For a whole hour I ate, and rested and cleaned my guns, rubbed down Sir Thomas, praised him, and loved him, as he well deserved. He had made a gallant run out of that camp, and he had marched on steadily ever since.

With the end of my hour of waiting, however, I saw a shape come wavering toward me over the level of the prairie. Then I made out the form of a man on horseback. I thought that, even in the distance, by the great, easy sweep of the gallop of the horse, I could tell that it was Lost Wolf on his charger. There was another token which I did not miss, a great, white buffalo wolf sat down on a hummock a hundred yards away, and watched me.

That beast always sent a chill through me ever since the day that I learned it belonged to Lost Wolf himself. The greatness of its size, and the calm disdain it had of humans and human ways, the perfect understanding which existed between it and its master, made it a little more awful to me. I could not help feeling that while the closeness of relation between the red stallion and Lost Wolf showed all that was noblest and bravest and truest in his nature, his control of the great timber wolf showed his cunning, his cruelty, and all the wild Indian traits in his character. Something of this flashed through my mind. Then here was Lost Wolf before me. A moment more, and he was sitting cross-legged on the farther side of the story and listening to my tale of how I had managed to break away from the caravan. It seemed to interest him deeply and to make him very thoughtful.

"But," said I, "if they come hunting me, you will find ways of making them lose the trail, Lost Wolf!"

"The white men never forget," said he. "And after the Indian has forgotten, and after he has gone to sleep, the white men come and tap him on the shoulder and take him away to hang. So it will be with me, some day, and perhaps it may be with you, also, my brother!"

At that moment I was so immensely flattered by the respect and the intimacy in the tone of Lost Wolf, that I had no regard for future dangers. The dangers of the present delighted more than alarmed me when Lost Wolf pointed to the side and showed me what I really had not expected for a long time—a scattering of half a dozen horsemen coming toward us across the prairie.

I had not expected it, because I had not dreamed that they would be able to follow my trail through the night. As a matter of fact, they must simply have ridden blindly to the east and then come toward the direction of the twin columns of smoke in the dawn.

22

I was not alarmed, at first, only excited. The alarm came fast enough, I can assure you. There were seven forms riding in that party, and the rate at which they approached us was a pretty convincing proof that they were not riding horses which were staggeringly tired. As a matter of fact, we learned afterward that they had started out with ten in the party, each man with a led horse. When they sighted that smoke, they sent back the tired nags on which they had been riding all the night, and they went forward on their fresher horses. If Sir Thomas was somewhat recruited by the rest of an hour, *they* had been rested, too, by a halt about dawn. Now they came up on us hand over hand.

We shot off away from them, and for ten minutes it warmed my heart to see the manner in which Sir Thomas left them behind. That was not a true token of what was to happen. So long as he could raise a gallop he could distance the caravaners, but the strength that he was putting into that long stride of his was plainly killing him. He could not keep it up indefinitely, and presently he was swerving a little. I knew what that meant, and so did Lost Wolf: When I looked across to him, with the perspiration running down my face, he nodded and said: "Get off and walk that horse for a way. I'll ride back and watch the rest of them!"

I did not understand exactly what he meant at first. In another moment he wheeled the red stallion and went whirling away toward the rear. He had gone to throw himself between me and the seven riders. I turned in the saddle and yelled to him; it made no difference. He rode on all the faster, and then a low gully shut me out from the view of what was happening in the rear.

I got off obediently and walked my horse along, watching the weak trembling of his legs, which showed how far spent he was. No mere moment or two of breathing would give him back his strength. And yonder those fresh horses were sweeping up on us.

Then a rifle began to talk behind me in the silence of the prairie—the rapid talking of a repeater which had never been heard on the plains before the Winchester came out there to amaze men and slaughter man and beast.

That was Lost Wolf at work. When I walked up on the other side of that shallow swale, I saw that Lost Wolf and the seven had disappeared. No, yonder were the last two or three of the seven riding hard to get to the shelter of a gully, into which they now dropped.

By the time they had got back to shelter, Lost Wolf had moved back again out of their effective range. Indeed, by the manner of his shooting, I suppose he convinced them that as far as that strong-shooting rifle would carry was a convenient range for him. He kept pushing into their faces an arm longer than theirs would reach.

As my fear died down, and my senses grew clearer again, I began to enjoy that wild game more than a little. One needed one man in a million for one's partner in such

117

work. However, when there was a Lost Wolf along, the danger diminished enough to let the fun appear.

For ten miles the seven followed us across the prairie, burning up pounds of powder and slashing the air with pounds of lead in the hope of bringing down Lost Wolf, or his horse, at the least. He kept slowly retreating, moving in a zigzag from side to side and back again, shooting only now and then. Apparently he was close enough to his goal each time to take the breath of some of those living targets. Something told me that he was not really trying to kill. He was simply carrying on a gigantic bluff.

At length, they seemed to decide that it was useless to wear themselves out and tire their ponies to helplessness at this dreary game that never got to any point. They scattered out, leaving three men behind and two on each side. Those on the fastest horses, I suppose, began to rush around on the flanks. They obviously wanted to encircle us and hold us there in the palms of their hands.

Lost Wolf called to me: "Can that horse carry you another five miles?"

I shouted back that he could—or for ten. That walking retreat had occupied a full two and a half hours, and Sir Thomas had recovered so much of his spirits and his strength that now he was biting at the grasses as he wandered along. By the time I was in the saddle, Lost Wolf was beside me.

As he came up, he said with a groan; "Now, if we wanted to kill, we would ride straight back!"

I stared at him.

"We would right straight back," he explained, "and kill the three who are straight behind us. Then there would be four left—but they would be in two couples, far apart. First we would wipe out one pair and then hunt down the last two! Would not this be an easy game, my brother?"

He raised his head a little, so that his great, massive chin thrust out, and he laughed with a brooding savagery. More than the skin of this man was red as an Indian?

We gave those fellows behind us a good half-hour's gallop. Before it was half over, we were drawing far ahead of them. When it ended, they had drawn together in a little dark group of riders on the edge of the horizon.

Then Lost Wolf paused and with my help—working at his direction—gathered three small heaps of brash and grass and lighted them. We rode on, and the three thin columns of smoke rose up into the sky.

"You are signaling to friends that may see it?" I asked Lost Wolf eagerly.

He only smiled.

"That is what *they* will think," said he. "Since they are tired already, perhaps that thinking will be enough for them, and they will be glad to turn back toward the caravan. It is a great distance from this place, now!"

Oh, wise Lost Wolf! Whether they paused to think all these things out or not, I can give my word that not one of the seven advanced beyond the three pillars of smoke that rose out like a signal out of the heart of the prairies. I have no doubt that when they put their heads together, they simply decided that it would be useless to follow a man who shot as well as the rider of the red horse and who, in addition, was now calling for Indian allies—or for vagabond whites, who were even more to be dreaded.

We two were left to go on together. Very soon there was nothing behind us to tell of the end of the chase, except the three little arms of smoke now rapidly gathering together and merging into one. Lost Wolf would not halt to rest, however.

He said: "It is better to ride a tired horse outside of danger than it is to ride him to the edge of it and leave him there. When we are on the other side of trouble, then we can halt for two days, insted of for two minutes."

There was logic in that, as there was in most of the sayings of Lost Wolf. For two days, in fact, we camped where we finally halted that afternoon. It was only when Sir Thomas was thoroughly recovered from the strain of his long journey that Lost Wolf would permit me to go on. Then he chose a course which did not point straight back toward Zander City. He asked me if I would visit him in the Cheyenne village which he called home, and I readily accepted the invitation. Who would not have been glad of such an opportunity?

On the way toward that village, Lost Wolf referred twice to a theme which I could see was lying heavily upon his mind; he wished to know what I thought the attitude of the people in Zander City would be, if he went in among them?

It was rather a stickler to me, that question. I was not familiar enough with the ways and the thoughts of Westerners to tell just what was going on in their minds and I had to answer out of my own store of ideas. I knew that to a great many prairie dwellers, all Indians were abhorrent. They blindly detested every creature whose skin was copper colored. These same fellows would hardly be willing to forgive a white man who had lived most of life among the Cheyennes and posed as the greatest champion in that formidable tribe for years.

These men would make trouble for Lost Wolf, if they could. But I thought that the majority of the people in the town would look upon him very favorably. What Lost Wolf particularly wanted to know was if he could visit the town for a short time, in safety. This I thought that he could certainly do, because the townsfolk could not but remember that he had been of the greatest service to them of late and had resolutely kept his plighted word to them.

I repeated all of these reasons to Lost Wolf, just as they occurred to me, and my very heart swelled with the desire to ask him what on earth made him want to come to pay a visit in Zander City? I was too much in awe of Lost Wolf to ask impertinent questions. That subject had to remain a closed book to me.

After a whole week of travel we came, one day, in the sight of three Indians who rode out of the morning horizon at us. They barely caught sight of us when they wheeled away with loud yells and rushed off out of sight.

"Lost Wolf, are they Pawnees?" I asked.

Instead of answering, he simply dismounted, stripped off his deerskin shirt and his trousers. When he was dressed only in the loin strap and the light deerskin robe which he carried in preference to the thick-folded buffalo robe, he took from the little pack behind his saddle a small box. Out of this he brought oil, greased himself from head to foot, taking colors such as would serve to paint the inside lining of a grown-up nightmare. Red and raw green and flaming orange and blue. He had a little mirror which he hung on the pommel of his saddle. By the reflection in that he was guided as he proceeded in his work of art.

A work of art you could call it, too—or of horror in art. Before my eyes I saw a man whom I looked to as a friend transformed into a frightful demon. I really trembled as I looked at him!

When that streaking and smudging of his body with those pigments had ended, this white barbarian combed out his long black hair, thrust half a dozen eagle feathers into it, their tips stained various colors. That seemed enough, but it was not. He continued his decorative efforts on the red horse, and that glorious animal became rapidly a monster worthy of its master.

Still the work was not ended!

When he had finished the painting, Lost Wolf took out another small packet; from it he took out what looked to me at first to be rags. As he fastened them to the reins of his bridle, my blood curdled and nearly stopped flowing, I can tell you. They were human scalps, not overold!

23

Two human scalps hung at the reins of a man I was about to have called my friend. What I saw was a scene about twelve years before. I was standing at the knee of an uncle in front of the great fire in the library and asking him if it were really true that there were anywhere in the world people so terrible that they *did* take scalps. The grim smile with which my uncle answered me that sometimes fairy tales came true, came before me.

I saw that picture now. By contrast there were the two scalps, dangling from the reins of the red stallion, close to the bit. It ripped through me like a saw. I stared at Lost Wolf as if he were a specter. But he was one hundred per cent alive. When he vaulted back into the saddle, he made a funnel of his hands at his lips and sent a wild screech winging across the prairie.

Out of the horizon came half a dozen far-heard echoes of goblin shrieks in reply. Those yells redoubled and multiplied as we cantered ahead; then I saw one of the wildest sights that any man could ever have witnessed—that is to say, I saw about five hundred men and boys, and women mounted on Indian ponies with weapons in their hands, tearing toward us as fast as they could beat their ponies along over the plains.

There was a host of dogs, too, yelping and yelling as though they were running on cactus thorns. The whole procession looked to me like enemies, if there were ever hostile people upon the face of this earth. I had a wild notion that Lost Wolf may have decided that it was impossible for him to add any glory to his past life, and so he was going to die fighting a whole nation of his foes.

That idea of mine grew brighter and more certain as I heard the yelling of those five hundred fiends ring louder and louder. Others were coming up from behind, as fast as horseflesh could take them over the ground.

They came closer and closer; just as I felt that the wave of living flesh was about to break over us and dash us out of life, it broke into two sections and roared past us on either side. I have never seen such frantic faces as those of the Indians who streamed by us. You could have called it terror or joy or sorrow or despair or exultation. All emotions presented in something past all ordinary stress appear a good deal alike.

Dropping their ordinary pitch of screaming, they redoubled a noise which I thought could never be equalled again by them or by any others.

They had seen the two scalps! Five hundred steam whistles were turned loose to celebrate the happy event.

I did not exist. I was no more than a wooden image of a man. Lost Wolf was the whole center of creation. I suppose that, as they brought him into the village in this fashion, many a young brave who stood by and watched must have vowed that he, too, would go forth on the warpath and bring home scalps, and become, for a moment or two, the greatest man in the world.

Yes, I could sit back like a man in a theater and gape at that performance. And a performance it was!

First of all, the whole rout went milling over the edge of a shallow little valley, with a brook cutting through the midst of it. On the shore of the brook there stood a whopping big Indian village, with the tepees marked out in a great circle around some central lodges.

The lame and the halt and the leftovers, down to the toddling children who could not ride and the mothers with young infants to tend, now came streaming out to greet us. They made the outer fringe—the foam, as you may say—of the pool of noise that surrounded Lost Wolf, as he cantered into the Cheyenne village.

I drifted out into that fringe, myself, because I had no business there. As I wandered there, gaping at what I saw, I marked out a short, wide-shouldered man with grizzled hair who, his arms folded, looked on at the affair.

The whole lot of warriors had formed in a circle. They began the queer, jerky steps that are called dancing by the redskins, and in the middle of the circle appeared Lost Wolf.

I stared hopefully at the other white man near me. He was dressed very much like any of the other inhabitants of that town, but there was something about his air of detachment that promised me he was different from his appearance. He met my stare with a grin and then a nod. Of course, I was out of the saddle instantly and standing by his side.

"What in the world does it mean?" I asked.

"Is it all new to you?" said he.

"As new as you could possibly guess."

I had to stop, there, because the yelling of the men who were dancing in the circle came in pulsations, as answers to the voice of Lost Wolf. Here Lost Wolf had reached a point in his impromptu talk that set the women and the children all screeching like hunger-maddened wolves.

"Look here," said the stranger, "you came in with Lost Wolf?"

"I did."

"Your name is Rivers, then?"

I said it was and asked after his own name. He said that his was Danny Croydon. I remembered the name because of its queerness. Danny Croydon was that same white trapper who had taken charge of a section of the education and attempted to bring Lost Wolf back to the ranks of the people of his own race and his own blood. He had failed, almost as a matter of course.

"Well," said Danny Croydon, "if you've been out on the prairie with Lost Wolf, you ask as a friend, of course."

"Of course, I do," said I, seeing his point. "He's the most considerable man that I've ever met."

Danny Croydon nodded.

"And yet there he goes making a fool of himself, eh?"

"It looks that way to me," said I, "but I don't understand what it all means."

"You have a grain of sense, lad," said Croydon. "*You* couldn't do it, and *I* couldn't do it, but it means something to the rest of them. Even Lost Wolf can't go the whole way with them, though he was raised just like the rest of those critters. He doesn't dance, you see, but he talks— and what a lingo! He makes up for not dancing by that talk, I tell you!"

"What does he say?"

It was all Cheyenne dialect in which Lost Wolf was talking.

"All he's done so far is to tell them the names of the bucks that he has killed and scalped. They're both Pawnees —as you can tell by the look of the scalp, if you have an eye for such things. Those Pawnee wolves have a special way of wearing their hair to make it pretty for the lucky devil who wears it in his belt or over his lodge fire. Well, the name of the first of these fellows I didn't quite get. It was something about buffalo. But the other is the one that they're raising the ruction about. That one is Lame Eagle. He's taken so many Cheyenne scalps, at one time or another, that you may say he is a pretty familiar household word among the Cheyennes, particularly among these braves who are following young Running Deer. He used to haunt their trails. Listen to Lost Wolf turn loose on the yarn, now. Strange that a modest fellow like Lost Wolf is willing to talk like a book, as soon as a dance starts around him!"

In the middle of the dancing circle, with his big, painted shoulder muscles leaping and writhing as he made his gestures, Lost Wolf orated. Danny Croydon picked out snatches of the talk and translated it for me, in a murmur at my ear.

"All day the white wolf ran back and looked over the hills and then came and ran beside me, talking, and what was it that he said?

" 'Two Pawnees are following you, O Master, and one is a great warrior and a great chief. Let their scalps hang at your belt before night!'"

I could not help breaking in: "Confound it! I thought that Lost Wolf would be above such nonsense as that. They'll break out laughing at him in a moment, I suppose."

"Not a bit of danger of that," said Croydon. "They'd a lot rather laugh at the devil in person. Besides, this whopper that he's telling is just the sort of a diet that they thrive on. They *like* it. Animals talking? Well, for my part I think that great white devil *does* bring in gossip to his boss!"

He went on with his running translation:

"I said to the white wolf: 'My son, go back and mark them down for me. They are hunting me, as they think, and they must still think it until the night comes. Because, not until my white brother sleeps, can I hunt the hunters!'"

"That means you, Rivers, I suppose."

It had never occurred to me that this devil of a man could have done such a thing while he was with me. This seemed to be the case. He went on to describe how, when the darkness came, his white wolf marked the two Pawnees and kept running back to him, giving him word of the danger that was coming, but how he would not leave the camp fire until I was actually fast asleep. Then he went back.

"Like a snake through the green grass, that makes no sound. It was not Lame Eagle that I met first, but his friend. I leaped on him from behind, and he died in my hands, making no noise but a little whisper in the end. At that, Lame Eagle said: 'Did you speak, my friend?'

"I let the dead man fall from my hands.

"I said: 'Yes, I have spoken. Can you hear me, Lame Eagle?'

"He had not time for a gun, but his knife was out as he turned on me. But what is an eagle when the teeth of a strong wolf are in its throat? Then I went back to my own camp fire—and the white man still slept. He had heard nothing and dreamed nothing!"

There was a wild outburst of applause at this, but Lost Wolf went on to scoop up the rifle of Black Elk and shake it above his head, while he thundered forth an oration in a new key.

"Humph!" said Danny Croydon. "I think that this is a part of the story that you know pretty well. It's *your* story, Rivers."

24

That amazing fellow was talking about me, dressing me up in a style so gorgeous that my own mother in her most optimistic mood would never have recognized her boy. It appeared that I was the man whose rifle could not tell a lie. It was as easy for me to shoot from the sky a hawk that was barely visible, as it was simple for another man to tap a friend on the shoulder.

When he got this far, every dancing Indian in that circle looked aside at me and gave a "woof!" that sent a chill up my spine.

I exclaimed to Danny Croydon: "They act as if they *believe* this awful rot. What will happen if they come and ask me to show off for them?"

"That's easy," said Croydon with a stretching grin. "All you have to do is to pick up some sand and throw it in the air. When you see which way it blows, say that it is bad medicine for you to shoot this day. Besides, they're not even apt to ask for an example of what you can do. Hearing Lost Wolf tell about you is just as good to them as seeing it. Beyond all that, you *did* bring down a hawk with a lucky shot not so long ago. According to scalp-dance lingo, Lost Wolf isn't lying at all. He's just telling the bald facts!"

That was only the beginning. There was a lot more—a very great deal more. It appeared pretty soon that I was a white man with the heart of a Cheyenne in my bosom. I had heard from Lost Wolf about the disappearance of Black Elk, and the story had left me pretty sick. I couldn't get the idea out of my mind night or day, and I had sworn that I would never rest until I had killed the men who had killed Black Elk. He, Lost Wolf, who had loved Black Elk, had begged me to give the pleasure of killing the hounds into his hands.

I finally had consented, very unwillingly. Then I joined the caravan and found the guilty pair of men who had killed Black Elk by treachery at the fording of a stream. I brought these two men out and gave them into the hands of Lost Wolf, who killed them both, bringing away Black Elk's rifle.

"But," said I to Croydon, "these fellows will want more proof than this. They had the scalps before, but now they have nothing but a rifle that might very well be just stolen. They have only the word of Lost Wolf."

"He's a man that has never been known to tell a lie," said Croydon. "He does better with the Cheyenne than the Bible ever does with an earnest minister of the gospel."

"Never told a lie?" I said, groaning. "After I've stood here and listened to this awful guff, can you tell me that?"

"Never what the Indians would call a lie," said Croydon. "He says that he talks with his wolf. Well, behind that is the fact that the wolf probably *did* keep an eye on those two Pawnees all through half of that day. He says that you can shoot a corner off the sun. As a matter of fact you *have* brought down a hawk out of the sky. No sir, you can't catch Lost Wolf doing more than putting *embroidery* around the truth."

He had to shout the last half of this. When the Cheyenne braves heard this last performance of mine they let out such a roar that a whole herd of grizzlies couldn't have improved a bit on it. On the heels of the roar of the men, the women and children sent lightning after thunder, and simply split our eardrums.

It was a great event, that arrival of mine in the camp of the Cheyennes. Before Lost Wolf got through, I was a hero worth any nation's pride. The way he used a magnifying glass on my deeds was worse than shameless. I can't repeat what he said even now, without blushing. I'll only give as a sample that he said fifty white men on chosen horses followed us across the plains for a whole night and a greater part of the next day; that I had frightened the whole caravan badly when they tried to kill me. When I broke away and licked nearly everybody in the outfit, they didn't dare to come within rifle range of us.

Tremendous inventions like this slid down the throats of those Cheyennes like buttered mouthfuls. They balked at nothing, and when that speech of Lost Wolf was over— and it took the greater part of an hour for him to let his invention mill work itself out—some of the other braves were drunk with emulation. When Lost Wolf retired, another brave leaped into the center of the circle and told about the last scalp *he* had taken.

It began to be pretty foolish, except that the dreadful faces and the reputation of these warriors gave a nightmarish point to all that they did.

Then they broke up that dance and began to scatter through the village, first crowding past me and shouting gibberish at me which, Croydon said, was all to wish me well and tell me that I was a brother—and would I come to take a meal in each one's tepee?

Croydon answered for me that I was already invited to the tepee of Running Deer. When he told me this: "Why, Croydon," said I, "I haven't so much as *seen* Running Deer since I came to this village!"

Croydon declared that this made no difference, because

128

Running Deer was there, was leading the dance, and in the thick of everything, though I hadn't spotted him.

Croydon said: "Why, man, if you were to go to some lodge other than that of Running Deer, he would cut his throat in shame. You've just come in from the warpath after rendering a great service to the whole Cheyenne nation and to Lost Wolf in particular. Black Elk was the great friend of the Wolf, and the Wolf is, of course, something more than a brother to Running Deer. To top it all off, Running Deer, himself, is under a great obligation to you. Don't make any mistake about these things. To one of these Indians an obligation is something that's a part of his flesh and blood!"

Right after that Running Deer came and shook hands with me. It always seemed a freakish thing to see a robed Indian shaking hands. He gave me a welcome to his tepee, his village, and his people in terms that didn't have to be translated, because his voice and his eyes were speaking to me at the same time.

I never saw any man, red or black or white, that I liked so completely, quickly, and without reserve as I liked that same Running Deer. He would have stood for a gentleman in any language and in any society.

He took me toward his lodge, and Lost Wolf broke away from the admiring braves to come after us. He couldn't free himself from the children. No matter where he went in that village, he had to go slowly, wading through whole drifts of the little Indian boys and maidens. It was a sight, after having heard him shouting out boasts about his murders, to see him smiling and gentle among those children, while they laughed and shouted and danced around him.

There was so much Indian atmosphere in the village that night that I couldn't digest all of it at a gulp, as you might say. The last thing I saw, before we turned in at the open flap of Running Deer's tepee, was a whole string of other braves standing in front of their own lodges. They were all so heated up and filled with the warm blood of self satisfaction and pride in their tribe, that when one of them began to solemnly go around in a circle in front of his door, may I be blasted if fifty more of them didn't start in doing the same thing!

Have you seen a rooster showing off in front of a hen that he wants to strike with awe, dragging his wings, cocking back his head, and walking in a circle? Those dancers were for all the world just like roosters. Now and then they would give a convulsive little sort of kick and hop, but on the whole that dancing just consisted of a sort of jerky high step, like a rheumatic old man walking on red-hot stones.

I never in my life have seen anything sillier than those Cheyenne warriors pirouetting singly up and down that village. They got a lot of satisfaction out of it, and after all, when the beat of a drum is added to it, I suppose it is just as graceful and sensible, and quite on as lofty a moral and aesthetic plane as the dancing that I have lived to see.

We turned in at Running Deer's lodge, and Danny Croydon turned in with us.

He didn't dream of stopping to be invited. I said to him: "Man, can you come in here without an invitation from the chief? Won't it be dangerous to you?"

He only grinned at me.

"Thanks," said he, "but it would be dangerous for me, if I went to any *other* lodge. This is Lost Wolf's place just as much as it belongs to the chief, himself!"

I found out afterward that Danny Croydon would have been pretty welcome at *any* of the lodges in that town, without an invitation. He was a great trader, and his reputation for honesty was so great that the only thing that would take the Cheyennes away from his trading stock was the appearance of firewater in the stores of a rival trader. Danny Croydon was one of the few good souls who refused constantly to let whisky come into the possession of the Indians, through his means.

This lodge of Running Deer's was a whacking big one. It was about twice as big as the lodge of any other chief that I was ever in; yet it was put together so that it could be dismantled and packed away on the travels very handily. This was due to some of the inventions Lost Wolf had applied to the living quarters of his friend. However,

130

though the wits of Lost Wolf had made the lodge a bit more spacious and comfortable than the usual tepee, the place was typical enough, with its fire in the center, and fenced-off sleeping quarters around the wall, and the feature which interested me most was the great pot which was steaming over the side of the fire and filling the tent with the fragrance of the best school of Indian cookery.

I noticed that pot first; then through the smoke and the steam that were stinging my eyes, I began to take in some of the other details.

I knew not a great deal about buffalo robes, but enough to understand that these with which I saw the place furnished were of the finest size and quality and curing. Those paintings that covered the walls of the tepee must have been worth an Indian fortune. There was a particularly slashing picture of two fighting buffalo bulls that was really recognizable. It was up to the standard, say, of the work of a fifth-grade boy in a public school.

Then I saw the squaws of Running Deer, and I forgot the stinging of my eyes.

25

They were a prize lot. The average Cheyenne girl exceeded the other prairie girls in good looks as much as they exceeded them in chastity. Take them all in all, they were a very good lot, and Running Deer had taken the pick. The average price of a squaw ran from one pony to five; Running Deer's five wives had cost him more than a hundred horses! He told me so himself!

Of course, he could never have stood such an expense out of his own possessions, but Lost Wolf came to his help and paid for two of the best of the lot. That was considered no more than fair because Lost Wolf insisted on living in the lodge of his friend. He had a big corner reserved to himself, heaped around with his little comforts and possessions, of which he had enough to make a whole tribe envious. His horse stealing from the Sioux and the Pawnees and the other enemies of the tribe, according to Danny Croydon, had made him a rich man. The peculiarity of Lost Wolf was that he refused to take a wife out of the tribe. Having paid the price of a pair of Running Deer's finest wives, Lost Wolf had the right to live in that big tepee, whose manufacture he himself had overseen. All of his cooking, matching, mending, sewing, and the manufacture of his buffalo robes was understaken by the wives of Running Deer.

Certainly he was a most welcome part of that family. The first thing that happened after he came into the tepee was that the children rushed for him. Running Deer had married for the first time when he was very young. Now he had a son seven years old, another boy and two little girls—a whacking big family for any brave, young or old. They were all big enough to toddle or creep, and they swarmed for Lost Wolf.

He seemed to be delighted. It looked as though they were dragging him down to the ground. There he sat in the firelight pretending to be very angry and pretending to fight them away. A muscular young scoundrel, four years old, took a black lock of the Wolf's hair in either fist and tugged as hard as he could; Lost Wolf roared as if he were in torture, to the huge delight and merriment of all the rest.

They were diving into his pockets now, bringing out whatever they found—a pocketknife, a bright-colored silk handkerchief, strings of beads. There seemed to be a mine of everything that children could possibly want in the pockets of that monster.

Running Deer stood by with his nose a bit in the air and his arms folded.

"Is the chief jealous?" I whispered to Danny Croydon.

"Not a bit," said Croydon. "But this sort of thing makes the whole tribe look down on Lost Wolf a little. He's never been known to cuff a child or speak up rough to a

132

woman—except his foster mother, and that old witch deserved it double."

Now that I looked again, I could see that he was entirely right. Running Deer was fond of his big ally, but he was more than a little contemptuous of him, also. The good nature and the relaxation of Lost Wolf in that tepee of his friend seemed a pleasant thing to me—but then I had the white viewpoint, not the red.

"Look here," said I to Croydon, "what does all of this mean? The only time he has a red skin is when he's on the warpath!"

Croydon nodded. After that, I had no chance to discuss my hosts with the trapper and trader. We were too busy with supper. We sat down around that pot—just the four men, and we did enormous things in the way of eating, I can tell you! The women squatted behind us, ready to be useful in reaching things here and there. Most of their reaching was in the direction of Lost Wolf, who was eating enough for a whole company of soldiers. I have never seen a faster or more fluent destruction of solids. He didn't pause until that pot was scraped clean. Then he went to his corner without a word to the rest of us, rolled himself in his blanket, and was snoring in a moment.

It was very rude. The nose of Running Deer was raised a little again. He began to make conversation very pleasantly to me, using Croydon as interpreter. He wanted to know my plans for the future, and he intimated that, if I cared to become a trader, connecting with the Cheyennes, I could be sure of a monopoly of their buffalo skins. He, Running Deer, would answer for this tribe which was under his control, and his influence would spread to others, also.

This was extremely agreeable. I went to sleep on a big, soft buffalo robe, dreaming of myself as a merchant prince, returning to Charleston with so much money made out of the pelts brought to me by Indians that my worst enemies would not have the courage to raise that ridiculous charge of murder against me.

These were in my mind, when I fell into a sweet sleep and forgot all my troubles and all danger that I might be riding toward in the future. In the midst of these happy dreams, I awakened the next morning to find that the camp was already stirring. Running Deer was moving his tribe farther on, toward a new camping ground, and the work had to begin before the sun was up.

Lost Wolf was not interested in this maneuver. I saw him standing apart with Running Deer. The chief was in the greatest affliction of mind, apparently. He was arguing with much heat. Lost Wolf was merely shaking his head and returning a single massive monosyllable from time to time, thus beating down all of the appeals of the Cheyennes. I applied to Danny Croydon, when I got down to the river for a swim, finding him whipping the water from his body as he stood on the bank of the creek.

Croydon said: "I supposed that *you* knew. It simply means that Lost Wolf is going to head back toward Zander City, and that he's going along with you."

I was thunderstruck, not having the slightest thought as to what it could possibly mean.

"Well," said Croydon, "it seems that he's going to drive in all of his own horses, too, and take the whole lot of his baggage away from the tribe. No wonder that Running Deer is cut up! Lost Wolf has what amounts to about ten Indian fortunes in his hands. He's a regular millionaire!"

I could see that, easily, when I got back to the center of the village after my swim and saw Lost Wolf directing the removal of his belongings. He had led so many raiding parties, and he had scooped away so many loads of stolen merchandise that he could have set up in a very respectable business in any Eastern City, selling his goods. He had beaded suits—though none half so fine as the one which he had given me—and he had heaps of buffalo robes, painted and unpainted. He had beads by the hundreds, to say nothing of powder and lead. The horses, however, were his prize possession. He had a grand eye for horse-flesh, of course, or he would never have corraled such an animal as the red stallion which he rode always. And he had used the excellence of his horse judgment in picking out the cream of the ponies every time that he accompanied a raiding party.

Danny Croydon stood beside me while those little, thick-legged, hairy, lump-headed Indian ponies were cut out from the main herd of the village stock. The young men and the boys of the tribe were busy at this work, and they shunted the herd into two parts with wonderful skill, sorting out the possessions of big Lost Wolf.

The giant, himself, stood by and watched with an eye that missed nothing. As for the Indians, their faces were black.

"It hurts them," I suggested to Croydon, "to see all of this wealth leaving the tribe."

"They are disgusted," said Croydon, "when they see that Lost Wolf knows the face of every horse that belongs to him. These prairie Indians make a virtue out of giving. But Lost Wolf picks the places where he makes his gifts."

"Why," said I, "it seems to me that I have seen him give away like water."

"Only to people he honors. He makes his gifts not as if he despised the things that he was giving, but as if he wanted to honor more the people to whom he gave. But your perfect Indian brave, Rivers, gives away just for the sake of giving—just because, now and then, he wants to be poor and feel himself stripped of every advantage except his gun, his horse, and his native good wit. In Lost Wolf they see the business instinct of the whites dropping out."

"He's a god with clay feet, then?"

"He is."

However, the work proceeded. The most docile of the horses were gathered together and packed high with the goods which belonged to Lost Wolf. The rest were scattered on ahead by the Indian boys as herdsmen. Then Lost Wolf announced to me that he was ready to proceed.

Saying farewell to Croydon, to Running Deer and his squaws and children, I started back across the prairie with Lost Wolf. Half a dozen of the young braves rode along as herdsmen, because it would have been a sacrilege for so distinguished a character as the Wolf to have had to do any manual labor—even so much as herding his own horses!

There were a hundred and thirty of those ponies, every one was a chosen beast. Those little horses would outsprint any thoroughbred for two hundred yards, and wear down most thoroughbreds in a day's march. The material out of which they were made was nothing but iron and leather—iron bone and leathery muscle. I suppose that no creature ever lived, so well adapted for foraging on the plains in winter, and scouring them in huge marches in the summer as were those same Indian ponies.

We marched along far enough behind the horse herd to keep out of its dust. For five long days I endured the silence of the prairie and the silence of big Lost Wolf, until once more I saw the low line of Zander City rising out of the prairie ahead of us.

It was late in the afternoon—the quietest time in the town, with the life of the day dying down, and the night life hardly begun. When Lost Wolf asked me if he could ride safely through Zander City, I told him that I thought he could, and that I would go along with him as an escort.

He looked over his ponies and had his herdsmen separate a section of twenty of them. Tying them together with rawhide lariats, he drove that little mob of ponies into the town of Zander City.

I thought, at first, that he was simply intending to sell the ponies for cash or trade them in for goods, but there was something about the air of Lost Wolf that told me he had other intentions. While I was still in confusion, he brought his little herd to a halt squarely in front of the house of the minister, Charles Gleason!

26

He secured the ponies in front of the house and walked up to the door, leaving me outside to guard the little herd. What happened in that historic interview, I could not relate as an eye witness. I heard it afterward in detail. When his voice at the front door was not answered at once, he went around to the back door; the great, white buffalo wolf leaped the tall fence that surrounded the Gleason garden and went with him.

There he encountered Mrs. Gleason in the domestic act of hanging out the tag-end of a washing which she had rubbed out while her roast was simmering in the oven with the rest of supper waiting for the return of her lord and master from the church.

Big Lost Wolf heaved up one of his gigantic hands and growled: "How."

Mrs. Gleason, for almost the first time in her life, was speechless. She had the heads of half a dozen clothespins in her mouth, and they fell out and rattled on the ground around her. Then she thought of self-defense, and she shouted for Rollo.

Rollo was a giant dog, half mastiff and half St. Bernard. He had been with the minister for a little more than a year and in the first month of his stay he had established himself as the boss of every dog in the town of Zander City. After that, Charles Gleason felt a good deal more comfortable when he had to ride off on a long trip to visit some sick parishioner. If the ruffians of the town should bother Mrs. Gleason while he was away, Rollo was sure to bring them to good account. There was about a hundred and fifty pounds of Rollo, and they were all hard pounds, kept in good trim by the fights he had with the other dogs in the town. Just enough new dogs came to Zander City to keep Rollo in trim. Now he had advanced to such a point that he taught a new dog to know him, by killing the foreign fool.

He had no fear of men, either. Altogether, as he came bounding along with his lionlike mane bristling, he was a picture that was enough to have spoiled the sleep of a very brave man for many a night.

However, a white flash leaped in from the side. Its teeth gleamed and ripped up the side of Rollo like a long knife stroke. Rollo turned to take the strange, wolfish creature by the throat. The throat was not at hand. Wherever Rollo rushed to get at the stranger, he was met by a crashing fence of teeth and a weight as great as his own, plus a power a good deal more. In fact, Rollo was on the verge

137

of having his own gullet opened with one rip of the wolfish teeth when Mrs. Gleason saw what was about to happen and decided to take a hand.

The first glimpse of Lost Wolf had given her a start and made her call for her dog. After the first shock, there was hardly anything in the world that really worried Mrs. Gleason. When she saw Rollo rolling on his back, the split part of a second from a miserable death, she snatched away the long heavy pole which she used to support the clothesline in the center, and she came charging with a war cry.

White Wolf was not a blind fighter. He had taken the edge off of Rollo's fighting hunger, by this time, so he left the big mastiff sprawled upon his back and turned to take care of the human enemy. Mrs. Gleason's courage held good even then. She swung the pole with a weight that would have scrambled the brains of the wolf as far as the barn if he had only remained in a straight line at her. He didn't; he twitched to one side—the pole hummed harmlessly past his head—and the next instant poor Mrs. Gleason saw a double row of frightful teeth open before her very face.

It would have been her last moment, perhaps, even though she flung up an arm to save herself, for jaws which could rip the side of a running buffalo were apt to find the throat of the woman at the first snap. Just here, the voice of Lost Wolf came with a bark like the explosion of a revolver—the grinning teeth closed on empty air, and the wolf sailed harmlessly past Mrs. Gleason.

Once more Lost Wolf spoke; that syllable of rasping Cheyenne made his wild ally crouch in the shadow by the fence, not daring to stir again until permitted.

Rollo got to his feet by this time. He was in no hurry to examine that gray, panting patch in the shadows by the fence, but he was willing to have a flyer at the man. He was in mid-air, with his jaws gaping, when Lost Wolf stepped neatly in. His long arms shot forth; his huge hands clutched the mastiff by the throat, and now he was carrying the brute toward Mrs. Gleason.

"What shall I do with him?" he said in perfectly good English. "Or shall I just choke him until he goes to sleep?"

Mrs. Gleason could not answer. She looked from the calm face of the big man to his forearms where the enormous bands of muscle stood forth. She decided that she had never before seen his like, and never would she see it again. Then the protruding tongue of Rollo warned her that her dog was about to die.

"For Heaven's sake!" said Mrs. Gleason feebly. "Don't kill the poor dog!"

Lost Wolf carried the mighty Rollo to the barn, threw him into it, and closed the door upon him.

"He will get back his breath, and he will also live," he said to Mrs. Gleason.

She had recovered herself a little by this time. How bitterly I have wished that I might have been present to see the face of that good lady! For once in her life, her vocabulary failed her, but only for a little time.

Then she said to this mighty destroyer of men:

"Young man, how dare you come into my back yard with your infernal wolves? Get out of here, and get quick!"

Lost Wolf regarded her for a moment with a weary indifference. Then he turned from her and spoke a single word—not to her, but to the gray brute under the shadows by the fence. The wolf came instantly slinking to his heels. They strode down the path to the back steps of the house and then up those steps.

"Heavens!" cried Mrs. Gleason. "Peggy—"

Then she yelled to Lost Wolf: "Keep out of that house!"

She charged as she spoke, but when she came near, the white wolf turned and gave her a single snarl. It nearly made Mrs. Gleason collapse, but when she saw the big man and his wolf stride through the kitchen door and into her house, her despair became greater than her fear.

She leaped up the back steps of the house, and she caught up a big double-barreled shotgun that always leaned against the wall in the little cupboard near the kitchen door. Armed with this, she rushed through the house, ready to fight and die. Peggy was somewhere in that house, and if Peggy came within the sight of this red-skinned monster—

As she passed the door of the library, she caught sight of the copper-faced stranger sitting cross-legged upon the bearskin rug in front of the fireplace, in the act of cramming one of the minister's long-stemmed pipes with the minister's best tobacco. The great wolf dog lay stretched before the feet of his master, ready to guard them.

Mrs. Gleason paused, made sure that her daughter was not in that dreadful room, and then threw her shotgun over the crook of her left arm. She was not a bad shot, for she could go out with any man and drop her bird on the wing. It was her way of taking a little vacation from her household duties.

She said: "This gun is loaded. It shoots straight and mighty hard, and it scatters its fire. Are you going to stand up and step out of this house?"

The man on the rug simply finished filling the pipe; then he lighted it and grunted through the thick haze of smoke:

"Send Gleason. I cannot talk to a squaw."

That was all—all that he said in answer to Mrs. Gleason plus a shotgun. I suppose that she must have trembled with her anger. To be called a squaw! Oh, to have been there to see and hear it!

She started to threaten him again but he finally blew a puff of smoke insultingly at her, with that outburst of the lower lip that Indians use when they wish to be totally annoying.

He said: "You shoot the dog and this will finish you."

He tapped the handle of his hunting knife.

Then he added: "You shoot me, and the dog will finish you. Go, squaw. This man wants to smoke in peace!"

Mrs. Gleason may have wanted to pump the two barrels of that shotgun into man and beast, but what he said made her pause to think. Shooting at Lost Wolf at close range was very much like planning to pelt a loosed tiger with stones. It was too exciting a prospect to be pleasant. She backed out of the door and sat down in the hallway to wait and to guard. While she sat there, Peggy came and in whispers was warned to go back.

So Peggy came flying out of the house to get help, for her mother would not move a step away from the place to allow it to be plundered and perhaps set on fire, as she said, by a wild Indian. When Peggy came racing from the front door, the first thing that she saw was me.

She was white as snow and prettier than any picture that has ever been painted when she rushed to me to beg for help. When I found out what had happened, I wanted to laugh, and yet I was worried, too, because I did not know what deviltry might come into the mind of that wild man in the house. I started for the front door, in spite of Peggy holding onto my arm and begging me to be cautious, and saying that she would never forgive herself and—

Just then Mr. Gleason came up and dismounted from his horse. He was with us in one jump, and when he found out what was wrong, he didn't hesitate an instant. He wasn't exactly a hero, but I suppose that he had never done any harm in his life, and so he was not going to take a backward step from anyone.

He pranced right into that house and I got along after him as fast as the girl would let me. He and I got to the door of the inner hall at the same moment. There Mrs. Gleason met us with:

"A fine man you are, Charles Gleason, to go off and leave a wife and child at home to be murdered and scalped by Indians! A fine man to be—"

I didn't think that Gleason had it in him, but in this emergency, he said: "Put that gun away, woman, or we'll *all* be scalped and murdered, perhaps. Put that gun away and please keep still!"

He walked toward the library door.

27

This may not sound as though it were a very great thing that Gleason had done, but considering the nerve strain of the moment, it *was* pretty brave. The instant that he got to the door of the library, with me at his side trying for the tenth time to explain that everything was all right, the instant that he got to the door of the library, the tenseness went out of the minister with a shudder of relief. He cried:

"Why, it's only my friend, Lost Wolf!"

Lost Wolf got up and stretched out his hand:

"You have good tobacco, Mr. Gleason."

"Heavens," cried the minister's wife from the background, "is it the same young wild man that ate up all our best ham and—"

"But you have a bad squaw," said Lost Wolf, "which is what the Great Spirit has sent you so that other men should not envy you. I am happy to see you again!"

This was as queer a mixture of boldness and frankness and courtesy as I had ever listened to. Mrs. Gleason was so completely paralyzed by what she heard that she staggered away for the kitchen to recuperate, only muttering as she went that she hoped Charles would break the Indian in two; he would *have* to, if he wished to have the world consider him a man!

I could not help chuckling at the thought of the minister laying hands on the giant bulk of Lost Wolf. Here they were shaking hands, and at least I could heave a sigh of relief when I saw that I had not introduced a murderer to the Gleason household.

Gleason was inviting Lost Wolf to sit down. When he had finished off his pipe he got up and announced what he had made this visit for, by leading the minister out onto the front porch and pointing out the twenty ponies which were tied up there.

He said: "When the Cheyennes want a good wife, that works hard and sews well and makes buffalo robes for him and keeps the fire warm in the tepee, he takes a pony to the lodge of her father and leaves it there."

I stared at him; Gleason stared at him. We understood what he said, but somehow, neither of us could permit the real meaning of his words to get into our minds.

"When a man sees a girl whom other braves want, and who is young and strong and pretty and has never been married before—a girl that knows fine beadwork, and how

142

to make the softest robes, and cook very well; then he takes three ponies to the lodge of her father and they talk together. If they are wise people, they take the three ponies and are glad of their good luck.

"But sometimes there is a great beauty. Braves have seen her and wanted her for their wife. Her face rides with them on the prairie. They are sick for her. And one man brings five ponies and ties them at the door of her father's lodge, and another man brings six horses. But a third man is very rich, and he brings ten horses and ties them all at the door of the lodge of her father, and her father gives the young girl to him.

"There are twenty horses standing at your lodge door. They are not common ponies. They are all chosen from the Sioux, from the Pawnees, who are born to know good horses, and from the Cheyennes themselves. Where is there a war party from the Cheyennes that has done great things, unless Lost Wolf rode with them? From every raid I have brought home fine ponies. Here are twenty, then.

"There is a young girl in your lodge. I do not ask if she is strong or if she can make beadwork. Does she work well? Are her hands hard? I do not ask why she has reached this age without finding a husband. Among us, the finest girls are married by the time they are fourteen. Your girl is much older, but I do not ask any questions. I give you twenty ponies. So give me the girl to take back to my tepee to be my squaw."

There it was at the last, all as clear as day and extremely bitter to Gleason and to me, also, because I was the man who had, in a way, brought this misfortune upon that house. If it had not been for me, he would never have come into the house, and if he had never risked his neck to see me and to get my help in his projected revenge, he would never have laid eyes on the girl.

Only that one look at her, and that had been enough! I could not understand why, well enough. Had not the same thing happened with me? What baffled me was that Lost Wolf could have gone coolly ahead with his plan of vengeance and never faltered for an instant until he had finished his task and laid the two murderers of his friend dead. Not that he loved the girl less, but that he loved his honor more. He felt that his honor was pledged to the revenging of his friend.

Respecting Lost Wolf for these things, at the same time, I was very much afraid of him for the same reasons. You could see that he was a fellow who kept himself perfectly under self-control.

The minister flashed one wild glance at me; I could only stare blankly back at him. Gleason said, at last, faintly: "That is a great price to offer!"

I would never have thought of even *that* time-serving reply. It did not keep Lost Wolf back. It never occurred to him that there might be a shadow of sarcasm in such a remark. He simply smiled and said:

"I am a rich man among the Cheyennes. The horses which I own are many enough to seat the warriors of a tribe. Many a time the chiefs have come to me and said that it was time for me to take squaws and so have my own tepee and let my children grow up to enjoy my wealth after me. But I have waited. And at last I have found your girl. Tell her that this is a happy day for her. Let her be brought to me at once, and carry the ponies to your own stable. They are yours."

From the expression of Gleason, I saw that he expected a knife in the hollow of his throat if he refused pointblank. He mustered his courage and said that he would have to consult with Mrs. Gleason.

Lost Wolf threw his robe around him. It was a near approach to a gesture of disdain.

"It is true," said he. "I have forgotten that the white men take the squaws into their councils. I shall go back and wait, and my friend, who stays with you, shall bring on the news to me of what you and your squaw will do with your daughter."

This was enough retort for the day from Lost Wolf. He strode away from the house, leaped on the back of the red stallion and was gone. He left the rest of us to brood over what had happened. Mrs. Gleason, her husband and myself, sat around the table and talked the matter over. For once, Mrs. Gleason was frightened enough to give up her overbearing manners. She only remarked that I had

144

brought a great deal of good fortune into their house, and then she got down to the serious consideration of their problem.

At first, she suggested calling out all of the townsmen and falling on Lost Wolf. It was no good telling her that this was not exactly a moral course of action. I simply showed her that if they went to take Lost Wolf, they were more than likely to collect nothing more than a handful of bullets and not very much fame. Then she suggested that we simply wait until he appeared again, and have armed men in waiting for him. Here Mr. Gleason put down his foot and said that he would not permit her to turn his house into a man trap.

You can gather from this that the twists and the turnings of her mind were not exactly honorable. At the same time, I could not help having a great deal of sympathy for her. She had her back to the wall, and she loved her daughter more than she would have loved the world, had it been made of gold and silver.

Finally, Gleason and I worked it out that I was to go out to Lost Wolf and tell him that Peggy had been consulted and that she had decided that she would not even *think* of such a thing as marriage for several years, at the least. Neither the mother nor the father wished to cross her desires on this vital point.

Before I started, I could not help showing the two of them that I appreciated the fact that I had brought in Lost Wolf to have a glimpse of Peggy in the first place, but that by going on this errand I was running a lot of danger of having my neck twisted off. That was just about what I figured would happen if Lost Wolf found out that I was, myself, a suitor for the favor of dear Peggy.

"So!" muttered Mrs. Gleason. "This is the fine young hero! Do you *admit* that you're really and truly afraid of him?"

"Oh," I told her, "I haven't any shame in that. Lost Wolf is not like the rest of men."

I went down, took the twenty ponies, and led them away through the dusk of the evening. By this time the sun had set and Zander City was growing dark fast. I took the river road, because I felt that by following this course,

145

there would be less chance, by far of coming in contact with the wakening life of the night in the town. I most certainly did not wish to be recognized with that mob of horses behind me.

I took the quieter river road, because there were fewer saloons and gaming halls and lodging houses facing that way. There were the docks where the river steamers were unloaded and the storehouses on the pierheads, where the goods were stored when they were waiting for further shipment up the river in lighter draft boats, or when they were to be taken to the stores in the town. There were offices and the beginning of the lumber yard, with a scanty supply of sweet-smelling timber in it. That street was always deeply gouged by the grinding wheels of heavy wagons.

More than halfway out of the town, I happened to ride in fairly close to the lights of almost the only drinking place at the river along that way. It had *real* lights, however, and over the door were two big lamps, throwing a single column of gold far out on the black of the river. "Buck" Raridan shot out those lamps, one night, and set fire to the place. It was thought that Zander City was about to go up in smoke, but the flames were put out. This was about two weeks before Buck's party.

As I came in a little closer to the lights—just *smelling* the damp alcohol breath of that saloon's insides—who should come sashaying out but a big man with a swagger to his shoulders that looked familiar to me. There was a sort of a sailor's roll to his walk, and when I got a squint at the side of his face, I knew him. It was Jock McKay!

The pull of my eyes made him jerk around quick and stare straight at me. I froze onto the handle of a Colt, ready for the gun play. Though he looked into the darkness toward me, he didn't see my face. There was too much light close to him, I suppose, and he was dazzled. For I saw him walk on down the sidewalk, and knew that I was safe for the moment.

28

When I got out to Lost Wolf, I found that he was with the remainder of his horses near the place where we had originally left them. I gave him the message as cheerfully as I could. He listened to it and shook his head with wonder.

"There is something wrong," said he. "I cannot tell what it might be, but I know that there is something wrong."

He sat for a long time in thought.

"It is simply that they do not wish to force their girl to marry before she begins to think of it herself," I suggested.

He dropped his chin upon one fist, corrugated with knuckles as hard and as rough as knobs on a rock.

"That can not be right," said Lost Wolf. "People would not listen to the voice of a child in such a matter. What is her voice to them? It is only her happiness and the ponies that she brings that counts with them. With a man who can pay twenty horses for a wife, how could she be anything other than happy? No, it is not that. And the fault must be with my price. Twenty horses was not enough. But tomorrow I shall show them that I *am* a great man and a rich man. I shall offer her double that number. Forty horses for a mere girl!"

I felt that I was in the oddest position in the world. I had to spy upon this man on the one hand, and on the other hand, I had to pretend to him that I was spying on the girl and her family. Somewhere, my game was almost certain to go wrong, particularly since Jock McKay was thrown into the picture. He was sure to make things hot for me sooner or later. I saw that about my only way out of this trouble was to rush matters through to a conclusion with Margaret Gleason. If I could turn her head completely with a whirl of romantic arguments, I made up my mind, while I listened to the deep stern voice of Lost Wolf in the light of his little camp fire, to run away with Peggy Gleason, marry her at the house of the first minister, and then start out to carve a way to fame and fortune for both of us.

I told Lost Wolf that I had better go back to the house of Gleason and see if I could not learn more exactly just what was holding them back from his offer. He thanked me most heartily for this offer, saying that my friendship was better to him than gold. Of course, I felt very cheap when I heard him carry on like that about me, and I was glad to get away and ride on back toward the town.

On the way, I turned over my recent resolution. The more I looked at matters, the more convinced I was that I was right. It was far the best to carry Peggy away.

Perhaps it was selfishness on my part, when I had practically no money, no position, no influence to help me along through the world and really no one of power interested in me—except enemies! I guess all young men are grandly blind egoists and egotists. If a young man were not so high headed and smilingly confident that he is going to show the world a thing or two, how *could* he ever dare to accept on his shoulders two prodigious burdens— the making of a career on the one hand and the provision for a family on the other? His confidence in his unique talents is so great that he pities the girl who refuses him, and rarely finds a gray head that he is not tempted to look down upon with contempt for all that is in it.

As for me, there seemed nothing particularly difficult in making a handsome income in a very short time, and then in establishing a safe and bright home for my wife and the children who were to come.

The little troubles with the Federal government, which made me wanted in Charleston for murder and which would shortly make me wanted in Zander City also, with the deaths of the Henlines saddled upon me, did not seem to me at the moment worthy of the slightest consideration.

A mere change of names seemed to me a simple way of dodging the trouble.

Then, a young man always feels that trouble will "blow over." Of course, they don't. Evil rumors never sleep, and most tongues are never sharp in praise. How little cleverness would there be in the conversation of all people if it were not that they have subjects for scorn and mockery and contempt!

I did not care to dwell upon such subjects. All that I knew was that pretty Peggy Gleason loved me, or smiled at me with her eyes, as though she did. It seemed to me that all that was sacred in human law and divine would be blasphemed if I did not marry that girl straightaway!

You will say that I surely remembered how often I, myself, had been falling into love and out again all my life. I assure you that I didn't. It was quite all right for *me* to do such a thing. A woman must love once, once only, and die like a plant without water if she cannot marry the first, the right, the only man!

I was young. As I look back on the affair, I am simply flabbergasted to think how fearfully, incredibly young I was—selfish and egoistic. I could not have wished for Peggy a better model of a husband than I was!

Getting back to the Gleason house, I found Mr. and Mrs. Gleason putting their heads together and conning the difficult affair over and back and forth. They welcomed me with enthusiasm and carried me in to participate in the council. I told them how I had left Lost Wolf, and what he had said to me.

Suddenly Mrs. Gleason spoke out of a depth of silent thought:

"Look here, this Lost Wolf is not an Indian, after all!"

I stared at her lighted face and suddenly saw the direction in which her thought was tending. Her husband did not see; he was joyously blind to all of such matters. He never saw trouble until it was brought up and introduced to him by inherited and given name. Even then he was hardly able to believe in it, most of the time.

"Well?" said he. "Well, I have never doubted that. I have *seen* his white skin. But what of that?"

"What of that?" cried Mrs. Gleason. "Why, it seems to me that just *everything* comes out of that!"

"Marcia," said her husband, "I trust that you are joking."

"Charles," said she, giving him back a glare, "I trust that you are not fool enough to call this a joke or a joking matter. What I say is: A red or a white skin makes all the difference in the world."

Gleason leaned back in his chair and smiled faintly across the table at me, as much as to say: "Let us humor the dear child." Seeing just where her ideas were tending, I wanted to throttle her. Plainly, I hated that woman. She was framed to irritate me in everything that she did.

"Won't you explain to us?" said he.

"You ninnies!" said the gentle Mrs. Gleason. "In the first place, will you please tell me which of the pair of you have it in your power to offer forty picked Indian ponies for *anything?*"

The ground was cleft before Gleason. He could not have looked more horrified.

He was able to say at last: "You may also ask which of the pair of us can show a scalp taken in fight—or raid—by day—or night. It doesn't matter, in Indian fighting, you know. The scalp is the thing, and I'm sure that Lost Wolf is a famous hand at harvesting them!"

You would think that this would have taken the wind out of the sails of Mrs. Gleason. A woman always has a facility for turning an argument so that she will answer only a part of what is said, a part which had no real bearing on the logical points which you have just advanced. A woman is not beaten until she is silent. I have never yet seen more than one woman who was silent until she was beaten!

Mrs. Gleason said: "I am sure that there are a great many people in the world who *should* be scalped. I could name a hundred in this very town of Zander City, and so could you, Charles Gleason, if there were any frankness about you!"

Raising his hands and his face—he was really a very good man, though a rather simple soul—he said:

"Marcia, I trust that you don't understand what you are saying. I trust that!"

"Rats and fiddlesticks!" said Marcia. "I understand every word that I have said, and I've talked the only good sense that has been heard in this room this night!"

Mr. Gleason smiled terribly and enduringly upon her. She didn't mind being endured. She minded nothing except a voice that rattled in her ears.

"I say," said Marcia Gleason, "that this same Lost Wolf is a man who has done a great deal of fighting all his life but—so did Samson, for that matter. So did a lot of your other old Biblical heroes with unpronounceable names. I mean, the ones that the books were named after. Particularly the—"

"Woman!" said Gleason, standing up from his chair. "Let not the Bible be blasphemed by being adduced—"

I wish I could say that this silenced that shameless woman. But it did not. She merely cried: "Oh, bosh! You can't talk down to me, Charlie Gleason. I know too well where the patches are on the toes of your socks!"

Nobody could do anything with a woman whose mind was like that. Nothing! It made me mad. If she had been a man, then I wouldn't have said a word. I would just have reached across the table and hit her as hard as I could.

She went on: "Forty horses—and other things to equal that, I'll wager. Look here, Mr. Missionary Gleason, here is a chance for you. Why not *consider* this affair. Why not take a look at it and see if the Lord hasn't put in your way a chance to save the soul of this poor Lost Wolf —this poor white boy who has never been mothered. I could cry over the poor child! Besides, Charles, how can you tell? He might have the making of a perfectly good trader in him; he might be rolling in good trader in him; he might be rolling in good American dollars, one of these days, and giving our girl a home for her to proud of."

She would have gone on indefinitely in this way had not Gleason held up his hand to the ceiling and cried out! "Fleshpots of Egypt! Fleshpots of Egypt!"

That was his last resource. It was apparently not the first time that she had heard this taunt. She banged her

151

big fist on the table and stood up and laughed. She said: "I'll beat you yet! I'll beat both of you. I dare you both, because I tell you, I have an idea that my girl was meant to be the good little wife of a real *man!*"

29

She flung out of the room after she had said that. I was glad to see her go, because tingling in my wrists and at the roots of my tongue I could feel that I was about to do or to say something very unbecoming the scion of an old family of Charleston's best gentility.

When she was gone, the minister jerked up the windows in the rooms and began to walk up and down.

He kept saying: "Nineteen years! Nineteen years!"

Of course, I understood what he meant. He had gone through nineteen years of that sort of thing. All at once he stopped, leaned a hand on the table, and got a foolish look in his eyes.

He said: "Still, there was something almost glorious about her when she stood up there and blasted us, wasn't there, Rivers? Wasn't there, my boy?"

"I suppose there was," said I.

"Something," said Gleason, "that made me start in and look all over my life and wish that I *had* improved on a lot of things that I had done. Didn't you feel that way?"

I said: "I confess that I was wondering what she would say when she went on to see Peggy. That is where she is now, I suppose!"

"Good heavens!" muttered Gleason. "I had not thought of that!"

The poor old thickhead! Of course, he would never have thought of anything as logical and to the point as that.

He went at once to see Peggy, but she was talking with her mother. When the talk was over, Mrs. Gleason came down the stairs and said to the pair of us, as she snapped her fingers in the air:

"Well, young man, I may not have found the right man for her in the painted skin of Mr. Lost Wolf, but you can bet your bottom dollar that I've put a few spikes in *your* name and fame that will keep you for a while. Now she's coming down to see you, and you can talk as you please. Only—what I've said has shocked her so badly that she can't *help* thinking over what I've said!"

She switched around and strode out of the room, swaggering her head a little from side to side in a rather masculine way that she had. Just like an old-time sea captain, half full of grog and all full of battle, pacing up and down his deck and bellowing: "Give them a round of red hot shot, boys!"

That was the way that Mrs. Gleason was when she got worked up to the proper pitch.

After a little while, Peggy stopped in the doorway with her hair down over her shoulder and her big, round eyes looking at her mother very childishly. Her father went to her with tears in his eyes and drew her to a chair. I began to love her with such violence and pity, and to mourn over her childishness, that I thought that my heart would burst.

"There, there!" said Gleason. "Don't you pay any attention to all of this nonsense, my child!"

"Only," said Peggy, "mother seemed to think—to wish, that I should think about—about—about—"

The word failed her. She flashed a hand up in front of her eyes and bowed her head a little. She wasn't crying. That would have been self-pity, and she wasn't that kind by a great distance, I can tell you. She was simply trying to understand and she was beat.

I could stand it no longer. Forgetting all about her father being in the room, I fell on my knees beside her, and took the hands of Peggy, staring at her with very moon-struck eyes, and saying:

"Peggy, your mother is talking simply to be queer. But what really matters is that I love you, dear, and that I intend to marry you—and that I *shall* marry you, no matter

153

what other people may think and no matter how they may try to interfere and—"

I don't know what I should have continued saying, here, but Mr. Gleason hastily interrupted me before Peggy could answer me in any other way than by the great flush that burned suddenly over her face and throat. Her father sent her away at once to her room. By the time she had gone, my senses returned to me a little, and I apologized to the minister for the manner in which I had acted. He was extremely kind about it, however, and told me that he had been young and impatient once, himself, and that he thoroughly understood. However, he could not help hoping that hereafter I would use a little more discretion. Of course, I promised that I would do so.

As for the problem of Lost Wolf, we advanced no farther toward the solution of it on this night. I went off to bed and left the poor minister patiently walking up and down and up and down, conning his worry backward and forward.

For my own part, I was rather happy before I closed my eyes. No matter in what bad taste I may have acted, I had at least blurted out my passion to Peggy Gleason in words, and I had received from her an answer that was a great deal more eloquent than words. I was fairly well satisfied with that day's work.

What tomorrow would bring, with Lost Wolf, Mrs. Gleason and Jock McKay all to be feared, I really did not wish to imagine. When I woke up in the morning, it was well after sunrise, and I had slept myself numb—as a person in good health will usually do when he has become too tired in the body or in the brain.

I got ready at once to see Lost Wolf, but before I could start, he was already in the town. Before I could leave the house, there came a trampling of horses, and there were the ponies of Lost Wolf flooding the street, tied together in knots and groups of half a dozen for convenience in handling. Some of the tamer horses carried the loads. No doubt the young Cheyennes had attended to the packing of the horses, but Lost Wolf himself had managed the rest of the work. Of course, he had not been able to get such

154

a mob of horseflesh into the town without attracting a lot of attention.

There were about a dozen men and boys following that herd and pointing it out to others in the houses that they passed. If the day had been a little older, there would have been ten times as many observers; already that crowd of witnesses was growing. It grew and grew while I wondered how long it would be before Jock McKay was included in the list.

Lost Wolf was stripping the packs from pony after pony, then throwing those packs into the rear yard of the minister's house.

Before he ended that work, the entire household was roused, and Mrs. Gleason flew about in great excitement.

"There's a fortune being thrown in right under your nose, Charles Gleason. I don't know what is in those mules, but *that* man wouldn't carry them around if they were not worth while. But you'll find a way of letting the wealth slip out of your hands again. I can trust you for *that*!"

"My dear," said the minister, "because that is the only man in the world who has ever frightened you, is there any real reason why you should admire everything that he does in this life?"

He went out to see big Lost Wolf, and we went with him—that is to say, Mrs. Gleason and I, for Peggy was much too frightened to go into the yard. She remained in a corner, very scared, her face pressed against the windowpane, observing and trembling.

In the yard, Lost Wolf met us and threw open the bales of his merchandise. He greeted the minister with his lifted hand and his deep-voiced "How!"

He pointed to the milling scores of Indian ponies; then he said: "These are for you to make you a great chief instead of a medicine man. When you have all of these horses, men will follow you to battle and you will take many scalps."

He strode back toward one of the opened bales and tossed wide the topmost of the robes with which it was piled full. That robe was one of the Indian masterpieces of painting.

"Your squaw," said Lost Wolf, "has never had a finer robe in her house."

You would think that Mrs. Gleason would have taken offense at this, but she didn't. She seemed determined to like that fellow, if only to spite her daughter and her husband.

She said: "And that *is* true, for I've never seen one *half* so good! How in the world were they ever made so soft and supple?"

She began to finger the edges of the robe and to admire its painted surface.

"See!" said Lost Wolf, who was certainly a fine hand at brightening the value of his goods. "When a goose sees corn it will come to eat, and when a squaw sees a good robe, she cannot help quacking!"

The minister had to turn sharply away, crimson with swallowed laughter. For my part, I was rather awestruck. I stood by, waiting for the anger of Mrs. Gleason to blast Lost Wolf.

She gave one flashing glance at Lost Wolf, which I thought meant that the storm was about to break. It appeared that she was only looking to see whether or not this was earnest or mere game. When she saw that Lost Wolf was not making a jest of her, Mrs. Gleason chuckled with the most perfect good nature.

She said: "All right, Charlie. Don't try to imitate him. I don't mind a little talk from *some* men! But are the horses all a present to Mr. Gleason?"

Lost Wolf looked at her with a good deal of surprise, as if he did not expect to hear talk from a squaw on such an occasion. He overlooked her magnificently, then he turned to Gleason again. The minister had recovered a little from his stifling fit, and said:

"It is true that you have brought us a most amazing purchase price, but—"

"It is not a purchase price," said Lost Wolf. "It is a gift to you. It belongs to you because you are the father of the girl that I intend to have for my squaw."

This was a new phase of the matter. Certainly a most surprising one. Mrs. Gleason gasped; then she turned suddenly and popped out her forefinger at me, as much as to say silently:

"Now admit that I am a prophet!"

Well, she was not far from it. I never had expected such talk or such actions. Here the minister stepped in. He seemed to think that matters had gone so far that he would have to use firmness and frankness, no matter what was the danger. He said:

"My friend, Lost Wolf, this is a great present that you offer to make to me, but I cannot take it, and the reason that I cannot take it is because my daughter cannot be your wife—now or ever!"

30

I should not have made such a speech. Not if I had had such a wife as Mrs. Gleason.

"You *want* to live like a tramp the rest of your life!" she told him with a terrible ring in her voice.

He turned to her and said: "Go back into the house, and don't let me hear from you again until I ask your advice!"

Oh, it was sweet music to me to hear him talk up like that, and I wish she had been overawed for once in her life. She was not! Not Mrs. Gleason—not Marcia! She merely laughed with a note in her voice that made her laughter like a man's.

"I am not backing up just because you begin to bark," said she. "Because I have heard that voice before!"

There she stood. When he tried to wave her away again, she folded her arms and asked who was there that dared to try to budge her from the spot when the future of her daughter was being discussed. It was lucky for her just then that *I* was not her husband. She would not have used the same tactics though. She was too smart for that. Bullying worked with Gleason; so she used that handle to the whip. With another husband she would have used still another. At any rate, she would never have stopped her labors until she was driving the wagon.

I was only watching the minister and his wife from the corner of my eye, because what mainly interested me was how Lost Wolf took this direct repulse. The big wedge of muscle at the base of his jaw leaped out to a point, and his nostrils flared. That was all. He controlled himself like a man. He said:

"That is good. When a friend speaks to a friend, he is honest. Now tell me why I can never have your girl? Who will pay more horses for her?"

The minister made a speech. I was sorry for it, but he had been in the pulpit so long that I suppose he could not frame his ideas smoothly in any other way. He would make speeches to me, for that matter, or to his daughter, or to anybody except his wife, who generally said "Bosh!" before he got more than halfway started.

"She is going to be the wife of a man who can give her something more than horses. She is going to be the wife of a man who can give her a house like the one she has been raised in."

"I shall build one twice as big," said he. "They are full of bad smells, and they are dark. They are too big and heavy to move away. When the winter is cold, you cannot move South to a warm sun with such a house. When the summer is hot, you cannot move away to the hills where the breezes are always cool. But if she must be given a house, I shall build her twice a house.

"She must have a husband," said the minister, sweeping on past this point, "who will dress as I and other white men dress."

Lost Wolf said: "That is strange. You wear trousers which tie up the knees as if with ropes and make it hard to run or to jump, and very hard to sit down. When the enemy comes in the night, you must spend much time to get ready. I take my rifle, and that is my coat and trousers, too. But I can buy such clothes."

"She must have," said the minister, "a man who wears the same *thoughts* that she is used to."

"I do not understand," said Lost Wolf.

"Why, man," said Mr. Gleason, "if you came to her, she would look at your hands and almost expect to see the crimson stains from your last scalping party!"

"It is true that I have taken many scalps," said Lost Wolf complacently. "They have dried above the fire in my lodge. The Cheyennes have danced around them. It is true!"

"There is a book which means to her more than any man, and that Book says: 'Thou shalt not kill!'"

"It is a strange Book," said Lost Wolf, shaking his head, "but I, also, can read. I shall learn that Book. I shall speak its words to her. The scalps shall still grow on the heads of the Pawnees, if she wishes it so."

"She must have a husband," said Gleason, more and more hot with interest, "who will live in town among other white men—white himself!"

"So!" said Lost Wolf, sighing. "Then a man must give up all of that for this?"

He swept his arm toward the prairies; then, with a gesture of disgust, represented the town with the hollow of his hand.

"He must learn to live as his brothers live," said Gleason. "Could you do that, Lost Wolf?"

The big man lifted his head and took a deep breath.

"I shall see," said he. "I shall see what I can do."

"Do you mean," cried the minister, "that you will *try* to change yourself?"

"I mean," said Lost Wolf, "that I shall think of all of these things and try to understand."

He started away.

"And these horses and all these packs—take them with you, Lost Wolf," said Gleason.

"They are paid," said the big man. "I shall not look at them again. They belong to the father of my squaw. They are a part of the price!"

He went off without looking back over his shoulder.

"Go after him," said Gleason to me, "and persuade him to take them away. I can't have his property here. It's as if I were considering selling my own flesh and blood for a price!"

I went after Lost Wolf and caught up with him in another moment. As he leaped into the saddle on the red horse, I jumped onto Sir Thomas and rode after him. The crowd that had gathered to look at the Indian ponies—and filch a few of them from the outskirts of the herd—gave way before us. In another five minutes the prairie wind was before us, and nothing else.

Lost Wolf drew rein and said: "This is a good thing, my brother. When a man's heart is troubled, a friend at his side is better than cool water on a new wound."

We rode on in this fashion, silently. He said at last: "This medicine man talks much, but he is honest."

"He is honest," I admitted, and I waited for something more.

"His squaw," said Lost Wolf, "also talks a great deal."

"She does," said I

"But she, also, is honest," said Lost Wolf.

I made no answer, and he glanced at me in surprise. Then he added: "When the mare and the stallion are both true, the colt will be a brave runner, also!"

That was his way of reasoning matters out. I finally said: "But do you mean to go back into the town and try to live as the other men live there?"

There was no response to this for long minutes. Then he replied: "Have you seen the cities of the prairie dogs underground?"

I told him that I had.

"They, also," said Lost Wolf, "are in darkness and in dirt, like these towns of the white men."

That was his only comment, though I waited eagerly for more words. On the whole, I thought that this was comforting. It began to look to me as though the big fellow would give up the girl of his choice without any more struggle.

Just then, when I thought that his heart must be nearly broken, a rabbit broke cover near us and scooted away across the prairie. Lost Wolf was after it instantly with a yell, and I followed as fast as Sir Thomas could sprint.

That was not fast enough. Sir Thomas started fast and

ran as well as ever, but that red streak of destruction simply ate up distance with his enormous bounds. Even so, the rabbit had gained greatly on him. Of course, a good greyhound can beat any horse for the first two hundred yards, though the horse will gain fast after that. A strong jack rabbit will run away from a fast greyhound in the same fashion—for a furlong or so. In fact, I have seen jack rabbits that no dog could catch.

However, with a furlong behind us, I could see the red horse begin to catch up with the jack. It swerved and took a new course, but the stallion was so far behind that it was able to change, also. In a bound it was up with the little scattering fugitive. The rabbit dodged, but it had more than the flying hoofs of the horse to avoid. The rider swung out, hanging by his heels, and his scooping hand caught the jack up.

When I came up, my broken-hearted man was laughing like a child and smoothing back the flattened ears of the poor little beast.

"That will make us a breakfast," I said.

"No," said he, "because you cannot kill a thing that has made you happy. There was blackness in me like winter, my brother, but now the sun is shining again—and look!" He tossed the jack into the air. It struck the ground with a thump, remained crouched there for an instant, and then scooted away for safety, with Lost Wolf laughing more like a silly child than ever.

I rather respected this odd scruple of his. In some ways, there was more delicacy in Lost Wolf than in any other man that I ever knew.

Suddenly he turned on me with:

"You are thinking a great deal."

"I am worried for you, Lost Wolf," I lied to him.

He smiled upon me with a real affection. I felt ashamed of dreading him much more than I loved him.

"It is only a cloud on the face of the sun. There will be happiness again, somewhere. There is no trouble for yourself, then?"

"Only a small thing. A man from the caravan has come back to Zander City—the caravan of the two men whom you killed, Lost Wolf.

161

He uttered a loud exclamation, and then he began to nod.

"The rest have hunted on our trail and then gone back, tired out. But the wise man came straight down the wind to find our tepees and watch for us there. You have seen him, and he has seen you?"

I said that he had not.

Lost Wolf was pleased; because to see an enemy without being seen is the sort of cunning that a man with his Indian training could appreciate.

"Then," said he, "tonight we will go and hunt him, while he is hunting you. Why should there not be another scalp to dry in the smoke of my fire, brother?"

I wished, with a shudder, that the Gleasons could have heard that speech from their hopeful convert.

31

The next thing for me to do was to find out how close the mind of big Lost Wolf was sticking to the subject of the girl. I made little or no headway in that direction. He had not a word to say about pretty Peggy Gleason all through the day, and when the evening came, he started back with me for the town of Zander City.

On the river edge, close to a sizable clump of trees, we picketed our two horses in the dusk of the day and took a canoe which we found beached near by. There was good reason to think that she had been abandoned as useless, because the moment we put the little craft in the water, it began to leak like a sieve. However, that did not hold us back. There was half a broken paddle in the canoe, but that was enough for big Lost Wolf. He squatted in the stern and put me in front of him, just out of the sweep of his arms to bail out the water. I kept a steady splashing over the side, and Lost Wolf made that paddle bend and creak with the sway of his gigantic arms. With the current behind us, we simply boiled down the river. I could hear the big man behind me, reveling in his work and breathing hard as he took a joy in the use of his prodigious strength.

I was to see it used to the full in quite a different manner before that night was over!

When we got to the town, he turned in from the current to the shallows, and we landed under the lee of the lumber yard, slipping up into Zander City like two thieves. We were, in a sense, because we were aiming at the life of a man.

We got to the rear of that same saloon out of which I had seen my man coming. I knew that once a man drinks in a saloon, he is apt to come back and try the same place again. There is a sort of homelike quality about sawdust that you have seen before, and a bar where you are familiar with the unvarnished spots. Usually, a man would go back and keep on going back to the same saloon. Since this was fairly early in the evening, I had good hopes that we might be able to find the man who was back in Zander City hunting me, as I had every reason to suppose.

There were not many in the place, as we could see through the rear window. Lost Wolf was in no hurry. He was hungry, so he pulled his belt up a few notches and then squatted and went to sleep—all except one eye, as you might say. He actually lost consciousness of everything in the world except the inside of that barroom, where he was on the lookout for a man as big as himself, wearing a shock of red hair—Jock McKay, as I had described him to Lost Wolf.

It was harder for me. My idea of a torment is to wait for anything—from a partner's lead to a train. There we had to stay for two cramping, miserable hours, listening to the foolish talk and roars of drunken laughter as the place began to fill up and stir up higher spirits.

I was ready to quit; four separate times I leaned and whispered at the ear of Lost Wolf that there was no use waiting there, because our man would not come. He did not deign to answer me and my impatience. Once, to be sure, he looked up, but it was only to look at the stars far beyond me and to pay no attention to me and my words.

After we had suffered there for the full two hours, through the swinging doors at the far end of the saloon came a big man with a familiar swing to his shoulders. I knew at once, by the outline of him, long before I really saw his features, that this was my man, Jock McKay.

He came down and took a big hooker of whisky, putting it down raw. Then he splashed two more drinks right down on top of it. I saw that this was a man who could shift his red-eye like a man, and my respect for him went up. He didn't drink like a fool who was trying to get drunk, but like a fellow who knew his own capacity— which must have been that of a tank.

When he had washed down those three terrific jolts of fire, he wandered back down to the rear of the saloon where the card tables were and leaned against a wall while he watched a three-handed game. He was asked to join, and we saw him pass two hundred dollars over that table in less time than it takes to tell.

He lost as well as he drank, for he simply smiled and slammed his cards back on the table. I could read his lips as he said:

"All right, boys, you've cleaned me out, all except enough for me to pay board, and lodging for a little while. And I got to have chuck if I want to do my work."

"What's your work?" somebody must have asked him.

The next thing he said was: "Hunting down a man— or a skunk, whichever you might call it. The same murdering rat that I've told you about before. He gave me this!"

He touched the side of his face. I could not see past the flare of the lamps that anything was wrong with his face. I had no doubt that he had pointed out the mark that my fist made when it landed on him back there in the circle of the caravan, when I had stood so close to the hour of my death.

Big Lost Wolf seemed to know what the gesture meant, for he turned, and I saw the flash of his teeth in the dark of the night. Then we saw my man wandering slowly out of the saloon and toward the street. Lost Wolf did not

164

hesitate. He started along with me. When we got to the street, he began to walk slowly, reeling a good deal, with his blanket furled up close around his neck, the very picture of a very drunk Indian.

Of course, nobody stood in his way when they saw that. Sometimes it is safe to play with dynamite, but it is *never* safe to fool with an intoxicated Indian, because they are simply mad! While they melted out of his way and gave him a random curse or two, I said hastily to Lost Wolf:

"I haven't told you that this man mustn't be killed."

He started.

"Why must he live?" he asked. "Have you squaws to whose hands you wish to give him?"

How many victims, then, had Lost Wolf himself turned over to the savage talents of the women? That was misjudging him, as I came to know later. No man every had to suffer from the torment because he fell into the power of that giant.

I said that it was merely because Jock McKay was doing his duty, and no more, by his two dead friends. I could not see him mobbed and taken by surprise because he had been able to trace me. All that I wanted was a chance to put my story in front of him. Lost Wolf listened to me very intently. Then he said that he would see that I had the chance that I wanted.

Big Jock McKay came strolling down the street. He waved an arm, bellowed a greeting at some one, came swaying past us, and stopped just as he was in the act of passing by. The flare from a swinging doorway ahead of us flashed across my face, and he saw what he had been wanting to see.

Jock McKay showed that he was not a man who believed in delays. He did not stop to say how do you do, simply reached for his gun and yanked it out into the nice fresh air. Another instant and I would have been food for the coyotes and the buzzards, because I was slow on that draw, having been taken so thoroughly unawares. I did not need to worry. Lost Wolf was doing my thinking for me that night, and my fighting, too. There was never a more capable hand at the latter work, at least.

His arm shot past me like a great beam, and his hand fastened on the gun wrist of Jock McKay.

There was no shooting. The gun rattled on the board sidewalk, and Jock McKay groaned. I scooped the Colt up. By the time I straightened, Lost Wolf was disappearing around the side of the next building, and Jock McKay was being carried in his arms.

People saw us, of course, but since there was no outcry, this might be just a little sample of the horseplay such as was constantly in use around Zander City. Besides, every man had his own fun or his own business to attend to, and paid very little attention to others who were in trouble.

In thirty seconds we stood at the rear of that building—it was a black, silent warehouse—and I was explaining matters to Jock—explaining, I mean, that though we had him there at our mercy, we didn't intend to harm him. I gave him my word that there had been a reason for the killing of the two Henlines. I explained how Black Elk had been murdered by them in the coldest of cold blood.

McKay, breathing hard with the pain, and chafing his crushed wrist where the grip of Lost Wolf had first fallen on him, listened to all of this talk with only this comment:

"One Indian was killed—and so two white men had to go down?"

Lost Wolf put in his oar then. "It was I who killed them, Jock McKay."

"I've guessed that," said McKay, bitterly. "The killing of the two of them was a little too much work for one man like *him*!"

"Let that go," said I. "The point is, McKay, that this is the sort of scrape that we can't bring up in court, as you might say. You could raise the town on us in no time, if you wanted to. To stop you, all we have to do is to bring down the butt of a revolver on your head—and let you drop. People don't ask too many questions about dead men in this town, and you know it. But we don't want to finish you. We have no grudge against you. We know that the Henlines were your friends, and you've been doing what you could to put them right. Very well—but what we want now, and what we'll be satisfied with, will be

166

your word of honor to forget that you know that we are in Zander City or that you connect us with that double killing!"

Of course, it was a chance, but I felt that I had to take that chance. Jock McKay muttered: "There's nothing for me to do. I'll give you my word."

"Shake hands on it."

He put out his hand, after a moment, and shook hands with both of us in turn. After that, we watched him go away.

"Parner," said I to Lost Wolf, "will he keep his word?"

Lost Wolf hesitated and then he shook his head.

"No Cheyenne would break a word like that," he said, he said, "unless he were drunk. But this man—he is not a Cheyenne. I cannot tell!"

Neither could I. There was something about the thoughtful, fallen head of McKay as he went away that made me doubt it. We started to leave that place and go back toward the street. We hadn't taken ten steps, before we heard the start of a clamor and a shouting. Then about a dozen men came around the corner of the warehouse and headed straight down toward us.

It was plain that McKay was *not* a Cheyenne!

32

I found out afterward how McKay was able to raise his crowd so quickly. He had not time to explain how two friends of his had been killed and how he was on the trail of the murderers. He could not have held an audience for ten seconds, even if he could have gathered the audience in the first place, on that street in Zander City. There were too many such tales floating the rounds. Men told them over their drinks.

All that McKay cunningly did was to call as he rounded the corner of the warehouse into the street:

"There are Indians here mobbing whites:

That was enough, of course. Just as if a man should leap into the street of any Southern town in the States and call out that negroes were beating a white. No rallying call could be more instantly effective. A dozen stalwarts rushed to the charge—miners, frontiersmen, trappers, gamblers, tenderfeet, in a shouldering mob.

Two or three guns instantly gleamed starlike in the front of this advancing storm, and I called to Lost Wolf: "Run, man!"

I did not wait. I decided that the better part of good teaching was good example, and I sprinted for cover. About ten long jumps from that spot I heard someone shout: "No shooting! Get the big one and then we'll round up the little beggar."

The rest of that good advice was lost in a roar like the bellow of a bull, or the thunder of a giant grizzly as it closes in with a foe. I jerked my head over my shoulder, for I thought that I recognized something in that voice. I was in time to see the robe thrown from the body of Lost Wolf. He flashed into clear view as he leaped into the dull light from a distant lamp, like a shadowy statue of old copper. He met that lurching front of the crowd and a scrambling confusion followed.

Once I saw a great wolf who had ventured too close to the edge of a little village. The town dogs had rushed out in a joyous, yelling chorus to eat him. When they came close, that wolf, who had been running away in a halfhearted fashion, turned around and jumped into the middle of the pack. It was exactly as though each of them heard the strong voice of a dreaded master calling to home. They whirled, and all that could be seen were dark streaks scooting across the plain for home!

The confusion around Lost Wolf was just as great, although the men did not run. They had too much headway to make such a sudden change. They simply tumbled

168

all over each other. The one in front put on the breaks and the ones behind kept jamming forward.

I turned around as fast as I could and came tearing back for the fight. I felt that we were in for the grand licking of our lives and a rope halter apiece at the end of it, but one good fight is almost *worth* a hanging. As I came hopping, I saw Lost Wolf shake a couple of clinging men away and step in. The shoot of his thick-muscled arm was like the thrust of the walking team of a big steam engine. His fist cracked a big man under the jaw, lifted him from his feet, and jammed him into the faces of those behind.

Then Lost Wolf turned and crossed the other hand on a driving fellow to the side.

It was very sweet!

I have always loved to see good, clean hitting. That is the major half of any sort of boxing, and boxing is the king of sports, certainly. As I jumped into the fray, I could see that Lost Wolf was not milling blindly. He was picking his spots one by one.

No wild savage, exulting in his strength, was Lost Wolf! He fought silently, with just a purring snarl in the hollow of his throat now and then, as he struck home.

I would hate to say that any twelve men in Zander City were ever licked by two. On this night there seemed to be no other word for it. Lost Wolf ripped that battle front to shreds, and most of those he hit went down, and went blind. A few got up and stumbled in to take him from the rear. When they came in close, they got me, instead. Although I was no Lost Wolf, I was just about as effective when it came to polishing off the fragments of men that that big steam roller left under his wheels. I could take well-aimed shots at men who came in, wide open, and I slugged with might and main.

How they went down, and lay kicking—but not getting up again!

We fought our way to the corner of the warehouse and the street; there the remaining fringe of men before us wavered and gave way. They shouted as they ran: "Indians!"

That was poison for us, of course.

Lost Wolf and I could have got off without any more hurt, but that big fiend rested his arm against the corner of the building and drew in his breath through his teeth.

He said: "Brother, that was very good! That was very good!"

He draped his arm affectionately over my shoulders. How he loved a fight! He was simply trembling with the deep, silent joy of it. I knew then that his skin was white, and his heart was white, too, because no Indian could have kept from waving arms and yelling in a case like this.

"It is time to go," said I to Lost Wolf; "it is more than time. It's almost too late!"

"Ah!" said Lost Wolf.

Out of the street those bolting fugitives had gathered about half a hundred recruits with their way cry of "Indians!" Now the whole lot of them came sprinting to get in before the little party was over—came rushing and yelling.

I laid hold of my friend and tried to drag him away. I had to pull him forcibly backward for a step or two. Then discretion came to my help, and he saw that it was simply suicide to try to play with such numbers.

When it came to serious running, I was a pretty fast sprinter, and Lost Wolf did not look as strong in the legs as he was in the shoulders. Nevertheless, in two strides he was away from me, and I was floundering behind him, with my eyes half blind with effort. A tall board fence at the rear of the place was our goal. Once over that, we could have a very fair chance to get away, but in the van of that crowd there ran some sprinters who really knew how to move. I was not perfectly fresh, and fear, no matter what the books says, ties up a runner's muscles. They were gaining on me from behind, and gaining fast.

How well I can remember the agony! It fairly makes the cords of my neck ache, as I remember it. I recall, most vividly, how a wedge of moon was stuck somewhere before me in a steel-dark sky as I raced for the fence—only ten steps away now.

Pounds of lead weighed down my nervous feet. The muscles of my thighs turned to water; a mist of blackness crossed my eyes. I was exhausting myself to run across a back yard—for the simple reason that I felt that I was beaten. Two or three men behind me were gaining with terrible speed.

There was no danger for Lost Wolf. He gained on them at every leap. He sprang to the top of that six-foot fence and hung there.

I expected him to drop out of my view forever, while I went to fill a noose and stretch a rope on this gay night in old Zander City. He dropped—but not on the far side of the fence! Just as a hand reached for me, with such force that the palms cuffed hard against my shoulder and knocked me sprawling on my face, too weak with fear and exhaustion to stir.

The yell of triumph was crushed away in a gasp of fear and surprise. I lifted my head from the ground in time to see a monstrous shadow fly between me and the sky. Lost Wolf struck the first ranks of the throng. I think he literally threw himself sidewise at them from the top of the fence, and his weight smashed them down in a heap.

A needle prick of joy went through my brain, and then a hot flood of power. I heard Lost Wolf yell: "Climb that fence!"

I did not wait, although it seems now that I was cowardly to run away from him. At that moment, it did not. I really felt that, if I turned back to fight, I would only be clogging the power of this giant by making him defend both himself and me. I jumped at the fence, swung myself up to the top of it. As I hung there a long instant at the top of my vault, I saw Lost Wolf, rising out of the tangled mass, swing a man by the ankles. There was a frightful scream out of that human club. Then the unlucky fellow was dashed into the faces of his friends in the crowd.

As I dropped down on the safety side of the fence, Lost Wolf shot above the fence and struck the ground beside me.

A head showed instantly above the top of the fence behind him. I shot point-blank at it, meaning to hit, too. I didn't, though I came close enough to draw a yelp from the pursuer. There was plenty of shooting through that fence, for the next few minutes, but not a head showed above it, while Lost Wolf and I ran toward the next street.

As we shot out onto it, Lost Wolf dropped back and let my stretching legs bring me up to him. He said:

"The river! You, that way—I this and—"

He was off.

I was in half a mind to run after him, because he had been like a big brother to me during this frightful swirl of action; and I felt frightened and alone when he left me. However, I saw that his plan of action was the only plan. They were hunting for two men, not for one, and if we separated we ran only a tenth of the chance of being overtaken.

So I sprinted down the street two houses and then cut sharply in between two buildings, over another back fence, and then down an alley.

When I got to a little vacant lot, with the dark, looming form of a cow in it, I threw myself down in the dew-wet grass for a breathing space.

My heart was racing past endurance, and my muscles were leaping and jerking. I remember that I kept squeezing the handles of my gun for comfort. While I lay there, the pain left my temples, and my breathing grew easy. The taste of the air became sweet and clammy cold in my throat. I heard a tremendous outbreak of yelling and shooting by the river, and I sat up with a start, for I knew what had happened.

33

It had seemed pretty miraculous to me that none of the crowd had spotted me as we tore along. The answer must have been that the big, glimmering body of Lost Wolf was easier to see in that half moonlight. I had taken it for granted that he had escaped, because I knew how fast he could run, and any one raised among Indians can hold his speed for a long time. So I had lain there on the grass enjoying the coolness, getting the shake out of my nerves and muscles, and remembering very contentedly how those long arms of Lost Wolf had cracked over those wild, fighting men of Zander City. How much drinking and how much talking it would take to explain what had happened in that city at the hands of an Indian! A scoundrelly Cheyenne!

Naturally, I never gave a thought to the idea that Lost Wolf might have got back to the river only to be discovered there again. Now I saw that he must have got there, and while he waited in the little canoe, it had been spotted and searched. Hence this new outbreak of yelling—this crackling of guns. I stood up and listened and cursed my selfishness in causing the delay which, perhaps, would hang my friend before the morning.

They did not have him yet! The noise streaked rapidly across the town. Then it swerved and turned back. It made a corner and came suddenly at me with a roar!

First I saw a coppery glint—and then Lost Wolf had turned another corner, while half a dozen guns barked from the front of the pursuit and spurted deadly little tongues of flame after the runner.

That dark river of men rushed away after the fugitive; they turned the corner; they still sped on. Wearied runners kept falling back, and fresh men were working to the front.

There were no relays to help poor Lost Wolf, to take his weary place! Here was a horseman, there another—and more and more, cursing the pedestrians out of their way and begging for an open lane and a clean chance to run down the fugitive.

Standing against the fence, I heard the noise dying out toward the open prairie. Then I turned back toward the river. It was swept bare of men. Everyone except gamblers that had gone to join in the king of all sports—the man hunt—and I simply sauntered down to the edge of the water and found the canoe—not tethered with a strip of bark, as we had left her, and secretly afloat, but drawn halfway up the bank. There was no need to tell how she had been discovered, for here was another canoe—a new beauty—nosing the bank a few yards away. Those who landed from that canoe, as they came down the river, must have seen the big, naked figure glide into the other, the derelict.

I did not have to hurry. There was not a soul near and I knew that the silence around me was honest. Real desolation has a voice of its own. I simply stepped into the new canoe, and began to paddle up in the lee of the shore, keeping close to the bank where there was hardly enough current to float a feather a mile in a day. I eased the canoe along at a good rate through this water, only having to strain and tug for progress when I turned some jutting headland where the current was swift.

Getting back to the trees where we had left our horses, I found Sir Thomas, but no trace of the great, red stallion of Lost Wolf!

It was well beyond me—entirely beyond me. I rode Sir Thomas in little circles around the wood, and I ventured on a few whistles. All that I found, after a half hour or so, was a little runt of an Indian pony wandering over the prairie, so crippled with age or sickness, it seemed, that it could barely hobble out of my way. I came closer to the little pony, and as I got near I could see that this was neither an old nor a crippled Indian pony, but one who had just been ridden within an edge of death. Exhaustion made it stand in that fashion, with its head hanging toward the ground, not touching a blade of the night-cooled grasses which were under his nose. Someone had just finished giving that little beast such a ride as it was not likely to get except in a matter of life and death!

A new thought came to me. I made a light with a twist of dead branches from a shrub. With this, I searched the ground near the pony. Almost at once I found what I wanted—the numerous indentations on the ground where the grass had been beaten down and where many hard-ridden horses had recently passed over the surface.

After that, I knew pretty well what had happened—at least, I was able to guess. Lost Wolf had ranged across the prairie on that stolen horse. As it failed and staggered beneath his crushing weight, he whistled loud and sharp to bring the red stallion to him.

The stallion had heard, had come galloping, bringing exhaustless strength and speed to the services of its master. Indeed, I looked off through the night with a laugh, for I knew well enough that Lost Wolf was free.

With that, I headed toward the Cheyenne camp where we had left Running Deer and the rest of the Indians not so long before. They might have moved from that spot, but they would not be very far off, in the matter of day's marches. I felt that my next move must be to rejoin Lost Wolf. Certainly we could not comfortably foregather in the town of Zander City. There was, therefore, very little left to us, except to meet yonder in the camp of his Indian allies.

In the dawn I made my camp by a little stream. There I rested myself and my horse until noon, and began the long trek again. After several days, I found traces of the old Cheyenne camp.

I went in on them confidently. Two young braves who were scouting on guard—for Running Deer was not one of those poor tacticians who allowed surprise to play any part against them—came out and stopped me. They recognized me and were very friendly, asking no questions, realizing I did not have the language. When I got on into the camp, I was glad to see the white trapper and trader, Danny Croydon.

He gave me a friendly hail and stepped out at once.

"How does it come," said he with a smile, "that you are here without my friend, Lost Wolf?"

On top of all of my happy deductions, this question was pretty much of a staggerer. I said: "Well, I see that you are smiling as you say that!"

He seemed a bit puzzled. Then I exclaimed: "Man, man! Do you mean to say that Lost Wolf isn't here?"

"Not here?" repeated Danny Croydon. "Why, of course I mean to say it! He's not here, Rivers. Why should he be? Did he say that he would meet you here, then?"

I admitted that he had not, but I told the story of what had happened.

Of course, I didn't make a very heroic figure in that narrative, of which you have just read the true account. I had to tell the naked truth to those keen eyes of Danny Croydon.

He said when I had finished: "I think I would have done exactly as you've done—unless I had known him as long as I have."

"What do you mean by that, exactly?"

He answered: "You remember how he hated to back up—and how he stood to fight when you, like a perfectly sensible man, were taking to your heels?"

"Well, that's Lost Wolf from head to foot. That's the make-up of him. He hates to back up, and that's what has made him an unpopular war leader with the Cheyennes. They're brave enough, but they don't like the bulldog way. A slash and a leap—wolf style, is their way. It's a very good way on horseback on the plains, but that isn't the thing that pleases Lost Wolf. He prefers to sink his grip in something—and then he likes to hold on. Just as he waded back through those fellows and knocked them silly. Well sir, that's what he did when once he had the red horse under him. You can put your money on that!"

I gasped out: "Do you mean to say that he could have been mad enough to charge back through those scores of fighting men from Zander City—every one of them ready to shoot to kill?"

Danny Croydon shook his head.

"Not as bad as all that," he said. "He would ease away from them, but when they got strung out, he would circle back and cut off the leaders or the stragglers, here and there. I've known him to make life miserable for a whole half regiment of men, that way. To him, it was just a great game. Of course, he has the advantage of the speed of that horse under him. It's almost like fighting from the back of an eagle, you know. Also, he has the nose and the wits of that devilish wolf that trails him around the desert."

I was very bewildered, now. Yet I found that Danny Croydon knew his man a great deal too well, to be guessing in what he ventured as an opinion.

Finally I said: "Well, what do you really think has become of Lost Wolf? Where is he now? Doesn't he know that I'll probably come here, since I can't very well go back to Zander City?"

"He knows that," said Croydon gloomily. "And knowing that, he could have had his fighting party and come in here ahead of you, because he travels just a couple of notches faster than a wind blows. But since he's not here, I'm afraid—"

"Afraid of what?"

"That he's not in much shape for *any* traveling."

I asked with a groan: "Have they killed him?"

He sighed.

"Aye," said Croydon. "I'm afraid that Lost Wolf has fought his last fight."

34

When Lost Wolf rode his staggering pony toward the clump of trees that made a darker shadow on the face of the darkening plains, his whistle ran shrilling before him and brought the red horse back to him on wings. Lost Wolf was off the back of the played-out mount and in the saddle on the stallion in the smaller half of a second. After that, he was like a man mounted on the back of an eagle.

In one thing, Danny Croydon's guess was correct—the thought of further flight was not in the mind of Lost Wolf. Now that he was safely mounted on the red horse, he wanted action.

First of all, he opened up a great gap between him and the leading men of the pursuit—a gap so great that when he turned back to harry those riders from Zander City, he found that the leaders had missed the way and were shooting off at right angles to the direction in which Lost Wolf had fled. He sat there in the night, debating whether it was best to let them ride on, and laugh at their folly, or else to turn around and break in among the stragglers, dealing out death from either hand.

Lost Wolf was no random fighter when white men were his opponents. It was all very well for him to find Indian foes, and break and crush them on either side, but it was a different matter when he found the people of his own race before him. Through all the history of Lost Wolf, the Henline episode was almost the only one in which he had gone out deliberately to kill whites. In that case, he had to deal with a pair of rascals who richly deserved what they got at his hands. Here were a number of townsmen, unidentified to Lost Wolf—men who were hunting him merely because they thought his skin was red. He let them pass through the night, and after they were gone, he turned back toward Zander City.

He was still within the reach of the lights of the little town. They winked and blinked at him out of the distance. Scattered lights out of the darkness have a singular effect upon the stormiest of hearts, soothing them, and letting loneliness take the place of anger.

Lost Wolf, as he rode toward the town, meditating thoughts of vengeance which should be taken upon the townsmen for the manner in which they had driven him up and down through that night, felt the lonely years of his life behind him. The lonely years before him were like old wounds in the body of a warrior when the wind strikes out of the north. Lost Wolf, though he kept religiously turned away from such thoughts, knew well enough that he was neither white nor red, and that there was only the ghost of a chance for true happiness before him.

Thinking of these things, rage left him, and bitterness followed. On the heels of that bitterness, while his heart was softened and opened, the face of Peggy Gleason slipped suddenly in. He rode toward the lights of the town from that moment not thinking of the men who wore guns belted upon their hips, but of the minister's daughter.

There was little difficulty in getting through Zander

City unnoticed this time. Part of the men had ridden out to hunt him; and a greater part, by far, were busy in the gaming halls and the saloons. Having had its share of excitement for one evening, Zander City had settled down to drink over and think over the exciting little history and count its wounds. Every time the big, quick fists of Lost Wolf darted out, they had left a mark that needed nursing, to say nothing of some pretty hard blows that I, myself, had struck.

Straight to the house of Gleason went Lost Wolf. When he got there he found that the place was black inside, except for a single lamp which burned low in the front hall. Out of the church, near by, however, came a voice which floated clearly on the air of the night. Lost Wolf recognized at once the tones of Gleason himself.

The white red man went to the church and climbed up to one of the windows which had been opened in the warmth of that summer evening. He could see all that lay inside—the minister holding forth in his little pulpit, expounding an obscure text—and beneath the unvarnished pulpit there were three scant rows of worshipers filling the front seats.

Mr. Gleason was a hard worker, but his greatest influence could never bring out a crowd. His best was shown in his house-to-house work; there it was that he built in the cause which he served. However, in another moment Lost Wolf marked the big, strong nose and the jutting, rocklike jaw of Mrs. Gleason in the front row, and beside her the daughter.

After that, he saw nothing else. There was a hymn, and when the little audience stood up to sing, Lost Wolf, with the sharp ear of a wild creature, picked out the voice of Peggy Gleason and forgot all the rest. She alone made music to his seeming. The rest was merely noise.

He slipped down from his window and glided back to the house of Gleason. The doors were locked, and so were the windows of the first floor. The windows of the second floor were not, for the sufficient reason that even the suspicious mind of Mrs. Gleason did not attribute to any man sufficiently catlike powers to climb the sheer wall of the house to such a height, without the pillars of a porch to assist him.

Lost Wolf was not to be included in this category. Where his fingertips could find a place, he could climb. He worked his way up the sheer side of the house, clinging to crevices, until he got to the first window of the second story. Through that window he lifted himself and dropped into the interior of a room where there was a faint scent of tobacco smoke in the air.

That was not what Lost Wolf wanted. He passed from chamber to chamber, until he entered one where he was greeted with a fair breath of perfume, light as the fragrance of a garden in autumn when the last roses are dying. That was the place that Lost Wolf had wanted to find.

From the church the sound of singing or of a single voice ended; in its place there was a subdued but universal babel; from the window he saw the congregation pouring out of the front door, and at the same time the lamps in the interior went out one by one, and window after window was shuttered with soft waves of darkness.

Lost Wolf marked the window of the girl's room; then he lowered himself from it to the ground. There were two difficult places in the descent. At each of them he paused— clinging hard to the wall—and with the keen blade of his hunting knife he sank two deep impressions where not his hand alone, but even his toes, could get a comfortable purchase. A moment later, he was coiled up in the garden dews, waiting for the window high above him to be flooded with yellow lamplight.

After a time, he heard the voices of the family inside the house. Then the screen door to the kitchen opened and slammed.

Suddenly the tender passion in the breast of Lost Wolf was a little obscured. He remembered another time when years ago, Danny Croydon had brought him in to Zander City for the first free taste of the life of the white man. In that same kitchen, for Gleason had been a great friend of Croydon, Lost Wolf had helped himself to a generous portion of ham and chicken.

Remembering, he recalled, also, that it was long, long

since he had eaten. In another instant he had glided through the door of that kitchen, and as Mrs. Gleason hurried in for the last look to see that all was well and to secure the rear door of the house under lock and key, Lost Wolf that instant was slipping into the capacious pantry.

While he heard her key, turning in the lock, he stood in that pantry and, with half-closed eyes, inhaling the fragrances around him—spiced jellies to be eaten with meat, jams, dried fruits in the lower bins—and the heavy perfume of newly baked bread, now wrapped up in clean dishcloths and cooling on the shelf just beneath the window.

His regretful nose informed him that neither cooked chicken nor ham was at hand. There was raw ham near, but he was not a true redskin. He could not enjoy uncooked smoked meat. What he did find was a huge leg of mutton, from which only a single scant meal had been carved.

This mighty joint was clutched at either end by the great hands of Lost Wolf; presently he was ripping the meat away from the bone. He did not pause until it was finished. After which he found the water pail in the kitchen, drank, and returned for more plunder. Two jars of strawberry jam—a meal for three men—next passed into the paunch of Lost Wolf. He sat down cross-legged on the floor to wish for a smoke and to let his meal settle while he listened to the last sounds from the upstairs, as the minister's family retired.

When all was quiet, he started. At the kitchen door he remembered that his costume was a trifle less than ordinary among the whites. So he returned to the kitchen, where another thought struck him.

For five minutes he was busied with sand soap and the bucket of water. When he finished, his skin was half raw, but well cleansed. After this, he took the red tablecloth from the kitchen table and cast it around his shoulders as a robe.

He was now equipped, he felt, for the most decent and formal company in the world.

35

When he was halfway up the stairs, something stirred, and the big man crouched, the terrible hunting knife instantly bared in his hand. It was nothing.

Yet this was an uneasy place. It was like stealing at night into the camp of an enemy, where noise never ends, and always there is at least the stamping of some restless horse in the distance. Here there was the faint creaking of old timbers in a distant part of the building, as the wind pushed an invisible hand against the side walls, or else a swiftly running whisper that whirred through the building from top to bottom.

Lost Wolf thought of ghosts and trembled. He clutched a little bag which hung from around his neck. In that bag there were powerful tokens of good luck, and the bag and all of its contents had so often been soaked in the sacred smoke from the medicine pipes, that when he gripped the emblem, Lost Wolf's nerves regained their strength and he was sure of himself.

He went on and gained the second story.

More than once I have thought of that monstrous form of a man leaning at each door that he passed, knife in hand, listening, dreadfully intent. For he was bent on such a business this night that nothing in the world could have stopped him. Good luck kept the poor minister soundly asleep, worn out with the strength of his own sermon.

Lost Wolf came to the door which he had selected beforehand as the right one. As he laid his hand upon the knob, it made a little rattling. He instantly withdrew his touch. However, there was an answering rustle from the inside of the room. Lost Wolf was about to slip away,

182

but then he assured himself that it could only be the breath of the wind, passing through the open window.

He remained there—until the door was suddenly opened, and Peggy Gleason said softly: "Is it you, mother?"

Then she saw the monster towering above her.

She had not been ready to sleep when the rest of the family went to bed. She preferred to sit in her room with the lamplight turned low, dreaming over again a certain wild speech which a young man had made to her not very long before.

When her widening eyes gathered in the truth of this specter that stood before her in the dark of the hall, she tried at the same instant to slam the door in his face and to scream.

He defeated both efforts with one gesture. He knew that she was about to scream, and much as he loved her he wanted to stop that shriek. He had heard women scream before, sending little cold shivers all the way up his spine to the base of his brain.

He stretched forth his great right arm, and the edge of the closing door thudded softly against a cord of muscle in that arm, while the big, capable hand of Lost Wolf took his lady capably by the throat.

There are ways and ways of handling throats. Those ways are a lost art. There is a way of breaking the wind-pipe and insuring suffocation at one grasp. There is also a way of pressing the palm of the thumb into the little cup of the throat and shutting off all air without a great deal of pain. Now Lost Wolf was a master of these arts, for he had learned them among past masters—the youth of a Cheyenne village. As he caught Peggy Gleason by the throat, he closed the ball of his thumb over that same hollow and made her scream die still-born. After that, he tucked her under his arm and closed the door.

He sat down, cross-legged, on the floor with the girl stretched across his knees. Then he said, for she struggled and tore at his wrists with her fingers: "Be quiet, and make no noise. I am Lost Wolf, and if you do not do as I say, I shall break your windpipe like a tube of dried bark!"

So spoke Lost Wolf, the lover, to the lady of his heart.

She managed to reach the floor, and she struck it with her heel. It suddenly occurred to Lost Wolf that this tender girl had a greater fear than that of death. Also, these noises would bring upon him the embarrassing necessity of having to murder the entire family if he wanted to get Peggy away from them.

He acted a little faster than a panther acts with its flirting paws. With a fold of his red tablecloth robe he muffled and blindfolded the face of Peggy. He tied her hands and her feet together, accomplishing all of this before a door opened and the voice of Charles Gleason called wearily: "Peggy."

Lost Wolf could hear the minister's wife say sleepily: "It was only a clap of wind—nothing else, Charlie. Come back to bed."

There was the sound of Gleason's yawn, like a groan. Then his footfall padded down the hall, reached the door of his daughter's room, and paused there. Lost Wolf rose to his knees. His left arm, as thick and as strong as a coil of the python's body, held the helpless girl to keep her soft struggles from making a sound across the floor. His right hand held the hunting knife. There he waited in the dark—and the door opened.

The hushed voice of Gleason called cautiously: "Peggy, dear!"

Then a long pause—a murmur—the door closed. The minister turned away from the face of death which had been in breathing distance of him.

Lost Wolf waited until the door of the minister's room had closed and until the house was quiet. In the meantime, the struggles of his victim had grown less and less frantic, though as spasmodic as ever. She was strangling; Lost Wolf knew it, because he was not unfamiliar with how dying or fainting people act.

He placed his hand upon her heart and held it there. As he counted the racing beats, he nodded, contented. She still had plenty of strength.

At last, he picked her up, slid through the doorway, and glided down the stairs, stepping by instinct close to the wall, where there is a lesser chance of creating embarrassing creaks and squeaks. He gained the kitchen door once more and unlocked it with a stealthy hand. Finally, he stood under the stars again.

It seemed to Lost Wolf that they were shooting rockets of a blinding brightness at the earth; never had he seen such joyous brilliance in the night.

Then the tall body of the red stallion was beside him. He loosened the head wrapping of the girl to allow her a single free breath of air. It gave her a chance for life, but not for shouting. Before she could utter a sound, Lost Wolf had gagged her again and laid her before him on the withers of the tall horse, and they were moving away through the night.

Twice more, in that night, the minister of the church in Zander City, so the tradition told afterward, roused himself and sat up with a cry, and his wife asked him what ailed him.

"We're in danger, Marcia!" he answered her.

"Nonsense," said she. "You're growing light-witted. What could be wrong? Is the house on fire?"

The third time that Gleason wakened, he could not be stilled. There was such a weight on his spirit that he insisted on getting up. He went down to his library and sat there with a heavy sense of gloom in his heart. He could not explain it. It was not the usual sense of failure and guilt. It was simply the dread of danger hanging over him. At length, he got up and hurried up the stairs, without having lighted the pipe which he had packed with absent-minded care.

When he got opposite the door of Peggy Gleason, he tapped gently against it. When he heard no answer he said to himself, with a great sense of relief, that at least all was well with her. He decided that he would look at her in her sleep, a thing which he had not done since she was a wee, small thing. So he went in and looked down at the bed of Peggy—and found that it had never been disturbed that night.

A moment later, and he was trembling at the bedside of his wife. When he wakened her with his shaking hand and his uncertain voice, this time, she did not start into anger, as she had done on the other occasions. She merely stood up at once and said hastily:

"What's wrong, Charlie? Are you sick, man?"

He could not speak; he did not have to. She gave him one glance, and then she fled for the room of Peggy. They stood together, poor mother and father, staring helplessly at one another. Charlie Gleason was the most surprised man in the world to find that Marcia, now that the great blow had fallen, did not storm and rage at all, but simply said to him in a quiet voice:

"God forgive us for all our sins. All my sins, because what sins have ever been yours, Charlie?"

It was not said in a crying voice, either. As she was masculine and strong-headed in her ordinary life, so she was masculine and strong-headed in the way she took her loss.

The minister was still sitting dumbly beside the bed, his hands clasped, staring at it as though there were a sick person in it, when Marcia Gleason, having run out to the neighbors, came back with a dozen men, and more men to follow. The tramp of heavy feet passed in and out of the big front door. There was the flash and swing of lanterns everywhere as they scoured the place until somebody shouted: "Look here!"

Others came, and they stared at the scratched place on the wall of the house and the deep scar where Lost Wolf had prepared for himself an easy place of ascent in case he had to flee directly from the room of the girl.

"No man that's not a monkey," said someone, "could have carried himself—let alone a girl—down such a place."

Marcia, herself, had now found the stripped mutton bone and the emptied jars of sweets in the kitchen. When, in addition to all of this, it was found that the outline of a man's naked foot of the greatest size was printed dimly two or three times in the hall of the house, there was no doubt left.

"It's the red white man the—white Indian, Charlie! He's come to take what we would not sell him!"

Zander City, after that, knew for whom it had to hunt.

36

At the end of a mere five minutes of galloping, with the great red horse going strong and free under this double burden, Lost Wolf knew that he was out of earshot from the town. Therefore he slackened rein.

He knew that it was time, too, for he had watched the pulse of the girl as he rode, and he could judge that she was close to collapse. That was Indian style—to keep clear eyes fixed upon even those who are nearest to us. Lost Wolf handled the girl he loved with as calm an air as though he were a doctor taking care of the poorest charity patient.

He stopped now, and removed the gag from her mouth. There on the ground he squatted beside her and felt her pulse strengthen, then race, while her breath came back in deep gasps. She could brace herself upon her hands, at length. Although Lost Wolf did not touch her, it seemed to him that he could *feel* her tremor. For that moment he had saved his stroke which, he felt, would remove her last terror. He said:

"I am that man who brought the horses and paid the great price for you. I have given robes alone enough to buy twenty of the most beautiful girls among the Cheyennes. I have paid horses to buy twenty, also. And yet I am a man to whom the greatest chiefs have offered their daughters for nothing—as a free gift, because they wanted to have me in their lodges as their friend and their ally. But I shall have you as my squaw, and I have paid down the good price for you. There is one thing more, and that may have stood between you and me. It is gone now!

Look with your own eyes and touch with your own hand, if you wish!"

So saying, he scratched a match and held it. The rocky features of Lost Wolf were wonderfully changed. Of course, their form was identical with the form which they had always had since manhood, but all was altered by the change in the color of the skin. The stain which he had used had kept away the effect of wind and sun, and the hard scrubbing with sand soap, which he had given himself, had left his face pale indeed!

He came, you might say, at one stride out of the region of nightmares and into that of manhood, so far as the girl was concerned. She was still terribly frightened, but before this, she had looked upon him as a monster, accidentally cast in human mold. Now she felt in him a being who could speak her tongue and think her thoughts with equal ease.

He was no longer an insensate brute but a human being.

Yet she did not attempt to answer him for the moment. There was too much fear in her for that. She sat trembling on the ground, with one hand pressed against the base of her throat, wondering when this terror would end and blindly reaching toward the future. Lost Wolf did not ask her if she could find happiness with him. It would not have seemed logical or right to him. He had made her simply the captive of his hand. In addition to that, he had upon her the double claim of an enormous price offered and paid down.

Certainly the odd conscience of Lost Wolf did not trouble him a whit in this matter. He was at peace with himself, utterly. So, having made a halt until the girl had regained her breath and her strength a little, he mounted the red horse once more and made her climb up before him.

They journeyed on into the coming of the dawn, and all that time Peggy Gleason did not speak. Whatever terrible things came into her mind, she kept them to herself, for she felt that it would be useless to say them to the giant who carried her with him. It was like being transported into a terrible fairy tale, a thing of imagination too awful to be real.

In the morning, when they came to a water hole, the monster made his camp beside it. He made a fire, and over it he cooked the white man's ration—coffee and sliced bacon. With it he had heavy, soggy cold corn bread. He cooked, and he ate. When he had done, he showed her the remnants of his meal.

"Eat!" said the giant.

Eat? There was no desire for food in poor Peggy. There was too much salty taste of sorrow in her mouth, and she felt that she could not force a morsel down her throat. So she told him that she was not hungry.

At this, he regarded her curiously, sitting with his pipe in his one hand, and his chin supported on the other fist.

"I have seen this before," said he. "Oh, yes, it has happened in the towns of the Cheyennes when captive women were brought in from a war party. I have seen a Pawnee starve herself to death. But she was the captive of a weak, foolish brave. Are you ashamed to belong to Lost Wolf?"

He struck his arched breast as he spoke and scowled upon her. Peggy Gleason closed her eyes.

"So," said Lost Wolf, "now you are praying. And for what?"

"Only to die!" cried poor Peggy in a sudden frenzy of fear. "Only to die, if God please!"

If the ground had been ripped open at his feet, Lost Wolf could not have been more perfectly surprised. He stared at her with new eyes. Certainly he had not dreamed that such a thing as this could be!

He looked down at the great muscles of his arms, at his rifle lying beside him. He shook his head, and the feathers rustled in his locks. What was lacking in him? What was wrong in him that the perfect warrior should possess, except a red skin which had been, surely, the chief thing that frightened the girl.

Was she weak of wit? He had all the horror which barbarous people feel for those afflicted with light minds. It is a strange thing that civilized people will laugh at madness, but the savage sees in the half-wit only the afflicted of God. Lost Wolf took the hands of the girl very gently and drew them down from her face.

"Raise your head!" said he. "Look at me!"

"I cannot!" said Peggy Gleason.

He could feel her hands not tugging at his, not attempting to free herself by force, but shuddering in horror at his touch.

He put his great, hard-fingered hand under her chin, and forced her face up. At that touch she looked forth at him with such terror and with such loathing, that even Lost Wolf suddenly understood.

His first reaction was that of a brute. Scoff at a dog, and it will show you his teeth; scoff at an Indian, and he will show you his knife. Lost Wolf took her by the hair of the head.

"Little fool!" said he. "Do you think that when I capture a fine horse in a raid, I turn it loose because it lags and does not wish to go along, and fears the strange language? No! I send my young men with whips to beat it along the right way back to the village. And so with you. If you will not eat, I shall force open your jaws with my own hands, and with my own hands I shall cram the food down your throat. Will you have me do that?"

What could have been more horrible to Peggy than that thought of being mastered in the huge grip of this giant? She stammered out that she would eat if she could. And Lost Wolf showed a touch that was not Indian at all. He did not stay to gloat over her submission. He went off and left her to herself to eat her meal.

She ate—with horror and disgust, at first, finally with a wakened hunger. When that hunger was a little blunted, her mind began to work on her situation, again. Then she saw what she had not noticed before—that when he made the morning fire, Lost Wolf had loosened his belt and laid it on the ground. In that belt was a holster, and from the holster projected the heavy butt of a new Colt revolver!

She had it out instantly, feverishly, and pressed the muzzle against the base of her throat.

Lost Wolf saw at that instant, and paused in his walking to and fro. He thought, at first, of catching up his rifle and trying with a neat, quick shot to knock the revolver out of her hands. Then he told himself that if he fired the shot and took her by force, the spirit would still be within her. He could not watch her every moment of her life.

"And I thought," said Lost Wolf, when he talked to me of this moment, later on, "that a spirit like the eagle's ought to be as free as the eagle's spirit. What could make her free? Only death, because there was not enough generosity in me to let her go. I thought that if there was the courage in her, I would let her die. It was the only gift that I could make her!"

So thought Lost Wolf—like a brute, you will say. Brutal it was, but frank, at least. Certainly such ideas were never born in the brain of a mere Indian.

When poor Peggy raised the revolver and pressed it to the base of her throat, she had a glimpse of the black, deep mouth of the gun. She closed her eyes and shuddered when the cold lips of steel touched her flesh.

Then she thought: "If I fire through the throat, I may not kill myself at once but only tear the flesh and bring a horrible agony—and so perhaps not die at all! But through the heart—"

She moved the revolver again; once more, she saw the round, gaping muzzle, looking frightfully large. Why should guns be made so great in size? A pin prick through the brain or through the heart would end everything just as effectually. With these enormous bullets to break the bones and to tear the flesh—why should the coming of death be made so horrible?

A voice sounded at the side. She saw Lost Wolf coming slowly, saying: "Put down the gun and put the bridle on the horse!"

She said: "If you come closer to me—if you come only a step closer—"

Lone Wolf smiled. I have seen those mirthless smiles of his, and they were far from beautiful!

"You are not brave," said he. "You will not kill yourself. You are just a squaw. Put down that gun, squaw, and bridle the horse, and bring him to me. Also, clean the pot and the pan. I am tired of laboring for myself and for my woman, also."

He sat down on the ground, with his back turned

toward her, and jointing the long step of his pipe, he lighted it calmly and began to smoke.

37

I suppose that most domestic crises are like this—recognized in a moment of silence. It is not the loud wrangle that counts the most; it is not the bitter altercation; it is not the discovery of unsuspected unpleasantness. Worse than all these are the morning when the husband forgets to kiss his wife goodby for the day. What shall be said of the tragedy when he remains wrapped in his own thoughts, though the full, delightful narrative of baby's latest exploit is being unfolded for his indifferent ears?

Again, what thrill of terror goes through the heart of the husband, when that wife who sat in quiet opposite him at so many meals is now observed laughing and chatting so gayly with a dinner partner, looking up to the face of the stranger at the dance with some of the original mystery of girlhood brought back to her eyes? These are the blows that cut the deepest, and sink slowly into the heart and remains there forever.

In this matter of Peggy and Lost Wolf the frightful moment was not that in which he took her from her house at night, half strangling her. It was in that instant of calm contempt when he sat down and turned his back upon her.

I should not say that it was mere calm. It was the maneuver of a skillful general. Lost Wolf told himself that if there were viciousness mixed with cowardice she would seize upon this moment to put a bullet through the back of his brain. He cast great stakes—his own life—upon that hazard.

What shall I say of poor Peggy, my dear Peggy, as she

saw the broad, heavily muscled back of the big man turned upon her? To her own terror there was added the terrible burden of self scorn. For she knew that there was not brutality enough in her heart to kill the man, and there was not courage enough to kill herself. Most awful of all was the feeling that her captor knew these things! She was not only helpless in the hollow of his hand, but in the hollow of his mind, also.

Presently Lost Wolf heard a faint stir, and when he turned his head a little, he remarked the girl making vain efforts to get to the head of the red horse. She was playing with fire, there. He tossed his head high, high beyond her reach, and now with flattened ears, he threatened to give her his teeth.

One word from the master turned him to stone.

There was a frightened glance, a gasp of relief, and Peggy Gleason found that the great stallion was patient under her touch. She had drawn the stalls over his sharp ears, and was fastening the throat latch when another specter startled her. A monstrous white wolf, greater by far than any that she had ever seen before, sat down a hundred yards away, and with his red tongue lolled forth, seemed to laugh at her with a devilish self-content.

She looked back at Lost Wolf for help, but the giant's back was turned. The slow puffs of smoke ascended from his pipe one by one and melted to nothingness in the desert air.

When she led back the great horse to Lost Wolf, and he mounted and took her up behind him, she saw the slinking form of the wolf follow, unheeded, behind. It seemed to my dear Peggy that horse and man and wolf wre linked together in a grim alliance.

They went on slowly, that day. In spite of the enormous strength of the stallion, Lost Wolf appeared inclined to spare it as much as possible. First he, himself, dismounted and walked ahead.

The girl could not credit her senses. Much as he apparently despised her, yet it did not seem possible that he would not credit her with sense enough to attempt an escape. Such, however, seemed to be his idea. For he stepped off briskly, at a gait which the stallion could match only at a trot. When the horse trotted, Lost Wolf seemed in a humor for running, and headed across the prairie at a long, easy stride. He drew a little away. He drew still farther off—

Then she made her move. She pulled the red horse around—she loosened the rein—and she struck him silently upon the flank with her open hand. There had been only one doubt in her mind, and that was whether or not she would be able to keep her place when the huge animal struck away at his full stride. There was no doubt once he began at his matchless full speed. His great bounds were taken as smoothly as the running of water. She could hardly have known how fast she was traveling, had it not been for the sudden gale which began to cut through her hair and fan against her face.

She was free. Yes, and for such a horse as this, she was almost glad to have paid such a price of misery and terror as she had endured with Lost Wolf. She was free—as eagles are free in the central heaven.

Then a sound struck faintly against her ear through the roar of the wind of that galloping. If only she dared to turn her head, would she not laugh to see Lost Wolf shouting with dismay, to see the consternation on the face of that strange man?

Here was the great horse pausing in his stride, now veering to the side so swiftly that she was almost flung from the saddle. As it was, clinging by hand and foot, she barely managed to keep to the side of the monster. He turned and headed like an arrow straight back toward his master.

That was the reason for the indifference of Lost Wolf! It was because he knew the heart of his slave.

He might have disposed of her in still another way. The big white wolf came bounding beside her, fairly bristling with horrible rage and hunger. One leap, one slash of those dreadful teeth, and she would lie dying on the plain.

The voice of the master called again, and the white wolf shrank away as though a lash had struck across its face.

They were at the back of Lost Wolf, and here the stallion followed quietly, shaking his head up and down, rejoicing in his speed, rejoicing in his truth to his master, and fairly dancing with eagerness to be off again. Lost Wolf had no word or touch of reward, for he had turned his back before they came up, even, and was once more jogging lightly across the prairie.

So deep a contempt amazed her; so deep a knowledge of human nature amazed and terrified her, too! How could he know when, indeed, her hand was actually gripping the butt of the Colt, in readiness to draw and to kill?

That was not the end of the odd adventures of this day. For an hour or more, the man journeyed on foot. For another hour he rode before her on the horse. Then he stopped and told her to dismount and follow him.

Dismount she did, and here was the red stallion walking swiftly away. She strode to follow, but her stride was neither long enough nor strong enough to keep up with this pace. The red horse walked like a thing possessed. She fell behind. She began to run, and that moment, the heat of the sun ran up into her brain.

It seemed to her that she could endure no more, and she threw herself down on the grass, grasping for breath. Presently the hoofbeat of the stallion was beside her and the voice of the captor:

"Shall I catch you with the lariat and drag you behind me? Shall I whip you before me? Get up, and follow. The Cheyenne women shall teach you many lessons!"

Peggy Gleason stumbled to her feet. She cast one glance upward to ask of the blue sky if such cruelty could be permitted by God on earth. That sky was pale with the fire of the sun, and her dazzled eyes sank back to the ground once more. She was stumbling ahead once more. Since she *had* to run, she could. Necessity oddly lightened her feet. The dust which curled upward behind the horse no longer stung her nostrils so sharply.

It was a long time before exhaustion began to grow upon her again. Not exhaustion of the mind, this time; not a weakness in her imagination, but the true fatigue of the body. Before she was reeling, before she was stopped, the rider had made his horse pause and had taken her up.

For another hour they rode together; then the man ran ahead. They paused for a small noon meal, which Peggy cooked. Peggy ate in silence at the bidding of her master. Then they mounted and went on again.

Another hour, and Peggy must run once more.

A difference, now. Her feet were swollen and sore. Her legs were aching and tired. Her throat was raw with the whistling of the dry prairie wind. Still she had to try to make the march.

She felt that there was no more use in appealing to the mercy of the rider than to the mercy of a sheer devil. She stuck to her work until a swimming blackness rose before her eyes and the ground rose up around her.

When she came back to her senses, there was water in her face. And the shadow of Lost Wolf lay between her and the sun. There she lay, wondering, slowly and dimly coming back to the reality from the happy dream into which she had fallen.

"Get up," said the master, "and climb up behind the horse."

She got to her hands and knees. The blood seemed to rush away from her brain, and it seemed to my dear Peggy that she would fall sidelong to the earth.

"Look!" said Lost Wolf. "I am too kind. I have not used a whip to help you up!"

The ridiculous cruelty of it cleared her mind again, and she was able to stand, able to reach his hand, and to drag herself up to the appointed place.

That day came to an end, and as the sun sank, they reached running water and the chosen site for their camp. She was told to dismount, to unsaddle the horse, to build the fire, and to prepare the food.

She thought, as her weak fingers struggled with the cinch knot which that mighty hand of the giant had tied, that God had concealed one mercy in this nightmare, for she would die soon—since all her strength was running swiftly from her body!

The work was done. The merciless eye of the big man flicked across her and straightened her like a lash of a whip, when she staggered. The meal was cooked and eaten; the pan and the little pot were cleaned.

"Here," said Lost Wolf, "you will sleep."

On the ground he had spread the blanket that covered the back of the stallion during the day and protected it from the galling of the saddle. And the warm deerskin robe was above it. There she lay down and wrapped herself warm.

Lost Wolf lay on the other side of the fire, under the cold shining of the stars.

She was too weary even for wonder. She slept at once. The beating of her heart sent great waves of numbness across her brain, and she was unconscious.

38

The splashing of a raindrop and the rattle of a volley of that rain among the dried grasses of the prairie wakened the girl. My Peggy started from her dream with a gasp—and she saw above her only the heavy blackness of the open face of the night.

She turned her head toward the red light upon the side. There was the form of Lost Wolf bowed near the fire, his gigantic arms locked around his knees, and his head sunk upon his chest—sleeping and resting there in spite of the downfall of the rain!

It did not seem possible but all things which were strange in others were natural in this monster. He stirred and wavered in his place as a fresh torrent cut at his back; a faint groan came from his lips in his sleep, and the great white wolf, rising up before him, licked his hands, licked his face, and lay down once more to guard his feet. The red stallion came in from the black of the night and stood over the man and the wolf, with the firelight turning his rain-polished sides to a body of flame.

This picture Peggy Gleason stared at.

She was amazed to find that in her heart there was pity

for the brute who had tyrannized over her in such a manner through that nightmare day.

She lay down again and wrapped herself more closely in the deer skin. Her mind was busier with thought, than was the rain with her face, as she lay there. She was telling herself that it was strange if a man could be loved by dumb beasts, and yet have nothing worth loving in his nature. More than strange indeed!

That thought twisted and turned in the brain of the girl until at last she got up, and took the thick, soft saddle blanket, went to Lost Wolf and laid it over his shoulders.

After that, since the ground was growing wet, she huddled herself in the deerskin and sat down opposite the fire—with its glow and its smoke between her and her master. She could feel his bright, large eyes fixed upon her from the obscurity beyond, but he said not a word in thanks.

Had he said more than fifty words since he brought her out from the house of her father?

It was only a brief shower. The moon began to struggle through the eastern clouds. Those clouds were rolled apart in a broad gap, and like diamonds studding steel, the stars began to shine.

But on opposite sides of the fire they sat through all that night.

In the morning, they started while the dawn was red. They journeyed on all day and every day, heading toward the camp of the Cheyennes.

You will wonder, then that I should have come to the village first?

It was not because the stallion carried double that Lost Wolf had chosen to take a longer route. He wished to have his white girl know something of Indian ways and duties before he brought her into the village. Otherwise, she would be laughed at. He knew that ridicule cuts with a far sharper lash than any whip. She needed strength, too, and she must master some of the prairie ways with a prairie ability before she came to the Cheyennes.

There were other impulses locked up behind the will of big Lost Wolf. What they all were, I cannot pretend to understand. He was never a very great talker, and though he looked upon me as a friend who had proved my truth to him in blood, still he did not open his heart to me completely. He did not know how to open it!

Language had never become to him what it is to some people, a thing that even extends beyond emotions. I have known people who never can talk down to their real ideas, but cartoon themselves in their words, hinting at emotion far vaster than anything that ever entered their narrow minds. Lost Wolf was not that type. He was a man who found the action of a strong pair of hands much more to the point than any words. Since he had grown to manhood with fame and with fortune according to Indian lights, and without eloquence, it was rather late for him to learn new ways.

I do not think it is too much to guess that the big fellow was not unwilling that the girl should see him away on the prairie in the elements where he was strongest. Nothing could have made him seem more startling in his strength than the devotion of the wolf on the one hand and the great red horse on the other—each of them living for the good word of the master.

That was the environment in which, instinctively, he wanted Peggy Gleason to come to know him; so he strung the journey out day after day. Her shoes were worn to rags by the bitter work to which she had to put them, while she traveled with Lost Wolf. When that happened, he killed a coyote with a beautiful long-range rifle shot, and out of its skin made for her several pairs of moccasins, soft beyond belief.

Everyday the march was resumed in the same fashion. The halts were only for the three meals, unless it were to turn aside, and run down some red-hot scent of game which the white wolf reported to the master.

In this manner, they continued for nearly two weeks. Then, on a morning, a stir and then a rumor ran through the camp of the Cheyennes. As I walked with Danny Croydon to a feast which one of the braves was giving—consisting of more talk than good food—I saw Running Deer dash past me on a racing pony.

Danny Croydon took one glimpse of the speeding chief and said instantly: "Lost Wolf!"

Naturally, I started a little at this, but Danny explained that he had seen Running Deer in a good many tight corners, but he had never seen him show the slightest emotion except when something concerning Lost Wolf was brought to his attention. So Croydon was sure, and a moment later, as a hoarse yelling began through the village, he held up a hand and nodded.

"They're yelling his name right now!"

I myself could now recognize the Cheyenne phrase which was translated as Lost Wolf. Of course, I was tremendously excited when a little later Croydon translated some more shouts by adding: "He's bringing in a captive again!"

I wondered how even the red stallion could have carried Lost Wolf from Zander City to the hostile territory of any other tribe and back to the Cheyennes again in this interval, but it might be explained by the fact that he had encountered an enemy party on the warpath.

It was an odd way to gather information by standing still in the center of the camp and listening to all that was discernible in the confused and growing uproar of the crowd outside the village. All the living creatures in it, except a couple of infants who were crawling in the background, had staggered or ridden or run or crawled out to greet the hero.

Then Croydon cried: "By Heaven—it's a woman that he's bringing in. Do you hear? A woman."

He added: "Does it mean that Lost Wolf had found some pretty Pawnee that he intends to take for his squaw?"

I could not help a little shudder at the idea, but Croydon said: "You can't tell. The fact that she's a captured enemy maiden may give her, along with a little prettiness, just enough tang to make a point with him. You can't tell about these things. I've seen some copper faces that were as pretty as pictures—in their youth. Listen to the way the Cheyennes are whooping it up! They're partly delighted, and partly they're as mad as all sixty!"

There was no doubt about the anger; it came ringing and stinging at our ears.

"They want that Pawnee or Sioux girl for the torture stake," announced Croydon after another moment. "But they could pawn their souls and never get her for that purpose from Lost Wolf. He's not that kind of an animal!"

The crowd was bursting into the village again, bringing the warrior and his companion along with them.

Croydon said: "What I don't make out is that they seem to be angry with *Lost Wolf*. Why the deuce should they hate *him* for bringing in a captive?"

Of course, I had not been able to translate the exclamations as distinctly as that. Anyone can recognize anger in a human voice, however, as distinctly as one can feel the poison in the sting of a wasp. I knew the Cheyennes were wild with fury, but I couldn't tell why.

However the next exclamation of Croydon drove a knife into me.

"Rivers, it's a *white* girl!"

I cannot translate that effect for you. Very queer that a single word could have made such a difference in a hardened old frontiersman like Croydon and a good-for-nothing rapscallion such as I was at that time in my life.

I know that we were idling quite at ease, up to that moment, with just a pleasant expectation of seeing our old friend, Lost Wolf. That single word—white—stuck a knife through the small of my back. I felt quick for my guns, making sure that I had two Colts with me. I knew that they were both loaded, and that I had a long-bladed, heavy hunting knife, also.

Danny Croydon was feeling for his own weapons, and I knew that that instinct of mine had not been so very far wrong. There was danger ahead of us, *great* danger.

Croydon gripped my shoulder.

"It's not all the white girl, though," said he. "It's not all the girl. Lost Wolf has done something else; the raving idiot has taken the paint off his face and has dared to come into the village in his white skin!"

At that same instant, we could see Lost Wolf, towering above the rest of the crowd. His face was indeed white—almost pale, it seemed to me.

He saw us, too, and he raised his hand in instant salute. Then he turned the red stallion toward us, with the form clinging to him from behind—the form of a girl—his girth of shoulders blotted out all chance we had of seeing

201

her face. Here the stallion swerved a little as it picked its way through the writhing, squirming mass of Indians. As it did so, Croydon saw and with one breath he had drawn all the strength out of my knees, for he gasped out: "It's Peggy Gleason!"

39

I had not had much experience with Indians, up to this point, as you can judge for yourselves. Yet I knew a good deal more than to have committed the joint blunders of which Lost Wolf had been guilty on this day. When I remember that his entire life had been spent among the Cheyennes, except for the brief period when Croydon was able to rule the tiger by force, I am only able to explain his blunders by supposing that Lost Wolf had lived too close to Indian human nature to understand a great many of its phases.

Too, he had always been the petted darling of the Cheyennes. He was not a chief, to be sure, but that lack prevented him from being envied as other chiefs were sure to be. He was simply a mixture of great warrior and great medicine man, which was a union positively godlike in its efficacy in the Cheyenne tribe. I, personally, know that he had taken more scalps in the Cheyenne name than any other warrior that ever rode a horse. Wherever he appeared among the people into which he had been adopted, he was surrounded by respect, obedience, and affection.

These things make up a veil through which the average mind cannot see very quickly. In some respects Lost Wolf was far less than average in his intelligence, just as he was far above average in other respects.

However, Croydon was perfectly right. The giant could

not have joined two more incompatible actions than to bring in a white girl to the village. To have his own face in its natural color was adding the worst sort of insult to the injury of the Cheyennes.

It was just exactly as though he had shouted to them:

"You see that I have lived among you all these years, always refusing to take a squaw from among the daughters of your greatest chiefs. But now I show you the reason. It was not because I was not interested in women, but because I despised you and your kind. Now, however, I have found a girl to my liking, and I have brought her here so that you may see and enjoy the superiority which she possesses over other maidens—Cheyennes and all others. Furthermore, I reveal to you the peculiarity of her excellence, which lies in her color. In her honor, therefore, I have made my own face white, and from this time forward, my life shall be for her and for people of her color and my own!"

He could not have said in words as much as he now said in symbol, or so it seemed to the Cheyennes. That he should have ridden in among them in such a guise, in all innocence and frankness of spirit seemed to them absurd. I cannot blame them for their ideas. Really, it was one of the most gigantic bits of dangerous folly that any man could have imagined.

"Look at the face of Running Deer!" said Croydon.

It was a fine study, I can tell you, in shame and rage and burning grief. I have never seen such a mask of woe as that poor young chief wore, now that he saw that insult offered by Lost Wolf to the entire tribe and therefore to his own person, he being the head of the tribe.

Even Lost Wolf, dumb and stupid though his conduct had been, was now beginning to realize that he had been a fool. As we stood there at watch, a great hulk of an Indian, one of the leading warriors of the tribe, rode through the press of his companions, shouting to them words which I did not understand. The gestures, which said with perfect plainness, "Follow me and do as I am going to do!"

What he started to do was to lay hands on the girl

behind Lost Wolf. As he did so, I heard her cry out sharply in terror.

At that, her captor whirled in his saddle and struck at the head of the big warrior. I think I have said before that the thrust of one of those arms was like the play of the walking beam in a huge steam engine. It clipped the warrior on the side of the head and shot him off his horse with a force so great that it was actually hideous. One could hardly believe it unless it were seen—and hardly believe even after it had been observed. I heard the crunch of bone. I cannot say that the warrior died from the effects of the blow, but I know that he had not recovered consciousness at the last reports.

That blow was not all. Lost Wolf was like a madman; he dropped the reins of the red stallion and guided it back and forth with the mere pressure of his knees—a truly wonderful sight to watch. In each of his hands, Lost Wolf carried a heavy Colt of the most recent model. Every man in that tribe knew that in the fingers of Lost Wolf was being carried the death of twelve braves.

They shrank away, and as they shrank, Lost Wolf scourged them with words and flayed them alive. I didn't need to know Cheyenne in order to understand that perfectly! What he said to those Indians made even their red skins turn redder.

Running Deer covered his face with a blanket and turned away—a very sick Indian, indeed!

Lost Wolf came on to us. He took the girl in the hollow of his arm with a wonderful strength and gave her to us. She was a little out of her wits, I supposed, because she moaned as though she were afraid to leave him. As a matter of fact, she was so frightened that she hardly knew where she was. The nightmare face of that big Indian warrior was still filling two-thirds of her mind.

I took her in my arms as Lost Wolf handed her down, saying:

"My two friends, the devil is in all the Cheyennes, but the Great Spirit has sent you here to help me in this great time of my life. Be true to me, and I shall never fail either of you!"

I said in a whisper: "Peggy! It is I!"

She opened her eyes wildly mad, then she clung to me so that I had to whisper at her ear: "He's watching. Be careful!"

He was *not* watching; he was too busy in the earnest work of cursing the Cheyennes. In the meantime, he formed an escort that took us down the length of the village, the red stallion dancing around us in circles, and Lost Wolf begging any dozen of the braves to step out and engage him for the sake of love or honor—or any better reason, if they could only think of one.

I've never seen any man look half so terrible or half so splendid as that giant while he raged around in the face of those scores of practiced fighting men. Not that they didn't answer him back, because they did. The conversation might have been translated in a fashion something like this.

Lost Wolf, singling out a dignified and important warrior: "You, Spotted Calf—do I not see you standing there like a fool—or like a dying buffalo with an arrow sticking in its belly? So are you, Spotted Calf, bawling, and speaking little sense. But I, this day, see you and will remember."

Whereas Spotted Calf would merely say in response: "Is this well? Is this wise, Lost Wolf, to take a white woman into the city of the Cheyennes and disgrace our daughters and our wives? Or are there no other faces in the world except the white ones?"

It was rather mild talk, compared with the concentrated lightning which Lost Wolf was scattering around him with such a liberal hand. He got to the limits of his vocabulary; then he stretched those limits a good deal and went on into new regions, getting handy expressions to throw at the heads of the Cheyennes.

Before he was through, he had fairly well silenced the braves. Why did he not get himself murdered would have puzzled most people—but it never puzzled me. I had seen him in action; I had heard the bones crunch when he struck that other brave on the side of the head. The Cheyennes were letting a little discretion mix up with their courage. As a matter of fact, whisky is about the only thing that altogether robs an Indian warrior of his usual good sense.

The men were quieted by the ripping talk of big Lost Wolf, but the women were only getting fairly well started. They kept their rattles going while Lost Wolf drew off with Croydon and me, who were keeping Peggy between us.

We didn't want to show guns, but the crisis was so bad that we had to. Each of us had a drawn Colt in his hand. Of course that made matters even blacker than before, because any Indian hates to have it appear that he has been made to back down—or any white man, either, for that matter.

We headed through the camp, until we came to the lodge of Running Deer. When we got there, we found plenty of buffalo robes lying around, lots of food and utensils, and a fire burning very bright and cheerful. We didn't find Running Deer, though we knew that he had ridden that way ahead of us. We didn't find any of his squaws, either, which made matters a little embarrassing for us.

Lost Wolf looked matters over and strode up and down inside the tepee. He said to me: "Go stand at the entrance and guard the red horse. These Cheyennes may come and try to steal him. Didn't they try to steal my squaw?"

I stood at the entrance to the lodge as I was commanded. While I stood there, I could see the braves gathering into focal points for discussion, in the distance. They were talking about how they should dispose of this new tribal entanglement.

Then I heard Lost Wolf asking Danny, inside the tepee, what he thought the absence of Running Deer meant. Danny said solemnly that he thought it meant only one thing. Running Deer did not want to stay with his wives under the same lodge that contained Lost Wolf and his new bride.

It brought a little exclamation from Lost Wolf and he cried out loudly: "Running Deer is my brother!"

Danny said: "He is a lot nearer related to the Cheyennes than he is to you. This is the time for you to begin finding it out."

That must have hurt Lost Wolf terribly, having done for another man all that he had done for Running Deer. By his silence I judged that he admitted Croydon was right, and that Running Deer was breaking with him.

I was terribly sick; I hardly cared whether I lived or died. Yet, I didn't really hate Lost Wolf. I might hate the life he had lived that had made it possible for him to have treated a white woman as he had done, but I really couldn't blame him.

Then I heard him say: "She is not my wife until she is willing to be my wife. I keep her only until she will speak the word. Speak to him, girl, and tell him that I have spoken the truth."

Peggy said: "It is true."

40

When Lost Wolf decided that Croydon was right about Running Deer's leaving the lodge, he wanted to move right on, saying that he would take charity from no man, not even from a man who had owed life to him half a dozen times. Danny had the sense to point out that Peggy was not in a fit condition to march on.

He was right. She was thin and tired out from the terrible march that Lost Wolf had put her through. That iron man thought that it had been a mere nothing. He would have gone twice as fast and far with another man, of course. Just the same, he had punished her terribly. In addition, there must have been a frightful burden of suspense on the mind of Peggy, lasting whole days and days, until she found out that Lost Wolf would really respect her.

There was worry for her poor family, too. That was not the end, for now she was in this Indian village, surrounded by what perils she could only guess, with the stake and fire in her mind every instant.

All these things tied neatly together made a burden

that broke her. She lay stretched out on a buffalo robe with her arms thrown out crosswise, and her eyes closed. I turned from the door of the tepee, and I could see the trembling of her lips. Although her face was wonderfully tanned by that journey which Lost Wolf had made her take under the sun, I could see the pallor in her cheeks.

She was spent. Lost Wolf reached down, picked up one of her hands, and let it fall. It dropped a dead weight, as though there were no strength in that arm to check its fall. Her eyes barely quivered open and looked blankly up to the giant—as though she were too tired even to reproach him for having taken her into such troubles as these.

You could see that he was moved, too. He turned away from her with his face like stone. Under the stone, one could guess that he was boiling with emotion. His assurance was breaking down, too. Finally he muttered to Danny in a sort of hoarse whisper: "What shall I do, Danny?"

"There's only one thing that we can do, and that's to stay here and wait until she gets stronger."

"I am strong enough now," whispered poor Peggy.

"Can you march on—can you ride a horse?" cried Lost Wolf. He turned and stared at her.

"Yes!" said Peggy.

"Are you sure?"

"I'm sure!"

"It may be," said Lost Wolf. "Stand up!"

He talked to her exactly as he would have talked to his horse, and I saw Peggy rise and struggle from her knees to her feet. She did not stay on them long. The strength was simply not in her. She began to reel and stretch out her hands as though she were feeling her way in the dark.

Lost Wolf gave an odd little moan that came from the pit of his stomach, I could tell. He caught her in his arms.

"I can ride, tie me on a horse!" said Peggy. "Oh, they'll burn me at the stake. I could see it in their faces!"

That same moan came out of the throat of Lost Wolf, a very strange sound, particularly coming from him. I felt decidedly at sea.

He began to walk up and down through the tepee with

Peggy held at his breast, and he cradled her a little from side to side, exactly as a mother might walk with her baby and cradle it. The strength of that man was so enormous that the comparison was really not extreme. He supported her easily and entirely with one enormous arm and laid the other hand on the shoulder of Danny Croydon.

"Tell me, Danny," he begged.

Danny was feeling a bit mean, and you could hardly blame him.

He said: "You've got yourself and her into this devilish mess. Now get yourselves out again. It's no business of mine."

Lost Wolf gave him a snarl that would have done credit to his namesake. Danny didn't flinch, and the giant changed his tune at once.

"Will you leave me? Will you go away with me, Danny?" said he, begging, like a child again.

Danny Croydon cursed, then he admitted that he would stay with the game until the end of it. It was a hard thing to say, but, of course, there was nothing left for us. Lost Wolf did not ask the questions of me. I was to learn why later on. He resumed that walking of his, and he began to talk to the girl on his breast like this:

"There will be no stake. There will be no fire. It is all a joke. These Cheyennes are my friends. Besides, I can make a magic that will take us away. When you are rested and strong, I shall make a great smoke. We will step into it, and it will carry us away."

The eyes of Peggy opened, and she looked up to him.

"You believe me?" said Lost Wolf.

She smiled a very little at him—as such a story deserved. But she said: "I believe you." And her tired eyes closed again.

It was a sad thing to see. Yet I wondered at her, and her wonderful kindliness, that she would not hurt this great, savage, gentle child, and let him know that she was not quite so untutored as any Indian maiden.

I looked at Danny Croydon, and Danny Croydon looked at me, until each of us must have been a blur to the other.

He came over to me and stood at the door to the tepee.

"What will come of it?" I asked.

"We are all dead men, and that's what'll come of it," said Danny. "Listen to that jackass!"

Lost Wolf was walking again, cradling the girl in his huge arms and murmuring to her. He was so far lost in pity and in excitement, that the idiot was talking to her in gibberish.

"What is it?" said I to Danny.

"Cheyenne animal stories," said Danny. "His foster mother used to put him to sleep with the same yarns when he was a little shaver." Danny gulped. "He's just like that," said Danny. "A fool. But a kind fool! And how he loves that girl! And you, Rivers, were to marry Peggy Gleason?"

I had told Danny, of course, long before.

"I'd really forgotten about myself," I whispered back to him.

The giant frame and the giant emotions of Lost Wolf made me forget that anything I ever felt could be considered true suffering.

"There comes Running Deer," said Danny. "And now we'll hear something that will be worth listening to. He's the whitest Indian on the prairie, bar none."

Running Deer was always worth watching; he was always worth listening to. He came riding up on a fine-limbed mustang, a pure beauty that looked like an Arab. He had a buffalo robe thrown like a Roman toga about his shoulders, and in his hand there were some flaring feathers.

"War feathers!" said Danny to me.

When he said that, my heart dropped to my boots. And I already had a chill because Running Deer had not yet seen me, on this day, but still he had no word for me.

Danny Croydon translated as Running Deer talked. He cried:

"Is Lost Wolf in the tepee?"

There was no answer from the tepee.

Running Deer said: "It is Running Deer who calls."

No answer came forth from the tepee.

Running Deer cried: "Lost Wolf, I am calling to you

for the love I have for you. Are you *giving* yourself to the fire and the stake?"

This to his brother—this to Lost Wolf; even Danny's voice staggered as he translated that speech. And this time even Lost Wolf was fetched.

He cried from the lodge: "I am here, Running Deer."

Running Deer said: "Do you remember the battles where we have fought side by side?"

Lost Wolf answered: "I remember those battles."

"Remember them, Lost Wolf. The people are calling out against you, but I have thought of those battles. I have stood up before my people and talked for you and begged for you."

"The Cheyennes are not blind. They are not fools. They remember what I have done in their sight. They have smoked too many scalps of my taking to forget me now."

Running Deer said: "Step out, then, Lost Wolf. Step out and let the people see you."

Lost Wolf stepped into the door of the lodge. Instantly from a hundred throats of men there arose a harsh shout of rage. Then, as though only the permission of the men had been waited for, there followed the sharper, shriller yell of women and children. Croydon did not translate, but I knew that the phrase had something to do with the pale, white face of Lost Wolf, now revealed to all their tribe. Better that he should never have worn the red stain. Then the open sun and wind of the prairies would have so burned and browned him that he would hardly have been mistaken for another of the Cheyenne tribe. But the stain and the paint had turned the sun. He showed at the lodge door a face well-nigh as pale as that of some bookkeeper, who never faces an honest day of shining sun.

He straightened and stiffened as he stood there before the tribe. He threw up an arm as though he would break into curses against them; instead, he took a whole stride into the open and then stood there with folded arms looking around him.

That took their fancy. This sublime insolence—though there was not a sign of a weapon in his hands or at his belt—silenced them in a trice. In that silence Running Deer said:

"I have spoken to my people, Lost Wolf. They say that they are tired of remembering the great deeds of a dead man. They say that Lost Wolf is dead. He was a great Cheyenne. There is left only a white man, and that man has brought a squaw into the camp. They say, let us have them both to burn. Let us have their scalps to dry in the smoke of our fires. Let us have them, or else, let Lost Wolf prove to us that he has not changed—that he is yet alive—let him give us the white girl to do as we please with her. Then he may be among us again and we shall know him."

Here was the ultimatum of Running Deer, himself, and all the Cheyennes behind him. The shocking thing, somehow, was not that the tribe of barbarians should have formed such a decision, but that Running Deer, of all men, should have backed such a vote.

41

Sharply, Danny Croydon said: "Talk soft; give us time, or we'll all be dead—you and the girl, and the two of us besides."

I thought that the fury that was trembling in Lost Wolf would tear its way out of his throat, but he managed to master himself a little, with a frightful effort. He said:

"Running Deer, I have heard you. What you say comes to me as the voice of the whole Cheyenne people. Therefore, I listen."

You could tell that excited and insulted as the Indians were, they were extra hot to keep this great fellow among them. At this first token of concession on his part, there was a yell of approval that fairly echoed through the tepees. He went on at once, as soon as the racket allowed him time:

"I have come in from a long trail and a hard trail. A man cannot give up a new horse, or a rifle, or a woman, without some sorrow. Let me have time for thought. If the Cheyennes want the white squaw, let them take heed together and talk together and let them know how many ponies they will give for her. For who has heard of taking away a woman without a payment? This thing is not done among the Cheyennes. Mark me, Running Deer!"

Running Deer was so delighted that he shouted:

"Oh, brother, if horses will please you, you shall come to my own herd and you shall count out the ones that please your eye. Whose eye is so pleasant as the Lost Wolf's? He shall take the twenty best horses; he shall take the fifty best horses, and I shall be happy to see them in his hands. They will be a great price for the white squaw, but they will be a small price for Lost Wolf!"

Here and there other voices sang out from among the men:

"Here are twenty horses for Lost Wolf!"

"I have a painted buffalo robe. It is now Lost Wolf's."

"I have a new-made lodge. It shall be Lost Wolf's."

"There are thirty horses in my herd that belong to Lost Wolf."

"I have a rifle."

So it went on, most amazingly. You could see, now, that ready as they were to part themselves from a man who offended their dignity and their personal honor, as they considered it, still they would hardly less willingly have given up their scalps. Once the big hero conformed himself to their ways and their customs, he could have pretty much what he wanted.

In short, Running Deer told his "brother" to take until the next morning to make up his mind. And all would be well!

There were the four of us sitting in a whispering circle in the lodge of Running Deer.

"What shall we do?" asked Danny Croydon.

A weak voice said from the corner of the lodge: "I think I understand pretty well. There are three of you. There is only one of me. And—and you—"

She could not get any farther. Self-pity and weakness intervened, and you could hardly blame her, for that matter. I went over and sat down beside her and took her hand. I said: "You do not need to worry about this thing. We all are thinking of the best way. There is really only the one way for all of us."

"What will *he* decide?" whispered the girl.

She had been tender with me, before this. Now there was a change that even a blind man could have told by the mere sound of her voice. I was no more than a wooden peg to her. Here I was holding her hand, trying to reassure her in this Cheyenne tepee with a thousand wretched forms of death all around her, and all that she answered me was: "What is going on in the mind of the big man?"

That was all that she cared about. She sat there, staring and trembling, white of face, but what was beating her down was not, really, the fear of death. It was the fear that Lost Wolf didn't care enough about her to try to save her.

That was why she stared like a sleep-walker, straight through me, asking me a question, but really not hearing me as I answered.

Danny Croydon could not speak. He was a little harder than the pair of us, and Danny would have been closer to giving up the girl I think, fond of her though he was. He could not see the good sense in selling the lives of three white men—not that a white woman should be kept from death, but just for the sake of making an honorable protest.

Lost Wolf settled everything. He said, like a king who disposes of a matter of state:

"There are not four people here. There is only one. We have one skin; it is white. We have one heart; it is the heart of the white man. There is only one life for us; there is only one death for us. I have spoken!"

A flame came into the eyes of the girl. I had seen, a

214

moment before, that I was a very small sum in the life of Peggy Gleason—a hardly remembered shore, as you might say. Now I saw that she worshiped the big man.

There *was* something grand about him. I could never have got words to say things which he had just said. I would have profaned such a thought with slang, but Lost Wolf brought the thing out as it needed to be phrased.

The matter was ended.

The Cheyennes, naturally enough, thought that it was ended in just the opposite direction. About this time, there was a voice of a woman at the lodge entrance. Lost Wolf called out for them to enter. Here came two of Running Deer's squaws carrying two pots of cooked meats. Behind them a pair of their children gaped and stared in at us. They were pretty things, those youngsters, and the seven-year-old boy was as fine a looking child as I have ever set eyes on.

Lost Wolf reached into his pocket and brought out some shining trinket. I have forgotten what it was, but he dangled it toward the two little boys and said something in Cheyenne. They came in tiptoe—for all the world like little antelope fawns, attracted by some unexplainable sight. The seven-year-old went first, his face a picture of excitement, and the four-year-old toddled after.

The mothers stood by, nodding and smiling. In an instant those smiles went out, I can tell you, as the youngsters came within the sweep of the big man's arms. He caught them up and tucked them inside of the grip of an arm apiece.

That was the end of that business. There was an exclamation of satisfaction from Croydon. I shouted in surprise, and Peggy, of course, vowed that the big fellow was throttling the two youngsters.

The mother's faces turned a rather sickly green tint. They began to babble noises at Lost Wolf, but he shut them up with a roar. He nodded at his two little prisoners, and then at the white girl. I did not need to have a translator to tell me that he was saying:

215

"You want the white girl. But now I have two Cheyennes to pay for her. Go back and tell Running Deer!"

They went. One of them dropped on her knees to clasp her hands and beg Lost Wolf in a set of pleading murmurs not to harm her darling. A man child is an Indian woman's heaven. Then she scampered off after the other mother. As they ran, they began to raise their wails, their steady shrill voices broken by the jarring of their footfalls.

Rome would be howling in a short time now, I guessed, and I was not wrong.

While the tide of noise grew up, Croydon lay down where he could look out through the front flap of the tepee —his Winchester in the dust at his side to help him keep the watch. I went to the rear of the tepee to keep guard there.

"There is nothing to fear now," said Lost Wolf. "Running Deer now will hate me forever. But he will manage it that we shall all go free. These are his two sons. He would give his right arm for this bigger of the two—hah, you little snake!"

The seven-year-old prize had found a chance to work his right arm free. He snatched the long hunting knife from the belt of Lost Wolf and struck at his breast. Pain made the big man loosen his remaining grip. The little, treacherous rat leaped from the lodge wall—under which he would have rolled and been gone in another instant.

The reaching hand of Lost Wolf was just about as fast as the strike of a snake. He caught the flying heel of the boy and brought him to the ground with a thud. It was admirable to see the little demon when he felt the grip of that mighty hand. He expected to have his neck wrung at once, of course. Lost Wolf simply turned him over to me.

I was the only one with any spare hands. The minute Lost Wolf was stabbed, the girl came with a sudden scream and threw herself down beside him. Danny Croydon cut his shirt away.

It was only a scratch, or else this narrative would never have been written. It was only a glancing upward slash of the knife that cut the skin of Lost Wolf a little. He was bandaged and as much himself as ever when we heard the excited voice of Running Deer shouting in front of the tepee.

Lost Wolf went out and answered him.

He said, first: "Running Deer, while I talk to you, two men whose guns never tell lies are watching you, also. Their rifles are ready."

"Ah, traitor!" cried Running Deer. "You have murdered my two sons."

"They are safely here," said Lost Wolf.

"Let me see them!"

The boys were shown, and a wail went up, the voices of the two mothers leading, of course.

"Do not talk to me of treason," said Lost Wolf, "when you have stabbed at me because I changed the color of my skin? I do not like the red color. It seems to me, now, the color of rats. It is the color of sneaking coyotes, not of men. But I pay you the two young coyotes. You may raise them as you please. But the white squaw goes with me."

There was no use in argument. Running Deer tried it and attempted to point out that two children could not be used to ransom four adults. Lost Wolf silenced everything by saying that he would end the talk by wringing the necks of the boys, then let the Cheyenne rifles butcher us when they could. We would cost them dear enough before the end!

That was the closing gun of the discussion. Beyond a doubt, the Cheyennes wanted our scalps, now, but they did not want to to risk the lives of two prospective warriors in the act.

What you might call natural thrift stepped in between, here, and rescued Peggy Gleason from a frightful death. It was agreed that Lost Wolf and the rest of us should leave the camp, and that we should take Peggy with us. We should retain one of the Indian boys until we were half a day's march from the village, and that then we should give the boy up to the Indians who would accompany us at a little distance.

Such was the agreement which was made.

In the meantime, there was a night to spend in that Indian camp before we started on the march toward our deliverance and back to the land of our own people. I am certain that no hours ever moved more slowly than did that night over our head.

I should make an exception for Peggy, because she had no real worry. Mere life or death did not greatly concern her. All that she had been anxious to find out was whether or not Lost Wolf was really willing and ready to die for her. When she had learned that, she could have lain down and gone quietly to sleep even with the scalping knife hovering over her head.

In a way, it was a night more full of bitterness than dread, for me. My pride was terribly hurt. Many a time I decided that I could not endure the offense which big Lost Wolf had done to me daring to induce my lady to change her heart from me to him. Before the morning came, I had reached a little better sense in the matter. After all, the novelty of the thing amused me.

What other lover on the face of the earth would have dreamed of dragging his lady across the prairie on forced marches—treating her to a taste of slavery?

Well, there was precedent for the matter in my life. It was not the first time, as I have said before, that I had fallen in love. It was far from the first time that I had found another preferred to me.

I sought refuge in the knowledge that though I felt my heart was going to break, break it would not. In the course of another few weeks, I should be heartwhole and fancy-free.

Besides, I told myself that Peggy Gleason was never meant for such an undistinguished fellow as I. It was foredoomed that a great man—a Lost Wolf—should come and take her.

So I watched the dark hours of that night through and was a very, very glad man when the morning dawned, glad because I knew that the second day and the second night, would be far easier than the first.

When the first gray of the dawn came, a hand touched my shoulder lightly, and when I turned, there was the face of Peggy near me.

She whispered: "Do you understand?"

218

Oh, yes, I understood! For all her labors and all her exhaustion of only the night before, a single sleep had made her bloom. Her eyes were dancing. She was filled with happiness and was perfectly careless of her fate.

Such a woman was meant for Lost Wolf, it seemed to me.

I said: "I understand everything, and I forgive everything."

She explained: "I didn't want to do anything but dread and loathe him. But I couldn't help it. He doesn't guess that I care for him. He has not even *asked* if I care for him! He doesn't seem to bother about a little thing like that. When the time comes he will simply order me to stand up at the altar—and I'll do it! And he'll *never* suspect!"

42

When the dawn came, we were ready. Out of the pot, we had cold buffalo stew for breakfast, and though it was a greasy mess the prairies made the coarsest diet an agreeable thing. We dipped into the pot, sitting in a circle, ate from our hands, then washed them in a bit of cold water.

Everything was smoothly arranged, so smoothly that I thought there was an ominous hidden danger, at first. Only Running Deer and the five men who were to act as our escort appeared. The rest of the population remained inside the tepees—I suppose, to escape from the disgrace of standing by and watching the forced submission of the tribe to such an act of violence as this.

We got on our horses in due order. Running Deer led the way through the village, having first only paused to extract from Lost Wolf and Danny Croydon an oath that they would abide faithfully by the terms of the contract. After that oath, he made not the slightest objection to having his eldest boy ride along on a pony whose lead lariat was tied to the pommel of Lost Wolf's saddle.

In this fashion, we rode two and two out of the Indian camp, into the open arms of the prairie. When we had gone on for about a mile or more, it dawned upon us that there was no trick. Running Deer was living up to his reputation as an honest Indian.

After we had ridden along for about an hour, Running Deer stopped and pointed out that we were now alone in the middle of the prairie and could use our eyes for looking about us and descrying the slightest danger. We were all well-mounted, upon magnificent horses—as horses went on the prairie. Had he not fulfilled his contract with us to the letter?

Croydon translated the talk that followed.

Lost Wolf said that the promise had been fulfilled; that Running Deer was an honest man, and that he, Lost Wolf, would always keep the most friendly remembrance of him. In the meantime, he begged that Running Deer, if he were ever in great danger and required help, would think of Lost Wolf and send for him.

Running Deer smiled, and said:

"Your help is a thing that no Cheyenne shall ever need. You were once a great warrior. Tirawa and the water spirits listened to your voice, when you called. And there was good fortune when you rode on the warpath. All of the Indian tribes would listen to you and dread you. But now you are nothing. You are a calf with a wolf's head, and you are a wolf with a calf's feet. You are not an Indian, because we will not have you among us. The whites will laugh at you, and you will not live with them. For the sake of a squaw you shall have unhappiness that shall last for many years. You shall not sleep with the calves; you shall not feed with the wolves."

This was pretty stiff talk, and you could see poor Lost Wolf taking it to heart. He was superstitious enough to believe in even Indian prophecy.

Running Deer went on: "When you are in danger, do not think of me. Even if I am in the reach of your voice,

220

do not call to me. When you are sick, forget my name. When you are hungry, do not remember my tepee. Or if you speak my name, do not call me brother!"

I did not need to be told that this was the retraction of a sacred pledge of friendship among the Cheyennes. I listened and felt about as sick as Lost Wolf did. That speech from Running Deer meant that about twenty odd years of the life of the big man had been thrown away.

Then Running Deer rode off, and left Lost Wolf with bowed head, making no effort to disguise the frightful pain that he felt. We saw the Indians vanish toward the south and the west. We all kept on toward Zander City.

We would get to the river. Then Croydon would go in and see how the land lay for the pair of us. At the least, he must bring out the minister for the marriage of Peggy to Lost Wolf.

The giant and the girl rode on by themselves, drawing a little ahead of us.

"Do you think," said I to Croydon, "that Running Deer is right?"

"There is one thing that Running Deer left out," said Danny. "He forgot that Lost Wolf is a genius. The laws for ordinary men break down where he steps into the picture."

The big man and the girl dipped out of view in the gully of a stream.

"But you think that he will not be an outcast both from the reds and whites?" said I. "I tell you, man, that Lost Wolf is about two-thirds brute. He has dragged that girl away from the town and never so much as told her that he is fond of her."

"He has dragged her away from the town and made her love him for it, and that is the main test," said Danny, "and besides—back up!"

We both reined back our horses hastily, for coming over the edge of the valley, we looked down upon the surprising picture of pretty Peggy Gleason standing by the edge of the river, where I suppose she had dismounted to drink. On the river bank kneeled Lost Wolf, in the age-old attitude.

Said Danny Croydon: "What he doesn't know by teaching, he knows by instinct. I think that lad will find a way to get on with the whites, when he bends his mind to it!"

MORE MAX BRAND BESTSELLERS...

BORDER GUNS	(88-892, $1.50)
CHEYENNE GOLD	(88-966, $1.50)
DRIFTER'S VENGEANCE	
	(84-783, $1.75)
FIRE BRAIN	(88-629, $1.50)
FLAMING IRONS	(98-019, $1.50)
FRONTIER FEUD	(98-002, $1.50)
GUNMAN'S GOLD	(88-337, $1.50)
THE INVISIBLE OUTLAW	
	(88-705, $1.50)
MAN FROM SAVAGE CREEK	
	(88-883, $1.50)
MIGHTY LOBO	(88-829, $1.50)
OUTLAW BREED	(98 074, $1.50)
PLEASANT JIM	(86-286, $1.25)
RIDER OF THE HIGH HILL	
	(88-884, $1.50)
THE SEVENTH MAN	(98-105, $1.50)
SILVERTIP	(88-685, $1.50)
SILVERTIP'S CHASE	(98-048, $1.50)
SILVERTIP'S STRIKE	(98-096, $1.50)
TRAILIN'	(88-717, $1.50)
WAR PARTY	(88-933, $1.50)

THE UNSHAKABLE, UNSTOPPABLE, UNKILLABLE CAPTAIN GRINGO IS BACK IN: